WASH
and DIE

Books by Barbara Colley

MAID FOR MURDER

DEATH TIDIES UP

POLISHED OFF

WIPED OUT

MARRIED TO THE MOP

SCRUB-A-DUB DEAD

WASH AND DIE

Published by Kensington Publishing Corporation

A Charlotte LaRue Mystery

WASH and DIE

Barbara Colley

KENSINGTON BOOKS
www.kensingtonbooks.com

KENSINGTON BOOKS are published by

Kensington Publishing Corp.
850 Third Avenue
New York, NY 10022

All Kensington titles, imprints and distributed lines are available at special quantity discounts for bulk purchases for sales promotion, premiums, fund-raising, educational or institutional use.

Special book excerpts or customized printings can also be created to fit specific needs. For details, write or phone the office of the Kensington Special Sales Manager: Kensington Publishing Corp., 850 Third Avenue, New York, NY, 10022. Attn. Special Sales Department. Phone: 1-800-221-2647.

Kensington and the K logo Reg. U.S. Pat. & TM Off.

Library of Congress Card Catalogue Number : 2007934366
ISBN-13: 978-0-7582-2251-0
ISBN-10: 0-7582-2251-3

First Printing: February 2008
10 9 8 7 6 5 4 3 2 1

Printed in the United States of America

To Evan Marshall

Chapter 1

She was running late, and Charlotte LaRue hated being late for anything. Pulling on her sweater, she snagged her purse on the way to the front door. If she hurried, though, she just might have time to go by the bank before her ten o'clock client.

Her thoughts on the notice she'd received about a so-called bounced check, she threw the dead bolt and opened the door.

A strange woman, with flaming red hair, was standing on the other side of the threshold, and Charlotte gasped with surprise, momentarily speechless. All Charlotte could do was stare at the woman as her mind raced with all kinds of dire consequences for having been so careless. With all the crime in New Orleans, a woman living alone could never be too careful. She knew better than to open the door without checking out the window first.

"I'm so sorry," the woman blurted out. "I didn't mean to startle you. I was just about to knock when you opened the door."

She was as tall as Charlotte, but probably outweighed her by a good twenty pounds. There was nothing all that menacing or frightening about the middle-aged woman, but these days one could never tell. Out of caution, Charlotte eased back a step and kept a firm grip on the doorknob, just in case she needed to slam it in the woman's face.

"My name is Flora Jennings." The woman smiled and batted her heavily mascaraed eyelashes. "I'm with Big Easy Realty." She thrust out her hand.

With one hand still firmly gripping the doorknob, Charlotte ignored the outstretched hand and simply nodded.

When Flora Jennings realized that Charlotte had no intention of shaking her hand, her fixed smile wavered and she dropped her hand. "I probably should have called first, but I just happened to be in the neighborhood. . . ." Her voice trailed away.

Charlotte sighed, then shivered. "I don't mean to be rude, Ms. Jennings, but it's cold and I'm running late—"

"It is cold for November, isn't it? I can't believe it's already November. Thanksgiving will be here before we know it. Usually our weather doesn't get this cold until after Christmas. Why, I remember one year running the air conditioner—"

Would the woman ever shut up?

"Ms. Jennings!" Charlotte threw up her hand to silence her. "Like I said, I don't mean to be rude, but what do you want?"

For a second, Flora Jennings's expression grew tight with strain, but she nodded. "Sorry—I tend to rattle on and on. I'll try to be brief, then. Like I said before, I'm with Big Easy Realty." From the side pocket of her purse, she pulled out a business card and offered it to Charlotte.

Charlotte took the card and glanced at it. It looked legitimate, but anyone could have a business card printed.

"I'm not sure that you realize this," Flora Jennings continued, "but this part of Uptown has become quite desirable since Katrina, especially these old Victorian doubles. And may I say that yours looks to be in terrific shape from the outside."

It should, Charlotte thought, especially after what it had cost her to have it painted. She slipped the business card into her pants pocket, then gathered the front edges of her sweater together in an attempt to fight off the chill. She supposed she should be grateful, though. After Katrina, her insurance had completely covered the expense of a new roof. Others she'd talked with hadn't been so fortunate.

"Anyway," Flora went on. "As I was saying, a lot of people want to move back home to New Orleans, and I have a long waiting list of clients who are very interested in buying or renting homes in this area. What I'm doing today is going door to door and offering a free price analysis to anyone who might be interested. The process—"

Again, Charlotte threw up her hand, interrupting the woman. "Are you talking about an appraisal?" she asked.

Flora Jennings shrugged. "Not exactly. It wouldn't be official. More like giving you a ballpark figure. It would only take a few moments of your time," she hastily added.

And where would I live if I sold my house? Charlotte wondered, growing more impatient with each passing moment. Then suddenly, it hit her. Of course. The woman was probably under the mistaken impression that the other half of her double was for rent.

Charlotte opened her mouth with the intention of telling Flora Jennings that she wasn't interested, but at the last second, she changed her mind. Though she had never entertained the idea of selling the family home, where she had been raised and had raised her son, she had been curious about the market value, especially since Katrina.

Should I or shouldn't I? Charlotte glanced at her watch and decided that her visit to the bank could wait until that afternoon. "Okay," she finally agreed. "But you need to wait right here for a minute."

Without giving the Jennings woman time to reply, Charlotte firmly shut the door. Reaching in her pocket, she removed the woman's business card, then hurried over to the telephone and dialed the number listed on the card. It never hurt to be cautious these days.

"Big Easy Realty," a cheery voice answered.

"Ah, yes, I have a question for you. Do you have an agent named Flora Jennings working for you?"

"Why, yes—yes, we do. But Ms. Jennings isn't available at the moment. May I have her return your call?"

"No—no thanks." Charlotte hung up the receiver. Satisfied that the woman was who she said she was, Charlotte opened the front door. Motioning for the real estate agent to come inside, she said, "This had better be quick. I have to get to work."

Flora Jennings's face lit up. "Wonderful!" she exclaimed, and immediately stepped through the doorway. "I really appreciate this opportunity. What kind of work do you do?" But even as she asked the question, her eyes were eagerly taking in every nook and cranny of the living room area.

Charlotte placed her purse on the coffee table and pulled off her sweater. "I own Maid–for–a–Day, a domestic cleaning service."

"Oh . . . how interesting."

To Charlotte's ears, the distaste in the woman's tone belied her words, but after forty-something years of being a maid, she'd gotten used to it. The insinuated snub no longer bothered her as it had when she was younger. She did honest work for honest pay, and there was no shame in that.

"The house is about a hundred years old," Charlotte said evenly. "And the double on the other side is almost an exact duplicate of this side."

Flora frowned. "You and your husband do own the entire house, don't you?"

Unwilling to admit to this perfect stranger that she didn't

have a husband, Charlotte simply smiled, and said, "*I* own the house. Free and clear. I rent out the other side, and it's occupied right now."

Flora shrugged. "That doesn't matter. Just give me a minute to measure this room, and then you can show me the rest of this half." From her handbag, she pulled out a pen, a notebook, and a measuring tape; then, she placed the handbag on the chair near the front door.

Once Flora had measured the living room, Charlotte gestured with her hand. "Through this doorway is the kitchen–dining room."

Flora nodded approvingly. "It's nice and roomy." She began measuring and jotting down numbers in her notebook, and after a moment, she glanced up and said, "I noticed when I drove up that it looks like you have a nice deep backyard."

"Yes, I do," Charlotte murmured.

"Well, let's see the rest of the house."

Charlotte hesitated. "Don't you need to know the size of the lot or something?"

"Yes, but I'll measure that after we've finished inside."

Charlotte nodded. "Okay." She motioned for Flora to walk ahead of her. "Over here are the bedrooms. There are two bedrooms and a bathroom."

"This one must be the master bedroom," Flora said, her eagle eyes scanning the room from top to bottom.

"Yes, it's the larger of the two." Charlotte had just recently redone her bedroom décor and had settled on a country look. She was really proud of the butterfly-pattern quilt she'd purchased at the annual Destrehan Plantation Arts and Crafts Festival upriver. Using it as a bedspread had provided just the right inspiration for decorating the rest of the room.

Within a few minutes, Charlotte had shown Flora the other bedroom and the bathroom. Each time, Flora measured and jotted down numbers in her notebook. That she also insisted on measuring the closets seemed kind of odd to Charlotte, but since she had never had her home appraised before, she didn't say anything.

Back in the living room, Flora picked up her handbag. "I really appreciate you doing this," she told Charlotte. "And I'll get back to you in a couple of days with your free price analysis."

"No hurry," Charlotte assured her as she opened the front door.

"Talk to you later, then," Flora said, but she paused at the front door. "You did say that you and your husband both live here, didn't you?"

"No, I didn't," Charlotte replied. "But I don't see where that's relevant, one way or another."

Flora stared at her a moment, then said, "It's not." Then she smiled. "I was just curious. Bye now." Then she turned and bustled out the door.

Once Charlotte had closed the door behind Flora Jennings, she walked over to the birdcage near the front window. "Well, that was a bit strange," she told the little green parakeet perched inside. From the corner of her eye, she saw a cream-colored car back out of her driveway. Figuring it had to belong to Flora Jennings, she said, "Guess she didn't have to measure the lot after all, huh, Sweety. Funny that she would measure the closets, but not the property."

The little bird sidled over to the side of the cage and stretched his head first one way, then another, a sign that he wanted to be petted.

"Oooh, you're such a good little birdie," Charlotte said softly as she stuck her finger through the cage and gave the parakeet a gentle head rub.

Though Charlotte had never entertained the idea of having

a bird for a pet, after over two years of sharing her home with the little parakeet, she couldn't imagine not having him. Of course he looked far healthier now than when she'd found him. She'd discovered him after a deadbeat tenant had skipped out owing her money, and the poor little thing was in pitiful shape, half-starved and sick. Not anymore, though. Now he was as healthy as could be, and she'd even taught him how to say a couple of phrases.

Charlotte glanced over at the cuckoo clock on the wall behind the sofa. "Oops, time to go. Now you be a good little bird, and I'll see you later this afternoon."

As Charlotte hurried out to her van, she couldn't help noticing a black SUV parked diagonally across the street from her house. The lone man in the SUV didn't look familiar and he was simply sitting there.

So, why *was* he just sitting there?

What if he was a thief casing the neighborhood? Though her neighborhood wasn't a wealthy one by any stretch of the imagination, she and most of her neighbors still had a few valuables—TVs, stereos, jewelry, and such.

With an uneasy feeling crawling down her back, Charlotte pointedly glared at the man before she climbed into the van.

"Oh, for pity's sake," she murmured. "Get a grip. Not everybody is one of the bad guys." First Flora Jennings, and now . . . "Probably just another real estate agent looking for property," she grumbled.

Even so, once she'd backed out of the driveway, she made it a point to get a good look at the car's license plate, noting that it was a rental car. She also made sure that she got a good look at the man as she drove slowly past his car. Too bad she was already running a bit late, or she'd stop and ask him what he was doing.

Yeah, right, Charlotte, you big coward.

"Well, I would," she muttered, countering the aggravating voice in her head.

Getting her bank account straightened out that afternoon had taken longer than she'd expected, but then everything seemed to take longer since Hurricane Katrina. By the time Charlotte turned down her street, it was almost four o'clock.

She glanced over at the bag of used books on the passenger seat, a gift from her client Bitsy Duhe. Since the death of Bitsy's husband, the elderly lady had more time on her hands than she knew what to do with, and though she filled most of her time on the phone gossiping, she also loved to read.

Bitsy knew how much Charlotte enjoyed reading too, and they both loved a good mystery. Even though she had a stack of to-be-read books on her bedside table, she could hardly wait to get home and go through the books.

With a sigh, Charlotte shook her head and snickered. It had been a while since she'd cleaned for Bitsy Duhe, and though Bitsy was generous to a fault, she could also be a real pain to work for.

During Katrina, Bitsy had evacuated first to Shreveport, where she'd stayed with an old friend, and then, at the insistence of her son, she'd flown out to California and stayed with him for several months. But like most of the tried and true natives of New Orleans, and in spite of her son's objections, Bitsy couldn't wait to come back home.

Charlotte was just thankful that she'd had the good sense to hire Dale Brown, and that Dale seemed to genuinely care about the old lady. And she was also grateful that Dale would be finished with his semester finals in time to clean for Bitsy the following Tuesday.

Too bad Dale only had one more semester till graduation. She'd have to start giving some serious thought to hiring someone else pretty soon.

Though her mind was still on the bag of books and her employee, Dale Brown, she did notice that the black SUV that she'd seen that morning, along with its occupant, was gone just before she pulled into her driveway.

As Charlotte shifted the gear into park, her gaze strayed to her front porch. Then she froze, her hand hovering above the ignition. A woman was sitting on the front-porch swing. But not just any woman, she suddenly realized.

Joyce Thibodeaux.

Charlotte felt as if she'd just been sucker punched, and dread, like a slab of concrete, weighed down her insides.

"Dear Lord in Heaven, now what?" she whispered.

Chapter 2

For more reasons than she could count, the very last person on earth that Charlotte wanted to see was Joyce Thibodeaux, the ex-wife of her tenant, Louis Thibodeaux. Before Joyce had finally been forced to enter a substance abuse program at a local hospital, she'd caused enough trouble and heartache for ten people, including Charlotte.

Poor Louis. Charlotte sighed. Did he know that Joyce was out of the hospital earlier than she was supposed to be? More than likely, he didn't. If he had known, he would have said something before he left Sunday afternoon for an assignment in New York.

"Oh, boy," she whispered. Louis was going to be furious when he did find out. But who could really blame him after what Joyce had put him through. After abandoning Louis and their troubled teenage son years ago, she'd come back into his life and claimed to be dying. But it had all been a lie. Knowing how Louis felt about her alcoholism, and desperately needing to get out of California, Joyce had used the dying ploy to play on Louis's sympathies and to cover up the fact that she was still a drunk.

Charlotte switched off the engine. Not looking forward to

the confrontation with Joyce, she took her time gathering her stuff.

You did this. . . . This is your fault. . . . Joyce's accusation on the day she was taken away by paramedics whispered through Charlotte's head. Considering that she was partially responsible for helping Louis persuade Joyce to agree to a drug rehab program, Charlotte had a sneaking suspicion that Joyce wasn't there to pay her a social visit—especially since Louis hadn't given Joyce much of a choice in the matter. It was either agree to go into the program or fend for herself on the streets.

Knowing she couldn't delay the inevitable confrontation any longer, Charlotte finally climbed out of the van. Both women simply stared at each other, and neither spoke as Charlotte approached the porch.

The first thing that caught Charlotte's eye as she climbed the short flight of stairs was that Joyce had lost weight and was wearing the same clothes she'd had on when she had entered the hospital weeks before. Joyce was a couple of years younger than Charlotte, and according to Louis, Joyce had always been a thin woman, but now she looked even skinnier than before. Of course the fact that she had pulled her red hair back tightly into a ponytail made her look even more emaciated.

She must be cold, Charlotte thought, her gaze taking in the short-sleeved T-shirt Joyce was wearing.

The next thing that Charlotte noticed was the large bundle at Joyce's feet. It was wrapped in what appeared to be towels and tied up like a gift with a thin rope.

Since Joyce had nothing but the clothes on her back when she'd entered the hospital and had no income, and assuming that the bundle belonged to Joyce, Charlotte wondered how she had acquired anything during her time there. Of course it was always possible that Louis or Stephen had sent her a few of the clothes she'd left at Louis's house. And, too, it was possible that one of the many charities could have contributed clothes to the hospital.

The second that Charlotte stepped onto the porch, Joyce abruptly stood and took a step toward her. Charlotte immediately tensed, unsure just what to expect.

"Hi, Charlotte."

To Charlotte's surprise, Joyce's tone was subdued, as was the expression on her face. With a nod of her head, she returned the greeting. "Hello, Joyce."

As they stood staring at each other, an awkward silence stretched out into several long minutes. Joyce was the first to finally break the silence. "I—I know that I'm probably the last person on earth that you want to see, and I apologize for showing up without calling first. But frankly, I was afraid that you wouldn't take my call either. Neither Louis nor Stephen will answer my phone calls. And yeah, I know what you're thinking and you're right. After what I did, what can I expect?"

A tear rolled down Joyce's cheek, and Charlotte felt the resentment inside crumble.

"Truth is, I'm scared, Charlotte. I was just released from the hospital. They don't have enough beds for the psych patients as it is, never mind those of us with addiction problems, so they released me to free up a bed." Joyce shrugged. "And now I have nowhere else to go and nobody to turn to." Another tear rolled down her cheek.

"I'm scared, Charlotte. Scared to stay by myself. Right now, I'm clean and I'm sober, but I'm terrified of falling off the wagon again. The doctors told me that my fears were normal, and that after a few days on the outside, I'd get better. I do plan to get my own place as soon as possible, but I need somewhere to stay besides on the street until then. I know I have no right to ask you this, but could I please stay with you—just until I find my own place?"

More tears filled Joyce's eyes and spilled over, but Charlotte steeled herself against the pity she felt and reminded herself that Joyce had proven to be a habitual liar . . . and a consummate actress.

Let he who is without sin cast the first stone. . . . Judge not, lest ye be judged. . . .

When the Bible verses popped into her head, Charlotte knew in that moment what she had to do. Faults or no faults, she couldn't turn Joyce away, but try as she might, she couldn't stem the uneasy feeling in the pit of her stomach. Just because it was the right thing to do didn't mean she liked it.

Before she could change her mind, Charlotte forced herself to nod her head, and though the words were like chewing nails, she said, "Yes, you can stay here for a couple of days, but just until you find your own place."

The look of relief on Joyce's face was heart-wrenching. "Thank you, Charlotte," she gushed. "I promise I won't be any trouble, and I promise you won't regret it."

Yeah, right. Famous last words. . . .

Ignoring her inner voice of doom and gloom, Charlotte nodded again, then turned and stepped over to the front door of her half of the double and unlocked the door.

The moment that Charlotte entered the living room, her little parakeet, Sweety Boy, began to squawk. "Missed you, *squawk*, missed you."

Charlotte grinned. "Good boy," she crooned. "And I missed you too."

Joyce closed the door behind her, and upon hearing the exchange between Charlotte and the bird, she stopped in front of his cage and frowned. "Never have liked birds," she muttered. "Especially in the house." After a moment, she faced Charlotte. "Why on earth would you want to teach that wretched thing to talk?"

Oh, boy, here we go. Not only was it a rude thing to say, but it amazed Charlotte that Joyce would be so . . . so . . . inconsiderate of her feelings about her pet. Charlotte never had been the type who liked confrontations, so she counted to ten before she tried to speak. Then, swallowing back the sudden spurt of temper she'd felt, she chose to change the subject, instead of answering Joyce. "If you'll follow me, I'll show you the guest room. And by the way, I hope you like red beans and rice. That's what I was planning on eating for supper tonight."

"Oh, anything's okay with me, especially after that awful hospital food. One thing, though, you wouldn't happen to have some garlic French bread to go with the beans and rice, would you? I love garlic French bread."

Usually, Charlotte fixed her plate at suppertime, then went into the living room to watch TV while she ate, or sometimes she'd sit at the table and read, if she was into a good book. Since she had company, she decided they should probably eat at the table.

"That was delicious," Joyce told her after they had eaten and were clearing the table.

"Glad you enjoyed it," Charlotte said as she unloaded the dishwasher. "It's the recipe that my mother always used."

While Charlotte began stacking the dishwasher with dirty dishes, Joyce seated herself at the table. "Is your mother still living?"

"No." Charlotte shook her head. "She and my father both died in an accident while I was in college."

"You went to college?"

Joyce's astonished tone put Charlotte immediately on the defensive. Ever so carefully she closed and locked the dishwasher, when what she really wanted was to slam it shut. As she rinsed and dried her hands, once again she made herself

15

count to ten to calm down. Finally, she faced Joyce. "Yes, Joyce," she said evenly. "I went to college—Tulane University, in fact. But I never finished. After my parents were killed, I had to quit and go to work."

"Sorry, didn't mean to pry."

Charlotte shrugged. "It was a long time ago."

"I never went to college," Joyce confessed as Charlotte seated herself across from Joyce at the table. "But I did go to beauty school and became a cosmetologist. At first, that's how I made my living when I moved to California. I actually worked for one of the big studios for a while." Joyce sighed, then bowed her head. In a voice barely above a whisper, she added, "But all the glamour in the world can't take the place of family." She raised her head and looked Charlotte in the eyes. "Leaving Louis and Stephen was the worst mistake I've ever made in my life—that, and drinking. And not a day goes by that I don't regret what I did."

Charlotte could almost believe that—for once—Joyce was telling the truth. But then she remembered how convincingly Joyce had played the part of a dying woman.

"I don't know just how much Louis told you about me," Joyce continued, "though I'm sure that none of it was good, but I want *you* to know that I'm not all bad. You've been really kind to me—much kinder than I deserve or could have expected." She paused, then, with a tight-lipped smile and a shrewd look, she said, "Especially considering that you've got the hots for my ex-husband."

Charlotte's mouth dropped open, and all she could do was stare at Joyce speechlessly. Her immediate reaction was to deny Joyce's crude words, but the denial seemed to stick in her throat. How could she deny Joyce's accusation when, deep down, on a level she'd rather ignore, she knew it was true.

"Oh, don't look so outraged," Joyce told her with a laugh. "Lighten up. I can't say as I blame you. My ex is a good-looking man for his age. And if you can get past the male-chauvinist side of him, he's also pretty nice. Besides, as much as I regret what I did, I've tried to move on with my own life, and I can hardly fault Louis for doing the same."

"I guess not," Charlotte finally said, for lack of anything better to say.

Joyce shrugged, then sighed. "There's also something else I need to tell you."

Great! Just wonderful. It took every bit of self-control Charlotte could muster to keep from groaning aloud. *Why me, Lord?* she wondered. The last thing she wanted was to be Joyce's confessor.

"I tried to tell Louis, but after . . ." Joyce's voice trailed off, then she took a deep breath. "After he found out that I'd lied to him about dying, he wouldn't listen to anything I had to say." She twisted her mouth into a grimace, then shrugged. "Anyway, when Louis found me in California, I wasn't really a homeless drunk then. Oh, I'd been a homeless drunk before, but that particular time happened to be one of my sober periods." Joyce suddenly leaned forward and lowered her voice. "I was actually working undercover as a snitch for a police detective and just pretending to be a drunk."

Charlotte frowned and shook her head. "I don't understand. If you were working with the police, then why on earth would you lie to Louis to begin with?"

"Because the only way I could know for sure that he would bring me back to New Orleans was if he believed I was dying. You see, my cover got blown, and some really bad dudes were after me. I needed to get out of town fast."

Up until that moment, Charlotte had believed Joyce, but the snitch story was more than she could swallow.

"You don't believe me, do you?" Joyce said, her tone belligerent.

Time to take off the kid gloves. Charlotte leveled a no-nonsense look at her. "I'll be perfectly honest with you, Joyce. I truly don't know what to believe about you anymore. I want to believe you—I really do—but trust is a delicate thing. Once trust is broken, it's almost impossible to win back.

"And another thing, if you'd been honest with Louis in the first place about these so-called bad dudes, he would have helped you. For pity's sake, Joyce, he's a retired police detective, plus he works as a security guard now. Who better to have on your side? I'm telling you, he would have helped you."

Joyce simply stared at Charlotte with a pitying expression on her face, and then she slowly shook her head. "No, he wouldn't have, Charlotte. Not in my reality. Maybe in yours, but not in mine."

On Wednesday morning, Charlotte poured birdseed into Sweety Boy's feeder, then placed it back inside his cage. "There you go, Boy," she murmured, giving the little parakeet a head rub with her forefinger. "Now you be a good little bird today. We've got company, so none of that squawking and carrying on like you do when Madeline and Louis come over."

For the life of her, Charlotte had yet to figure out why the silly parakeet reacted like he did when her sister, Madeline, and Louis were around. There had been a couple of times she'd had to remove him and his cage from the room to keep him from injuring himself as he'd thrashed against the inside of the cage.

"Be good," she repeated as she rubbed his head one last time. Not for a second did Charlotte believe the little bird understood what she said, but she did believe he could understand the tone of her voice. Or was that dogs? Whichever, she thought. Talking to Sweety Boy beat talking to herself all the time.

She pulled her hand out of the cage and latched the door. Glancing over at the cuckoo clock, she decided that if she hurried, she could get the dishwasher unloaded before time to leave for work.

With a sigh, Charlotte hurried to the kitchen. Today was her regular day to work for Sandra Wellington. Sandra's Italianate-style mansion was gorgeous on the outside and exquisitely decorated on the inside, but cleaning it usually took her all morning and half the afternoon. Sandra was a really sweet woman who paid Charlotte better than any of her other clients, but she was a dreadful housekeeper.

Charlotte had just put away the last of the clean dishes when Joyce, fully dressed, entered the kitchen.

"Thank goodness," Joyce said. "I was so afraid I was going to miss you."

"You almost did. I'm just about to walk out the door."

"Well, if it isn't too much trouble, I was wondering if I could catch a ride with you as far as the streetcar line on St. Charles Avenue. I have several appointments lined up today to look at rental places. I'm ready to go," she added. "I just need to grab my bag and my lunch."

"Your lunch?"

Stains of scarlet darkened Joyce's cheeks. "Well—ah—I—I hope you don't mind, but—but I took the liberty of making myself a sandwich last night before I went to bed, so all I'd have to do this morning was grab it out of the refrigerator."

"I don't mind, Joyce."

"Oh, good. And I can ride with you?"

"Sure, just hurry," Charlotte answered. She'd be willing to take Joyce to Timbuktu if it meant getting her out of her house sooner. "I'll be in the living room waiting."

"Great, and thanks!" Joyce did an about-face and headed toward the guest room.

After Joyce disappeared through the doorway, Charlotte went to the living room. But as she slipped on a sweater and picked up her purse, she couldn't help wondering how Joyce intended to pay for an apartment. As far as she knew, Joyce didn't have an income, and it was unlikely that she had any type of savings account. After what Joyce had pulled, it was for sure that neither Louis nor Stephen was giving her money.

So why don't you just ask her?

Charlotte shook her head. "Nope!" she whispered. "Not gonna happen." Besides, it was really none of her business.

At that moment, Joyce appeared in the living room doorway. "What's 'not gonna happen,' and who are you talking to?"

Eyeing the red, white, and blue-striped tote bag Joyce was carrying, Charlotte chose to ignore the first question and answered the second one, instead. "Just gathering wool, as they used to say. Talking to myself." She purposely turned to look at the cuckoo clock. "Good grief. Just look at the time. I've got to go."

"I saw you looking at my tote bag," Joyce said a few minutes later when Charlotte backed the van out of the driveway. "I'm sure you recognized it, but I'm hoping you won't mind me borrowing it to carry my sandwich and things, just for today. My purse isn't big enough to put the sandwich in. I found the tote bag in the bottom of the guest room closet and figured you didn't use it much."

"I don't mind, Joyce, but next time I would appreciate you asking ahead when you want to borrow something of mine."

When Joyce didn't say anything, Charlotte figured she'd ticked her off. She glanced sideways, but Joyce had turned her head and was staring out the passenger window, so all she saw was the back of Joyce's head.

Yep, she's ticked.

Well, that's just too bad, Charlotte decided. Joyce could just stay ticked off. Just because she'd agreed for Joyce to stay with her a couple of nights didn't give the woman the right to take whatever she wanted without the common courtesy of asking first.

Shame on you. Shame, shame. Since when did you become such a grumpy, stingy old woman? Some grandmother you're going to be.

For several seconds, Charlotte grappled with her conscience. Just the thought of her yet-unborn grandchild made her ashamed of how she'd been feeling and acting lately. Any day now, her daughter-in-law, Carol, would have the baby, and after years of longing, Charlotte would finally have a grandchild.

Charlotte decided to vow, right then and there, to try to do better, to try to be more charitable and thoughtful, the kind of grandmother that her grandchild would be proud of.

When Charlotte approached St. Charles Avenue, she flipped on the right blinker and pulled over near the curb. "There's a streetcar stop across the street," she said. As soon as she stopped the van, Joyce opened the door and climbed out.

"I probably won't be home till late this afternoon," she told Charlotte, her tone cold enough to freeze ice cubes. Without waiting for a response, she slammed the door and marched away.

No thank-you or even a kiss my butt. "Humph! So much for manners," Charlotte grumbled as she shoved the gear into drive. And for a second, Charlotte was glad that she hadn't apologized to Joyce, but only for a second. After all, what good was knowing the Golden Rule if you didn't live by it and use it?

Charlotte was a bit later than usual finishing up at Sandra Wellington's house. Out of the blue, Sandra had decided that she wanted Charlotte to clean out all of the bedroom closets.

Charlotte grinned to herself. She'd chosen to start with the

21

walk-in closet in the master bedroom first. By the time she'd finished making Sandra choose what to keep, what to throw away, and what to give to charity, Sandra had changed her mind about cleaning the rest.

The day had warmed up considerably, and was so beautiful, that on her way home Charlotte lowered the driver's and passenger windows almost halfway down to let fresh air into the van. If not for the errands she had to run later, it would have been the perfect day to sit out on the front porch and read one of the books that Bitsy had given her.

Except Joyce will probably be there.

Charlotte groaned. Maybe not . . . Maybe Joyce was still out apartment hunting. She could always hope.

That's not very nice.

"Great," she muttered. "Here we go again." All day long, she'd been fighting with her conscience over Joyce, and she was good and tired of it. All she wanted was a little peace and quiet. Surely wanting some alone time couldn't be so terrible, she thought as she turned onto Milan Street.

She was several houses down from her driveway when she noticed the black SUV parked across the street from her house. If she wasn't mistaken, the SUV was the same one that she'd seen the day before.

Just before she turned into her driveway, she got a good glimpse of the license plate and the driver. Sure enough, it was the very same car and the very same man sitting in the driver's seat.

Maybe it was time to find out just what he was up to, Charlotte decided as she shoved the gear into park and switched off the engine. Between having to worry about everyone that came to her door and putting up with Joyce, she'd just about had enough.

And if he's up to no good?

"Time to find that out too," she muttered.

Chapter 3

Though determined to find out what the man was up to, Charlotte decided it would be really careless not to take precautions. After digging in her purse, she finally located the small canister of pepper spray she always carried with her.

Now what? She couldn't just walk up to the SUV with the pepper spray in full view. But how to hide it? Then, out of the corner of her eye, she spotted her sweater. Though the morning had started out cool, the day had warmed up considerably, typical New Orleans weather. She didn't really need the sweater now, but it would help disguise the pepper spray.

Pepper spray in hand, she pulled on her sweater. After slipping the canister into the right pocket of her sweater, she dug out her cell phone and dropped it and her van keys into the left pocket. Then she climbed out of the van.

Casually, she slid both hands into the sweater pockets. With her right hand, she took a firm grip on the pepper spray and positioned her forefinger on the release button. That way, the pepper spray was hidden, but she could pull it out quickly if she needed it. Squaring her shoulders, she marched toward the van.

Though the man's head was bowed, as if he were reading something, Charlotte knew good and well that out of the corner of his eye, he could see her coming.

Once she'd crossed the street, she was careful to stop just out of reach by the driver's window.

"Ah, excuse me," she said.

When the man turned his head toward her, the first thing she noticed was his coal black hair and the really dark sunshades he wore. Then she noticed his face, at least the part she could see. His smooth skin was tanned, and he had a square jaw, with a shadow of a dark beard. He had an aquiline nose and a strong but rigid profile.

Young and handsome, she thought. Too bad he was hiding his eyes behind the sunglasses. You could tell a lot about a person just by looking into their eyes.

"I don't mean to be rude, young man, but I saw you sitting here yesterday morning. And now, here you are, back again. This is my neighborhood, and I want to know what you're doing."

The man sat up higher in the seat, and when he pulled off his sunglasses, she couldn't help noticing that his eyes were the most brilliant blue that she'd ever seen.

"Ma'am, I apologize if I alarmed you," he said smoothly.

Then, before Charlotte could even think about pulling out her pepper spray, he slipped a badge from the inside of a jacket pocket and held it up at the window. It could just as easily have been a gun, she thought, feeling a bit unnerved. If she hadn't been so upset about Joyce, she would have used the good sense God gave her and called the police first to check the man out, instead of . . .

"I'm a police detective."

His statement interrupted her thoughts and she breathed a sigh of relief. Though she tried to read what was written on the badge, he quickly slipped it back into his jacket pocket before she had enough time.

"If you don't mind," he continued, "I'd like to ask you a

24

few questions pertaining to an investigation that I'm working on."

The moment the detective said "investigation," to Charlotte's chagrin, Joyce's name was the first one that popped into her head. Her next thought was that she should be ashamed for automatically assuming such a thing about Joyce. But she consoled herself with the fact that after all of the trouble Joyce had caused, her automatic assumption was just a natural reaction.

Suddenly, the detective opened the door and stepped out of the SUV.

He was taller than she'd expected. Keeping a cautious eye on him, Charlotte took a step backward and her fingers tightened on the canister of pepper spray. He'd claimed to be a police detective, so why was she still so jumpy around him? Maybe she should ask to see his badge again.

"Is there somewhere we can talk?"

Still not quite trusting the so-called police detective, Charlotte hesitated. What if this was just a ploy to gain entrance to her house? *So he could do what?*

Immediately, all of the horror scenes from the television series *Criminal Minds* flashed through her head. For more years than she cared to remember, Charlotte had been both blessed and cursed by her imagination. Now she felt it was more a curse than a blessing.

She finally motioned toward her house. "It's turned out to be such a beautiful day—how about we sit on my front porch?"

And what if he says no?

Before she could think of an alternative, the detective nodded his head.

"Your front porch will be just fine, ma'am."

Once on the porch, and wanting to keep a healthy distance

between herself and the detective, Charlotte hurried over to the swing and sat down in the middle of it.

The detective gave her a knowing look, and without blinking an eye, he settled on the porch landing near the steps. Once seated, he stretched out his long legs and leaned back against the porch column. "I'm looking for a woman who's a key part of my investigation," he said as he pulled a pen and a small spiral notebook out of his jacket pocket.

Disappointment ripped through Charlotte. *Has to be Joyce,* she thought. Even with all the problems that Joyce had caused, in her heart of hearts, Charlotte had held out hope that for once, Joyce had told the truth and was trying to get her life back in order. "Guess leopards can't change their spots after all," she whispered.

The detective frowned. "Excuse me? What was that?"

Charlotte shook her head. "Nothing important." She sighed heavily. "I guess you're here to talk about Joyce Thibodeaux."

Though the detective didn't verbally confirm her suspicions, he jotted something down in the notebook, then said, "And what about Ms. Thibodeaux?"

"Well, for one, she's a very troubled woman." Charlotte motioned toward Louis's side of the double. "You see, she's my tenant's ex-wife. You might have heard of him," she quickly added. "His name is Louis—Louis Thibodeaux. He's a retired detective with the NOPD."

Noticing the blank look on the detective's face, Charlotte waved her hand. "Never mind. Anyway, it's a long story, and to make a long story short, Louis works for Lagniappe Security, and after one of his trips to California, he brought Joyce home with him. He'd gone looking for Joyce to tell her about their new grandchild, but when he found her in a homeless shelter, she claimed that she was dying from cirrhosis of the liver. Feeling sorry for her, he persuaded her to come back to New

Orleans. Then, a few weeks later, Louis learned that all that was wrong with Joyce was that she was an alcoholic. After that, he had her committed to a substance abuse program. And now she's out."

"Do you know where she's staying?"

For reasons Charlotte wasn't sure of, she found herself reluctant to tell the detective that Joyce was staying with her. Instead of answering his question, she hedged. "Not with Louis, that's for sure. He said that he was done with her. And besides, he's out of town at the moment, anyway."

Suddenly, it occurred to Charlotte that Joyce could show up at any minute, and if Joyce did happen to show up, then the detective would know that she hadn't been completely truthful about Joyce's whereabouts. Of course Joyce had said that she would be gone most of the day, but Joyce said a lot of things that weren't true. Time to end the interview and get rid of the detective.

"I've told you everything I know." Charlotte stood, hoping that the detective would cooperate. *Liar, liar, pants on fire . . .* Ignoring the voice of her conscience, Charlotte continued, "So—if you don't mind, I have some chores I have to get done and some errands to run."

The detective hesitated, then finally nodded. "You've been very helpful, ma'am, and I appreciate the information," he said as he pocketed the pen and notebook and stood.

As he turned and started down the steps, it suddenly occurred to Charlotte that in every episode of *Law & Order* that she'd watched, the detective always offered his business card to the person he was interviewing, just in case they thought of something to tell him later. Come to think of it, he never had even told her his name.

"Ah, excuse me," she called out. "Do you have a card? You know—in case I think of something else to tell you?"

He stopped and threw her an amused look over his shoulder. "Sorry, I'm all out of cards, but I'll be back in touch again."

Unsure whether it was his smug tone of voice or the look on his face, Charlotte felt her temper spike. "Well, do you at least have a name?" she called out.

That brought him up short. A second later, when he turned to face her, his expression was tight with strain. "Yes, I have a name," he said impatiently. "Name's Aubrey Hamilton. Now, is there anything else?"

"No, nothing else," she answered, taken aback by his tone.

Once inside her house, Charlotte went straight to her desk and wrote down the name *Aubrey Hamilton* on the desk pad. Beside the name, she wrote *police detective*, followed by several question marks. Maybe she'd give Judith a call about Mr. Aubrey Hamilton. Having a niece who was an NOPD detective had its advantages. If Judith didn't know him, she had ways of finding out about him.

Thoughts of her niece reminded Charlotte of one of the errands she needed to run that afternoon, and she needed to get it done before the evening workday traffic.

It wasn't that often that Charlotte went down into the French Quarter. For one thing, finding a parking spot could be a real pain, depending on what event was going on or what convention happened to be in town at the time. Besides which, Charlotte considered the parking-lot fees to be outrageous.

But Madeline's birthday was coming up, and Charlotte had learned through Judith that there was a particular earring-and-necklace set that Madeline had admired in a small jewelry shop on St. Peter Street. Judith had already bought the necklace for her mother and had suggested that Charlotte might want to buy the earrings to match. Madeline could be picky and was hard to buy for, and for once, Charlotte was relieved to be able to get her sister something she knew Madeline really wanted.

Since the shop wasn't but a few blocks down St. Peter, Charlotte decided to park in a parking lot near Jackson Brewery and walk from there. As she walked along the sidewalk that ran in front of the huge Jackson Brewery mall, she eyed the window displays from the shops inside.

When she passed a particular display, her footsteps slowed, and she stopped to stare wistfully at one of the mannequins that was decked out in a beautiful sky blue sweater and matching slacks.

Sighing longingly, she shook her head. "Yeah, right," she murmured, and regretfully turned away and crossed over to St. Peter Street. There were only a few weeks year-round in New Orleans when the temperature got low enough to even wear a sweater, and since she already had a drawer full of nice sweaters, buying yet another one wasn't the least bit practical.

Glancing around as she walked along Jackson Square, she was glad to see that the artists were back at their usual spots along the fence surrounding the Square. It was also good to see that the mimes and the ragtag street musicians had finally returned as well. Everything seemed almost normal again.

She chuckled beneath her breath when she passed a mime standing statue still, his face painted to look like a clown's. Every time she saw a mime, the urge to stick out her tongue or make faces at him—anything to make him smile or laugh— would come over her.

"You're weird, Charlotte," she murmured to herself, and kept walking. The farther she walked up St. Peter, the more she began to notice that something was different. For one, the streets were fairly clean, cleaner than she'd ever seen them. Even before Hurricane Katrina, the Quarter had never been all that clean, and afterward, it was worse . . . until now.

She'd heard talk about the cleanup in the Quarter, and she'd read an article about it in the *Times-Picayune*, but this was one case where seeing was believing. The *TP* article had given most of the credit to a new French Quarter cleanup company, SDT Waste and Debris Services, and to its company president, a young entrepreneur who also owned a couple of hotels in the French Quarter as well.

Charlotte smiled. One thing she definitely remembered about the article was how handsome the young man was. Why, people, mostly women, even vied for his autograph. Even his own mother was amazed at all the attention her good-looking son the garbageman was receiving.

By the time that Charlotte finally reached the quaint jewelry shop, she was out of breath, a harsh reminder that she'd been neglecting her daily walking routine of late.

It took a few minutes of searching through the enclosed glass jewelry case, but Charlotte finally spotted a pair of earrings that looked similar to the necklace Judith had bought.

"May I help you?" the sales clerk asked.

"I hope so," Charlotte told her. "My niece, Judith Monroe, bought her mother a necklace for her birthday. I was hoping to buy the earrings that matched the necklace." She tapped her finger on the glass case right above the earrings. "I think those are the ones that match."

"There's one way to be certain," the young woman said as she stepped over to a computer. Her fingers flew over the keyboard, and within just moments, she smiled. "You're absolutely right," she told Charlotte as she turned away from the computer. "The earrings you picked out are the match to the necklace."

Once Charlotte had paid for the earrings, she tucked the small jewelry sack inside her purse, then left the shop. When Charlotte approached the first cross street, she had to wait for a line of cars to drive past. When the last of the cars drove by, Charlotte glanced to her right to make sure the street was clear. Just then, a familiar-looking woman emerged from inside a shop across the street. Charlotte froze and narrowed her eyes.

At first, she thought that surely Joyce had seen her—she looked straight at her—but when she raised her hand to wave, Joyce turned away and hurried on down the street in the opposite direction.

"Guess she didn't see me," Charlotte muttered as she watched Joyce disappear around the corner. But why the hurry? she wondered. And unless her eyes deceived her, everything about Joyce's body language screamed guilt. But guilt about what?

There you go again. Can't ever give the poor woman a break.

Now even more curious, Charlotte ignored the aggravating voice in her head and glanced back at the shop that Joyce had come out of. When she read the sign above the door, P & J PAWNSHOP, a sinking feeling settled in the pit of her stomach.

A pawnshop! And a seedy-looking one at that.

Suddenly, a vision from earlier that morning popped into Charlotte's head . . . Joyce and the tote bag she'd borrowed.

At the time, Charlotte had been more concerned that Joyce had "borrowed" the bag without asking, but now she wondered if maybe Joyce had needed it for more than just carrying her lunch.

As far as she knew, Joyce had nothing of real value, and renting an apartment cost money, so that left just one thing. Charlotte didn't want to think the worst, but she couldn't seem to tame her suspicious nature when it came to Joyce. All of her instincts were telling her it was highly possible that Joyce had "borrowed" something else from her without asking—something of value that she could pawn for money.

Charlotte shook her head and heaved a big sigh of frustration. There was only one way to find out.

After looking to her right again and seeing that the coast was clear, Charlotte stepped off the curb and crossed the street to the shop.

As she opened the front door of the shop, a bell jingled, announcing her entry. For several moments, Charlotte simply stood, her gaze taking in the crowded shop. Unlike on Royal Street, where the shops were well kept and contained beautiful antiques, the pawnshop was filthy. Most of the stuff in it looked like the kind of junk that would have been more suited to a flea market. Already, she felt the need for a bath, just being in the place.

Making sure she didn't brush up against anything, Charlotte chose the path of least resistance as she made her way to a glass display counter. Behind the counter stood a rumpled, unshaven man, who didn't look in much better shape than his dirty shop. Judging by the gray in his greasy-looking dark hair and the deep lines on his face, Charlotte figured the man was either in his late forties or early fifties.

"Got something to pawn, or are you buying?" he asked, his tone surly.

"Neither," Charlotte told him, "but I have a question. That woman who just left is my houseguest, and I'm afraid that she's stolen something of mine and pawned it."

The man narrowed his eyes and shrugged. "Not my problem, lady. That's between you and your"—he paused a moment—" 'houseguest.' " He said it like it was a dirty word.

Charlotte thought it was quite revealing that the one thing he didn't suggest was reporting the incident to the police. "Well, could you at least tell me if she pawned something?"

He squinted his eyes at her. "Look, lady, I've already told you that none of this is my concern, so stop asking."

"It is your concern if you're selling stolen property," she shot back.

His expression turned to stone. "Lady, read my lips. Not. My. Problem." Then, like Jekyll and Hyde, his expression softened, and although it seemed a bit forced, he grinned. "Besides, even us lowly pawnbrokers have a code of honor and confidentiality."

Yeah, right, she thought, quickly scanning the display case full of cheap-looking jewelry for anything that looked remotely familiar. Seeing nothing, she did an about-face and headed for the front door. "Thanks for nothing," she called over her shoulder.

Not expecting a response, she didn't wait for one as she exited the shop and pulled the door closed with more force than necessary.

" 'Not my problem,' " she mimicked beneath her breath as she marched down St. Peter. "What a jerk!" she grumbled.

By the time Charlotte walked all the way back to her car, she was too tired to be angry any longer. All she wanted was to go home, prop her feet up, and have a nice cup of coffee. And like Miss Scarlett O'Hara in *Gone With the Wind,* she'd think about everything tomorrow.

As Charlotte pulled into her driveway, she prayed that Joyce hadn't returned yet. Though she'd tried to put Joyce— and the problems she presented—out of her mind, all during the drive home she'd thought about the situation and tried to decide how she was going to handle it. So far, no miracle solution had presented itself.

Once Charlotte parked the van, she headed for the porch. As she climbed the steps, a noise reached her ears, a noise that sounded suspiciously like it was coming from inside her house. She had either left the television on, a burglar was stealing her blind, or Joyce was inside.

But how had she gotten inside without a key?

Charlotte sighed. Had she ever told Joyce about the spare key hidden beneath the ceramic frog in the front flowerbed? She couldn't remember doing so, but she must have. Since she was fairly sure that she hadn't left the television on, and no burglar worth his salt would take the time to watch TV in the middle of burglarizing a house, the intruder had to be Joyce.

Chapter 4

Following her instincts, Charlotte first tried opening the front door without using her key. Sure enough, just as she'd suspected, Joyce hadn't bothered locking it.

Careless. Careless and selfish. . . . But look on the bright side. Maybe Joyce found somewhere else to live.

"Yeah, and maybe pigs fly too," she grumbled.

With a shake of her head, Charlotte stepped inside the living room. When she saw Joyce sprawled on her sofa, sipping a cup of what smelled like freshly brewed coffee, it took every ounce of willpower that Charlotte could muster to hold on to her temper.

Joyce glanced Charlotte's way. "Hey, Charlotte." She held out her coffee cup as if she were making a toast. "Finally home from the trenches, huh?"

Charlotte chose not to answer, but asked a question of her own. "How was the apartment hunting?"

"I found a couple of possibilities."

Charlotte motioned toward Joyce's coffee cup. "Is there any more of that left?"

"Oh, sure. Help yourself. I always make a full pot."

"Help yourself"? In my own house, she's telling me to help myself to my own coffee?

Before Charlotte said something that she would regret, she forced a tight-lipped smile and hurried to the kitchen. A few minutes later, armed with her own cup of coffee and her temper once again relegated to the simmering level, Charlotte settled in the chair opposite the sofa. For several minutes, she tried to relax and ignore Joyce and the television while she quietly sipped her coffee.

But *trying* to ignore Joyce and being able to do it were two different things. There was just no way she could stop thinking about the police detective casing out her house or the pawnshop incident. Regardless of what the ill-mannered shopkeeper had said, she simply couldn't shake the feeling that Joyce had stolen something of hers and pawned it.

"We need to talk a minute," she finally told Joyce.

Joyce glanced at Charlotte and shrugged. "So talk," she said, turning her attention back to the television.

Charlotte glared at the other woman, and forced herself to silently count to ten. She tried once more. "I think you'll want to give what I've got to say your full attention. Could you please turn off the TV?"

Joyce rolled her eyes. Then, with exaggerated gestures, she held out the remote and pressed the power switch. "Is that better? Satisfied now?"

Biting back the stinging retort that was on the tip of her tongue, Charlotte took a deep breath and let it out slowly. Then, between gritted teeth, she said, "When I left for work yesterday morning, I notice a man sitting in a black SUV parked across the street. Well, he was there again today, so I decided to see what he was up to. Come to find out, he's a police detective."

Charlotte paused for a reaction from Joyce, but nothing in her expression gave Charlotte a clue as to what was going on in Joyce's head. "Aren't you the least bit curious as to why a police detective would be parked in front of my house?"

"No!" Joyce snapped, her tone defiant. "Why should I be?"

"You really don't know?"

"No, Charlotte, I really don't know," she drawled mockingly, "but I'm sure you're going to tell me."

Charlotte stiffened and saw red. "You've got that right," she shot back. "For your information, he was here looking for you. He said it had to do with an ongoing investigation."

Stone-faced, Joyce shook her head in denial. "That's ridiculous," she said evenly. "There's no reason for the police to be looking for me. No reason at all."

"And you don't know a detective by the name of Aubrey Hamilton?"

Charlotte could have sworn that for just the briefest of moments, something akin to fear flashed in Joyce's eyes, but then Joyce shook her head again and averted her gaze.

"No, I don't." Joyce stared at her hands as she picked her fingernails.

It was just a gut instinct, but Charlotte was certain that Joyce was lying through her pearly whites. For one thing, Joyce wouldn't look her in the eye. But other than outright calling her a liar to her face, and with no way to prove she was lying, there was nothing Charlotte could do about it . . . at least not for now.

Charlotte stood. "How do you feel about gumbo for supper? I've got some frozen and it won't take long to thaw it out."

"If it tastes as good as what you brought me that time when I was staying at Louis's place, then *yum-yum*. Is there anything that I can do to help?"

Charlotte was so shocked that it took a while for her to find her voice. That Joyce even remembered the incident—never mind acknowledging it—was totally unexpected. "Why, yes—yes, of course. You can cut up a salad while I put some rice on to cook."

Charlotte waited until after they had eaten and were cleaning up the kitchen before bringing up the pawnshop incident. She had just put the last of the dirty dishes inside the dishwasher when, as casually as she could, she said, "One of the apartments that you're considering must be in the French Quarter."

Joyce was wiping off the table, but paused. "No, not really. I can't afford any of those apartments." She resumed wiping the table.

"That's odd," Charlotte said, still striving for a casual, non-confrontational tone, "I could have sworn that I saw you this afternoon. It was right off St. Peter Street."

Joyce laughed, but Charlotte could tell it was forced and as fake as a three-dollar bill.

Joyce shook her head. "Nope. Sorry, that wasn't me. Must have been my double—you do know, they say that everyone has one. Besides, I've been right here since noon."

Liar, Charlotte wanted to scream, but when she opened her mouth to confront Joyce, she made a split-second decision against confronting her and closed it. For one thing, she'd had a long day and she was tired—not really up to arguing or confronting anyone. Besides, at this point, even if she did confront her, and Joyce finally admitted she had been at the pawnshop, there was no way that Joyce was going to admit she'd stolen anything. Better to wait until she had some proof. And better to wait until she was rested up.

With a huge yawn that wasn't faked, Charlotte said, "As soon as I fix the coffeepot, I think I'll go to bed and read myself to sleep. Who knows, since I'm off tomorrow, I might even actually sleep late in the morning." Charlotte didn't expect a response, but she'd wanted to let Joyce know not to disturb her in the morning.

Joyce's response was a shrug of indifference, and then she dropped the dishrag into the sink and headed for the living room.

Charlotte stared at the wadded-up, dirty dishrag. The least Joyce could have done was rinse it out and drape it across the edge of the sink to dry so that it wouldn't sour overnight.

Using the tips of her forefinger and thumb, Charlotte gingerly picked up the dishrag and took it to the laundry room. Back in the kitchen, as Charlotte filled the coffeemaker with water, she heard the sound of the television. Rolling her eyes, she spooned coffee into the basket and set the timer.

Once in her bedroom, Charlotte closed the door, then stood staring at the doorknob for several minutes, her thoughts on the lies that Joyce had told her.

Charlotte hated being so suspicious of every little thing, and she hated not feeling safe in her own home, but over the years, she'd learned to trust her instincts. She'd also learned that it was foolish not to take precautions. The one thing that she didn't want was to wake up in the middle of the night and find Joyce burgling her bedroom, or worse. At this instant, her instincts were screaming at her, *Better to be safe than sorry. Just do it.*

I didn't lock the door last night, she silently argued.

But you should have.

"Okay, okay," she muttered as she locked the door. Then, as an added safeguard, she wedged the extra kitchen chair that she always kept in her bedroom beneath the doorknob.

When Charlotte awoke on Thursday morning, she allowed herself the luxury of simply lying in bed a few minutes, and doing nothing more than staring up at the ceiling. After months of getting harangued by her son, Hank, to cut back her hours, she had finally given in and decided to take Thursdays off, as well as the weekends. Hank would have preferred that she retire, but Charlotte had put her foot down and flat-out refused.

"Humph, that's like 'the pot calling the kettle black,' " she grumbled. Her son should think about taking his own advice and cutting back, especially considering all the hours that he'd been working lately.

She might not be an important surgeon like her son, but she liked what she did for a living and she was good at it. As long as she was physically able to continue working, and as long as she enjoyed it, she couldn't see the sense in retiring . . . at least not yet.

A slow smile pulled at Charlotte's lips. Of course once her little grandbaby was born, she might have to rethink her position on the matter of retiring, especially if her daughter-in-law, Carol, decided to resume her nursing career and needed help with the baby. And who knows? Maybe Hank *would* consider cutting back his hours once the baby was born.

Spotting the beginnings of a cobweb in the corner near the window, Charlotte made a mental note to dust the edges of the ceiling when she did her weekly cleaning on Saturday. Then her gaze slid to the door. The sight of the chair wedged beneath the doorknob was an unpleasant reminder that she wasn't alone in the house.

Hmm, maybe she would confront Joyce today about all of the lies she'd told. Or even better, maybe she would work up enough courage to tell her she had to find another place to stay.

After a trip to the bathroom, Charlotte's nose detected the scent of freshly brewed coffee, and like a cat drawn to catnip, she headed for the kitchen. Her thoughts still on the situation with Joyce, she finally decided that she would give Joyce one more day to find her own place, and if she hadn't found somewhere else to live by then . . .

Charlotte sighed and shook her head. Who was she kidding? She couldn't just throw Joyce out on the street. She walked over to the cabinet and poured herself a cup of coffee. No, she couldn't throw her out on the street, but she could speed Joyce's departure by helping her find somewhere else to live.

With her thoughts occupied by possible places that Joyce could live, Charlotte didn't notice the piece of paper on the kitchen table until she sat down right in front of it.

"If it had been a snake, it would have bit you," she whispered as she leaned forward and read the scrawling handwriting on the piece of paper. It was a brief note from Joyce letting Charlotte know that she had left early due to an appointment to look at an apartment.

"At least she had the decency not to wake me," Charlotte muttered, her eyes straying to the Thursday *Times-Picayune* folded neatly beside the note. That Joyce had even thought to bring in the newspaper was another surprise. "Probably so she could look at the rental ads," Charlotte muttered again.

For Pete's sake, Charlotte, stop being so distrustful and such a cynic about everything.

Not liking what her conscience was telling her, Charlotte sipped her coffee. She didn't like being distrustful or cynical. She didn't used to be that way. So was it part of getting older, or was it from being around Joyce?

Charlotte stared out the window as she finished her coffee. She didn't have an answer, but, cynic or not, she couldn't shake the feeling that Joyce was stealing from her. With a sigh, she set down her cup. There was only one way to know for sure.

Charlotte didn't have a lot of valuables, just a few nice

pieces of jewelry that she'd inherited from her mother, a gold watch that had belonged to her father, and some silverware. She kept most of her valuables scattered in little hidy-holes throughout her house. That way, if a thief found one place, he might think that was all there was and leave the rest alone.

"Auntie, you really should get a nice strong safe. . . ."

Her niece's words played through her mind as she headed for the first hiding place, a bedside-table drawer in her bedroom that she'd lined with velvet.

When she first opened the drawer, she thought that her eyes were playing tricks on her, so she pulled it completely free from the table and set it on top of the bed to get a better look.

"Oh, no," she groaned.

Her mother's rings were there, and her own diamond pendant necklace was still there, along with her pearls, but where was her father's gold watch?

That watch is just the sort of thing that might bring a good price at a pawnshop. But are you sure that you put the watch in the drawer?

Charlotte's eyes squinted in thought as she searched her memory. She was 100 percent sure that she'd placed the watch in the drawer. . . . Well, almost 100 percent, but just to satisfy the tiny doubt niggling in the back of her mind, she quickly checked the shoebox in the bottom corner of her closet, where she'd stashed most of the silverware. Not finding the watch there either, and with just one last place to check, Charlotte headed for the guest room.

At the closed door, she hesitated. It was her house, so why did she feel like *she* was the intruder if she entered the room and looked around, almost like she was invading Joyce's privacy?

After a moment, she finally grabbed the doorknob. "Get

over it and just do it!" she retorted as she twisted the door-knob and shoved open the door.

But in the doorway, she froze, her eyes wide with disbelief. "What a pig," she whispered when she finally found her voice.

Joyce hadn't bothered making her bed, there were clothes on the floor, the closet door was standing wide open, the trash basket was so full that wadded tissues had fallen on the floor around it, and a dirty plate and glass . . .

"Oh, no!" Charlotte rushed over to the beautiful oak night table that her grandfather had built for her mother as a wed-ding gift. She snatched up the plate and the glass. Sure enough, beneath the glass was a huge white water ring.

Charlotte groaned. If only she'd known ahead of time just how carelessly Joyce would treat her things, she would have covered the tabletop with a scarf or hand towel, anything to keep Joyce from ruining the finish of the beautiful old table.

Plate and glass in hand, Charlotte hurried to the kitchen. After putting the dishes in the sink, she took out her special polishing compound and a clean polishing cloth from beneath the sink cabinet, then hurried back to the bedroom.

Grumbling to herself, she spread the compound and began rubbing it into the wood with the cloth. Though the water ring was slowly disappearing, Charlotte frowned when she saw the indentation in the wood.

"What on earth?" she exclaimed, staring at what appeared to be writing of some kind. Charlotte rubbed harder, but the indentation didn't go away.

Then it came to her. As quick as the sting of a bee, Char-lotte realized what she was looking at. Joyce had to have been using a ballpoint pen to write notes on the table, and of course it never would have occurred to her to put something under the paper to protect the wood. But what kind of notes?

Charlotte squinted and turned her head sideways. Sure enough, she could even make out some of the words. There was an address on St. Peter Street.

"Bet it's the pawnshop," she murmured.

Following the address, there was a dash, and after the dash, Joyce had written, *bughouse bluebird.*

"What the devil does that mean?" Charlotte murmured. "That can't be right." But no matter which way she turned her head, or how much she squinted her eyes, she still came up with the same words. But there was more—yet another address and another dash, then the word *daisy.*

For long minutes, Charlotte continued staring at the writing. What could it mean? she wondered. And what on earth was Joyce up to now?

There was one thing for sure—just standing there and staring at the writing wasn't going to give her any answers. On the contrary, the note etched into the tabletop, along with the missing watch, and Joyce's lies about being at the pawnshop, just fueled more questions.

Still thinking about her dilemma, and still hoping to find her father's watch, Charlotte checked the last hiding place, a box full of more silver, which was shoved under the bed.

She knelt beside the bed, reached beneath it, and pulled out the small box. One look inside the velvet bag in the box, and disappointment, along with a sense of loss, filled her. The watch wasn't there. She had been keeping the watch to give to Hank at the birth of his first child, and now it was gone, probably forever. . . .

After swallowing the lump lodged in her throat, Charlotte took a deep breath and sighed. Sitting there, feeling sorry for herself, wasn't doing anyone any good. What she needed was to find out what was going on.

She dropped the bag back inside the box, replaced the lid

on the box, and then she pushed it back beneath the bed. She dusted off her hands. Yep, it was high time she did some checking up on Ms. Joyce Thibodeaux. *Past time*, a little voice whispered in her head.

"Yeah, yeah," Charlotte grumbled, grabbing the edge of the bed for support. But as Charlotte got to her feet, a wave of weakness washed over her. She grabbed hold of the bedpost to steady herself. After a bit, she felt somewhat better. Even so, the incident was a stark reminder that in her haste to find the watch, she'd completely forgotten about breakfast.

As a diabetic, Charlotte knew she needed to eat regular balanced meals, and she also knew that stress wasn't good for her.

"Oh, well," she muttered, the two small words heavy with sarcasm as she walked carefully out of the room and headed for the kitchen. There wasn't a whole lot she could do about the present stress in her life, but she could do something about eating.

In the kitchen, Charlotte fixed herself a bowl of oatmeal and a piece of toast. She was almost finished eating when out of nowhere an image of Aubrey Hamilton popped into her head. Her expression stilled and grew serious. She'd wondered how to go about checking up on Joyce, and now she knew. At this point in time, who better to ask than a police detective?

Chapter 5

"Hello, I'd like to speak to one of your detectives. His name is Aubrey Hamilton."

"Who's calling, please?" a gruff voice asked.

"Charlotte LaRue."

"One moment, please."

While Charlotte waited, she drummed her fingers against the desktop. After giving the matter some thought, she'd decided to start calling all of the district police stations, starting with the Sixth, until she located Aubrey Hamilton.

"Ms. LaRue." The gruff voice was back. "You must have us mixed up with another district. We don't have a Detective Aubrey Hamilton working in the Sixth. Can someone else help you?"

"No—no, thanks." Charlotte quickly hung up the receiver.

After calling all eight district stations in the city, Charlotte finally gave up an hour later. According to the police, they didn't have a detective by the name of Aubrey Hamilton.

Still sitting at her desk, Charlotte tried to recall the conversation she'd had with Hamilton. He hadn't said that he worked in New Orleans, but then he hadn't said a whole lot. Like a babbling ninny, she'd done most of the talking. Come to think of it, she'd almost had to force him to give her a name, and she never did get a good look at his badge.

"Badge, smadge," she muttered. He might not even be a police detective. Nowadays an authentic-looking badge could be bought at almost any costume shop.

After a minute passed, Charlotte made up her mind. Picking up the phone receiver, she dialed her niece Judith's number. After six rings, Judith's voice mail picked up.

"Detective Monroe. Leave a message."

Disappointed that she would have to leave a message, Charlotte hesitated, then said, "Hi, hon. Aunt Charlotte here. Could you please give me a call when you get a chance? I need some information about one of your fellow detectives. Love you. Bye."

The second Charlotte hung up the receiver, she regretted leaving the message. "Hindsight's a wonderful thing," she grumbled, her voice dripping with sarcasm.

Judith would insist on knowing why Charlotte was interested in Aubrey Hamilton in the first place, and after Charlotte had explained it all, she'd have to listen to Judith lecture her about not getting involved in police business.

"Well, it's not police business yet," Charlotte argued, her words directed at Sweety Boy. Of course the little bird ignored her. "Humph! A lot of help you are. So, now what?"

She glanced down at her pajamas. "Get dressed—then decide," she muttered.

By the time she'd dressed, Charlotte had made up her mind that the only thing left was to return to the pawnshop. Surely, if Joyce had pawned the watch, the jerk that owned the shop would have it on display by now . . . unless someone else had already bought it.

The thought of someone else with her father's watch spurred a sense of urgency she hadn't felt before. Charlotte grabbed her purse and headed for the front door. If she had to, she'd buy it back, if for no other reason than to keep someone else from buying it. And if someone else had already bought it, she'd track that person down and buy it back.

Charlotte parked once again near Jackson Brewery. The sun was out, and the temperature had warmed considerably. Somewhere in the distance, a saxophone was belting out "When the Saints Go Marching In," reminding Charlotte of the wonderful season that the Saints football team was having.

The blue sweater and slacks were still on display in the window when she passed by in front of the Jackson Brewery building, and Charlotte sighed.

Keep walking. You're not here to shop, and you do not need another sweater.

After crossing Decatur, she sidestepped around a horse and buggy waiting for their next tourist fare, then hurried up St. Peter.

A few minutes later, when Charlotte approached the pawnshop, her footsteps slowed, and dread settled in the pit of her stomach. Giving herself a silent pep talk, she finally took a deep breath, straightened her shoulders, and went inside. Just like the first time she'd entered the shop, the bell above the door jingled, announcing her arrival.

Across the room, she immediately spotted the same rumpled, unshaven man that she'd seen the day before. Except for a glance her way, he ignored her and continued polishing what appeared to be a badly tarnished silver tray.

Making sure that she didn't brush up against anything, Charlotte ignored the man as well as she made her way to the far end of the glass display case.

As she scanned the contents of the display case, she was glad for once to be ignored by store personnel, especially since this particular one had been such a jerk. Unless she spotted the watch, she had no intention of even speaking to the man.

Halfway down the case, Charlotte's heartbeat suddenly quickened. Though she couldn't be sure without taking a closer look, she was almost positive that the watch prominently displayed against a black velvet cloth was hers. And she was equally sure that it hadn't been displayed when she was there the day before.

Charlotte cleared her throat to get the shopkeeper's attention. "I'd like to look at this watch, please."

The man shook his head. "Won't do any good. It's sold."

Charlotte went rigid and blood roared in her ears. "I still want to look at it," she retorted, her tone edged with steel.

"Nope." The man shook his head.

"Why not?" Charlotte shot back.

"Lady, are you deaf? I said it's already sold."

"And I said that I still want to look at it." She paused a second, then said, "Unless there's some reason you don't want me to look at it. I told you yesterday that I suspected my house-guest of stealing from me and pawning what she'd stolen, and that watch"—she tapped the glass case above the watch—"that watch is mine." Charlotte glared at him. "Or maybe you'd rather cooperate with the police, instead. I don't think they condone selling stolen merchandise."

Before Charlotte realized what the man was doing, he reached beneath the counter and pulled out one of the biggest handguns that Charlotte had ever seen. His unblinking eyes never left her as he placed the weapon on the counter in front of him. Though he wasn't holding the gun in a menacing way, he rested his hand on the butt of it. "Lady, I would advise you to mind your own business and stay away from the police."

Though Charlotte's heart was pounding like a wild thing, it

was on the tip of her tongue to tell him that this was her business.

Just keep your mouth shut and get out of here now!

Good advice, she thought as she eased a step backward.

"You don't really want to tangle with me," the man warned. "And the last thing you want is to cause me any trouble." He cocked his head to one side and narrowed his eyes. "Understand?"

When Charlotte didn't answer, but continued staring at him, he laughed harshly. "You best understand. You'd best go about your business and keep your mouth shut."

Again good advice, she decided, at least for now. Commanding her legs to move, Charlotte slowly backed away from the counter. Again the man laughed.

She was almost to the door when he reached over with his free hand and snagged the same cloth that he'd been using earlier to polish the silver tray.

Now what? she thought.

With a knowing smile, and as if that had been his purpose all along, the man picked up the gun and began polishing it. Come to think of it, had that been his purpose all along? Had she once again let her imagination get the best of her?

There was no way to know for sure, but she wasn't sticking around to find out, she decided as she turned and fled out the door. Still a bit shaken, with her thoughts on what had just happened, Charlotte took her time walking down St. Peter.

That watch was her father's watch—of that she had no doubt. She was especially sure after seeing how the jerk had acted. Thus, the reason he didn't want her looking at it any closer. Charlotte fumed. Why, she'd even be willing to bet it wasn't really sold.

Charlotte was almost to the end of the block when she saw

an attractive young woman step away from a store window and head in her direction. As the woman drew closer, Charlotte got the distinct impression that the woman somehow knew her.

"Ah, excuse me, ma'am," the woman called out, then smiled.

Charlotte stopped. "Are you talking to me?"

The woman nodded. "I might be able to help you."

"Help me?" Charlotte narrowed distrustful eyes, and wondered if after being threatened with a gun, she was now going to have to deal with a beggar. Funny, though, the woman didn't look like a beggar.

Again the woman nodded. "I know this sounds weird, but I was in the pawnshop yesterday when you came in. No one knew I was in there, though, because I came in with a small group, but when my friends left, I stayed behind to look at an old typewriter. And of course the place is so full of stuff, neither you nor Roy—that's the owner's name, Roy Price—saw me. And after I heard your conversation with Roy, I sure didn't want him to know I was in there, so I kind of hid in the corner until you left and Roy went in the back room.

"Anyway," she continued, "what I wanted to tell you was that everyone in the Quarter knows that Roy fences stolen stuff on a regular basis—everybody but the police—especially jewelry and other small things. It's just that he's so intimidating that no one will report him to the cops. After I heard the way that you talked back to him, I figured you might be someone he couldn't intimidate."

Ha! Charlotte thought. *You should have seen me shaking like a leaf in there a few minutes ago.* "Er, ah, well, I haven't quite made up my mind about that yet," Charlotte responded.

The young woman's face collapsed with disappointment. "You're not going to report this to the police?"

"And the last thing you want is to cause me any trouble."

Recalling Roy's implied threat, Charlotte shivered. Was he bluffing? Was his threat simply an intimidation tactic? Probably, she decided. An intimidation tactic that worked. At least on her it had worked, since she'd hightailed it out of there.

"Like I said," Charlotte told the woman, "I haven't made up my mind about that yet."

"Guess I can't really blame you, not when no one else will do anything either. But listen, you probably don't know this, but you might have more luck on Friday. Roy's partner works on Fridays and the weekends, and since she's never seen you, you might have better luck looking for your property then."

"Thanks, I'll keep that in mind. And if you don't mind me asking, why are you so interested in getting Roy busted?"

" 'Cause he deserves to get busted," she retorted, her tone full of venom. "I gotta run now. Good luck!"

With that, she turned and hurried up the street, leaving Charlotte shaking her head in bewilderment.

By the time Charlotte parked the van in her driveway, she'd made up her mind. She'd confront Joyce about the watch first. If Joyce denied stealing the watch, then she'd definitely talk to Judith about Joyce and Roy Price.

Charlotte climbed the steps to the porch, but even from outside, she could hear a TV blaring loud enough to wake the dead. Since Louis was still out of town, it had to be coming from her half of the double.

The loud TV, plus the fact that once again Joyce had neglected to lock the front door, was aggravating enough. Then Charlotte entered the living room, and the first thing she saw was Joyce sprawled on the sofa. When Charlotte spied several empty beer bottles on the coffee table, her temper flared.

Dropping her purse on a nearby chair, Charlotte stalked over to the coffee table, snatched up the TV clicker, and turned off the television.

"Hey, I was watching that!"

"Too bad," Charlotte retorted. Dropping the clicker on the table, she picked up an empty beer bottle, instead, and glared down at Joyce. "What's the meaning of this?" she demanded.

Joyce glared right back at her and struggled to sit up. "So I had a few beers. So what?"

Barely able to control her fury, Charlotte threw Joyce's words back at her. " 'So what'? 'So what'! Is that all you've got to say?" She slammed the beer bottle back onto the table.

A nasty smile spread across Joyce's lips, and clasping her hands together, she lifted them up to Charlotte. In a mocking voice edged with sarcasm, she said, "Oh, please, Miss Charlotte, please forgive me. I didn't mean to do anything wrong."

For a second, Charlotte wanted to slap her silly, or at the least, shake her until her teeth rattled. "Yeah, right, Joyce," she shot back, her voice rising. "And I guess you didn't mean to steal my father's watch either, did you?"

Joyce dropped her hands and her expression clouded with anger. "You're accusing me of stealing from you?" she yelled. "That's what this is about?"

Charlotte gave a decisive nod. "You've got that right," she yelled right back. "You stole my father's watch and hocked it, and now I want you out of my house."

Joyce stumbled to her feet, and Charlotte stepped back out of arm's reach. "You're a lying hypocrite," Joyce screamed. "That's not what this is about." Joyce pointed an accusing finger at Charlotte. "You just want me out before Louis comes home. And don't you dare try to deny it, because I was here when he called and left a message on your machine to tell you he'd be coming home Friday. And don't bother checking the machine. I erased his message. This isn't about some stupid watch. It's all about Louis. You just want me out of the way before he gets back, so you can have him all to yourself!"

Charlotte was so stunned and so furious that she could barely breathe. "Get out, Joyce!" She ground the words out between her teeth. "Just get your stuff together and get out of my house, or I'm calling the police."

The expression on Joyce's face turned vicious and was full of loathing as she glared at Charlotte.

If looks could kill, Charlotte figured that she'd already be one dead duck.

Then, without warning and without a word, Joyce turned and stomped off toward the guest bedroom.

Very briefly, Charlotte hesitated. Should she just leave Joyce alone, or should she follow her to make sure she didn't steal anything else? Before she even finished the thought, Charlotte headed toward the guest bedroom. No way was she going to give Joyce the opportunity to steal anything else from her.

While Joyce quickly gathered her few possessions, Charlotte watched from the bedroom doorway every move she made.

Once Joyce had her stuff bundled up, she turned to glare at Charlotte. "Satisfied?" When Charlotte didn't reply, Joyce flounced past her, heading for the front door, and Charlotte followed her again.

At the door, Joyce jerked it open, and with her hand still on the doorknob, she turned to Charlotte and yelled, "You're going to be sorry for this! I'll make sure of it!" With one last glare at Charlotte, Joyce stepped through the doorway and slammed the door behind her hard enough to rattle the windows.

For a long time, Charlotte stood staring at the closed door, Joyce's parting shot ringing in her ears. She wasn't afraid of Joyce, not really—so why the ominous feeling deep in the pit of her stomach? And why did she feel as if she were still waiting for the other shoe to drop?

Chapter 6

Charlotte put away the mop, her last chore for her newest Friday client, Joy Meadows, and then glanced at her watch. Since she was finished for the day, maybe she'd take a ride back to the Quarter and check out the pawnshop again. And maybe Roy Price's partner would be more accommodating.

Joy had left right before lunch and hadn't yet returned. Charlotte quickly scribbled her a note, then hurried to her van. Just as she climbed inside and fastened her seat belt, her cell phone rang. Once she'd retrieved it from her pocket, she squinted at the tiny screen on the phone. Immediately recognizing her son Hank's caller ID, she flipped the phone open. "Hey, hon, what's going on?"

"Just thought you'd want to know that Carol is in labor, and we're on our way to the hospital."

All thoughts of going to the pawnshop fled and Charlotte's stomach churned with anticipation and joy. "I'll be there as fast as the speed limit and traffic allows," she gushed. "Please give Carol my love and let her know that I'm on my way."

"Will do, Mom, and you be careful."

Charlotte folded the phone closed, her mind racing. She

should call her sister. Immediately flipping the phone open again, she tapped out Madeline's number.

When Madeline answered on the third ring, Charlotte barely allowed her time to say hello. "Carol's headed for the hospital," she gushed, unable to hide her excitement.

"Is it time already?"

"Time flies," Charlotte quipped. "Would you please call Judith, Daniel, and Nadia for me?"

"Sure, and as soon as the clan can get it together, we'll be there. And, by the way, congratulations, Grandma!"

"Madeline, you bite your tongue and save the congratulations for *after* the baby is born."

"I swear, Charlotte, you and your silly superstitions. That baby is going to be just fine—perfect. Well, maybe not quite as perfect as my Davy and little Danielle, but—"

"Okay, Maddie. You've made your point, and thanks, sis, for the pep talk, but I better get on down the road. Wouldn't want to miss the birth of my first grandchild. See you at the hospital."

Two hours and four cups of coffee later, Hank entered the waiting room, a bounce in his step and a huge smile on his face. Neither Hank nor Carol had chosen to be told the sex of the baby before the birth. Though Charlotte suspected that Hank knew, she could hardly contain herself waiting to hear if her grandbaby was a boy or girl.

Charlotte met her son halfway across the room. "Well?"

"Well, Grandma, you have a healthy, bouncing baby grandson."

"A boy?" Tears sprang in Charlotte's eyes. "Oh, Hank, that's wonderful."

"There's more," Hank warned, then quickly added, "You also have a healthy, bouncing baby granddaughter as well."

"Twins?" Charlotte cried. "Oh, dear Lord in Heaven. Are—are they okay? And Carol—is she okay?"

With an understanding smile on his lips, Hank placed his hands on Charlotte's upper arms and nodded. "All ten fingers and all ten toes for each of them. And Carol is just fine—a little tired, but fine. As soon as they get her and your grandchildren cleaned up, you can go see for yourself."

Charlotte gave Hank a suspicious look. "Did you know?"

"Know what?" he asked innocently.

"You did know!" she accused. "You knew she was going to have twins and didn't tell me."

Hank slid his arm around her shoulders. "We wanted it to be a surprise. And besides, we didn't want you worrying any more than you already were."

By that time, Madeline, Daniel, and Nadia had gathered around Charlotte and Hank, all offering their congratulations with a hug, a slap on the back, and a kiss on the cheek. Only Judith was missing, but Madeline had explained that she was tied up with a homicide case and couldn't leave the murder scene.

"Told you so," Madeline taunted Charlotte.

"Yeah, you did, didn't you?" Charlotte agreed as Madeline hugged her.

Thirty minutes later, Charlotte and the rest of the family stood outside the nursery staring at the two tiny babies in the cradles nearest the viewing window. "Oh, son, they're beautiful," she said with awe. "The little girl favors you somewhat, but that little boy," she added in a choked voice, "he's the spitting image of you when you were born. I can't wait to get my hands on both of them."

Hank chuckled. "Somehow I don't think that's going to be a problem. You'll be having ample opportunity to spoil them both rotten."

Charlotte grinned. "That's what grandmothers are for."

Hank nodded. "And speaking of grandparents, I need to call Mack."

Momentarily confused, Charlotte stared at her son, wondering why he would refer to Mack Sutton and the word "grandparent" in the same sentence. After all, Mack was no blood kin whatsoever.

"Now, Mom, don't give me that look. I know that Mack isn't the babies' grandfather, but he and my dad were best friends. To hear him tell it, he and you were pretty close too, right up until the time he introduced you to my father. Anyway, after our talk when he was in town last time and I realized just how good a friend he was with my father and with you"—Hank shrugged—"I promised him I'd let him know when the babies were born."

"You told Mack that Carol was having twins, but you didn't tell me?" Charlotte blurted out the accusation before she could stop herself. Then she immediately wished she'd kept her mouth shut. After all, besides sounding petty, it was none of her business whom Hank told or what he told.

Hank shook his head. "No, Mother."

Uh-oh. Most of the time, Hank called her "Mom." The only time he called her "Mother" was when he was irritated with her about something.

"I said that wrong," he continued. "I didn't tell *anyone* that we were having twins. I just meant that I promised Mack I'd let him know when the *baby* was born, but now there happens to be two of them."

"Of course—sorry." Charlotte reached out and squeezed his arm. "It's no big deal. Really, it's not. You *should* give Mack a call and let him know. And tell him I said hello while you're at it."

* * *

Charlotte was still walking on air later that evening when she left the hospital, and she couldn't seem to stop smiling. No words could begin to describe how she'd felt when Hank had placed her grandson in one arm and her granddaughter in her other arm. The awe she'd experienced holding both of those tiny bundles of life close to her heart and staring down at their perfect little face was indescribable. Even now, just the thought of the sudden rush of love that had filled every corner of her being at that moment still brought tears of joy to her eyes.

"Nothing like it," she whispered in a choked voice, and she knew that it would be an event that she would remember for the rest of her life.

Charlotte was almost home when her euphoria suddenly took a nosedive. Even three houses away, she could see lights blazing from her front window. Most of the time when she knew that she would be out after dark, she made a point of leaving the porch light on, but without fail, she always turned off all of the lights when she left for work each morning. So why were the lights on inside of her house?

"Joyce," Charlotte muttered, and in her mind, she could still hear Joyce's parting words: *"You're going to be sorry for this! I'll make sure of it!"*

Had Joyce come back to make good on her threat? And if she had returned, then *how* did she intend to make good on her threat?

How else? By stealing you blind or messing up your house.

Suddenly, visions of Joyce toting off all her valuables, and then coming back to smash or break the rest of her things, danced through Charlotte's head. She swallowed hard as she turned into her driveway.

To make things worse, now Joyce, like Charlotte's family, knew that she kept a spare key beneath the small ceramic frog in her front flowerbed, so there would be no reason for her to even break in. She could just open the door with the spare key and walk right in.

And so could any member of your family.

Yes, any member of her family could use the spare key, but since she'd just seen most of her family at the hospital, it was highly unlikely that any of them were there.

With her headlights still on, she craned her head and peered down where the small ceramic frog sat near the steps, but the frog was in the shadows of the hedge and there was no way of telling whether it had been disturbed.

Charlotte shut off the van and switched off the lights as her gaze slid to the front door. *What to do . . . what to do . . .*

She should probably call the police and let them deal with Joyce. But what if her suspicions were wrong? Though she didn't think so, it was always possible that she *had* slipped up and left the lights on that morning herself.

No, she wouldn't call the police, at least not yet. The easiest, simplest thing to do would be to check beneath the frog first, and if the key was missing, then she'd know. And then she'd call the police.

And what if the key is still there?

"Joyce could have put it back when she was finished," Charlotte argued.

Not likely. Since when has Joyce bothered locking the front door?

Most of the time, Charlotte tried to ignore the annoying voice in her head, but it was hard to ignore or argue with logic. She took a deep breath and let it out slowly. There was always the possibility that she was letting her imagination get the best of her. And again there was the possibility that she'd simply neglected to turn off the lights when she'd left that morning, and the lights being on had nothing to do with Joyce.

Feeling better already, and a bit foolish for getting all

worked up over what was probably nothing, Charlotte climbed out of the van. Just to set her mind at rest, when she neared the front flowerbed, she knelt down beside the ceramic frog. Even in the dark, she could tell that the frog had been moved and wasn't sitting where it normally sat. A sudden cold knot settled in her stomach.

Charlotte picked up the frog and felt all around the area where it sat. The knot in her stomach tightened. The key was missing.

Anger, hot and swift, knifed through her. Since no one but her family, Louis, and Joyce knew about the key, and since she'd just seen her family at the hospital, and Louis was still out of town, that only left Joyce.

Charlotte replaced the ceramic frog and got to her feet. Her eyes on the front door, she dusted off her hands, then climbed the steps. Even from across the porch, she could tell that the door wasn't even closed all of the way, never mind being locked. Without touching the doorknob, she easily pushed the door open.

She wrinkled her nose as a noxious odor hit her. What on earth was that smell? Growing angrier by the second, she pushed the door open even farther. Then, she gasped.

"Oh, dear Lord in Heaven," she whispered, her heart pounding like a bass drum beneath her breasts. Feeling weak in the knees, she grabbed hold of the door frame to steady herself. Chairs were overthrown, her coffee table lay on its side, and papers from her desk were scattered on the floor like dry leaves on a fall day. Even her telephone and answering machine were on the floor.

The floor . . .

It took only a moment for Charlotte to realize what she was staring at on the floor. Amidst the shambles of her living room, a woman's body lay sprawled in the middle of the mess.

A scream clawed at Charlotte's throat, and a wave of dizziness came over her. Beneath the woman's head was a pool of blood. Charlotte couldn't see the woman's face, and a good bit of her hair was matted in blood, but she immediately recognized the part that wasn't. She also recognized the clothes that the woman was wearing.

Joyce.

Had to be.

Chapter 7

Like a deer caught in headlights, Charlotte couldn't tear her gaze away from the lifeless body on the floor.

Don't just stand there. Do something. Call the police.

Jerking herself into action, Charlotte stumbled backward toward the steps. Her knees weak, she sank down to the top steps and then pulled out her cell phone. In spite of her fingers trembling, she was finally able to tap out Judith's phone number. "Please answer," she whispered while listening to the phone ring. But in her mind's eye, she could still see Joyce lying in a pool of blood on her living room floor.

Judith answered on the fourth ring. "This is Monroe," she snapped.

"Oh, Judith, thank God—"

"Auntie, what's wrong?"

"You've got to get over here as soon as possible," Charlotte told her. "There's a body on the floor in the middle of my living room, and I'm pretty sure it's Joyce Thibodeaux."

"Whoa, Auntie, back up a minute. Are you sure she's dead?"

"No, but there's an awful lot of blood. I should check. Maybe she's not dead, after all." Buoyed by the thought, Charlotte got to her feet.

"No!" Judith shouted in her ear. "Do not go inside, Aunt

Charlie. I repeat, do not go inside that house. The killer could still be in there. I want you to lock yourself in your van and wait for the police to get there. I'm on my way."

Charlotte sagged against the porch column. "But what if she's still alive and needs help?"

"She'll get help. Help is on the way. I'm radioing dispatch right now."

Charlotte could hear Judith rattling off her address and a bunch of number codes. "Humph! Your so-called help might be too late," she muttered. "I'm going in." Charlotte pushed away from the porch column and headed for the front door.

"Aunt Charlie, don't—"

"Too late, Judith. I'm already inside."

"Son of a—"

"Don't cuss, Judith."

"Oh, for crying out loud! At least watch where you're stepping. You're going to contaminate the crime scene."

"I'm not going to contaminate anything," Charlotte insisted. "For one thing, the place is a wreck already. I think Joyce must have trashed it before—before . . ." Charlotte's voice trailed away as she concentrated on where she was stepping.

"Why would Joyce have trashed your house?"

"It's a long story," Charlotte answered. The argument she'd had with Joyce, along with Joyce's threat, would have to come out, but Charlotte had no intention of explaining it over the phone. Better later than now.

"She's on the floor facing away from me, and, like I said before, there's a lot of blood around her head." Careful to avoid the blood, Charlotte knelt down beside Joyce and felt for a pulse at Joyce's neck. Joyce's body was still warm, and Charlotte had seen enough *CSI* episodes and read enough mystery books to know that meant it hadn't been that long since she'd been shot.

"There's no pulse," Charlotte said, "and it looks like she

was shot in the forehead, just above the bridge of her nose. Probably a small-caliber gun, maybe a twenty-two."

"Thank you, *Detective* LaRue," Judith snapped sarcastically. "No offense, but I think I'll wait for the crime scene team's opinion. Now get out of there or I'll be forced to arrest you for interfering with a homicide investigation."

"Okay, okay, I'm leaving," Charlotte grumbled, a bit miffed that Judith would so easily dismiss any observations she'd made. "See you when you get here."

"One more thing, Auntie. You'll need to be able to identify yourself, to prove that you live there. Just show the officers your driver's license when they arrive."

Judith hung up and Charlotte flipped her phone closed. Her mind racing, Charlotte slipped the phone inside her pants pocket as she headed for the front door. She was almost to the door when she suddenly stopped in her tracks and went stone still.

The birdcage door was wide open, and the cage was empty. Where was Sweety Boy?

At the doorway, Charlotte turned around, and holding her breath, she listened for even the slightest sound that might indicate that the little bird was still somewhere in the house. The only sound she heard was the ticking of the cuckoo clock.

For several moments, she debated going back inside to search for Sweety Boy. Then, in the distance, she heard the warbling wail of a police siren.

Her time was up. Unless she wanted to get arrested, she figured she'd better be in her van with the doors locked when Judith showed up.

On the slim chance that the little bird was still inside, Charlotte pulled the front door closed as best she could without touching the doorknob. Then she hurried to her van. But as she sat waiting and the sirens grew louder, visions of Joyce raced through her head: Joyce sitting on the porch swing;

Joyce sprawled on the sofa; Joyce wolfing down gumbo like it was her last meal. . . .

Charlotte sighed heavily. The worst vision of all was the last time that she'd seen Joyce alive: the look of pure hatred on Joyce's face when she'd screamed her threats.

A shiver ran down Charlotte's spine and she squeezed her eyes tightly shut, as if doing so would shut out the images. But instead of images of Joyce, all Charlotte could see were scenes of Sweety Boy being gobbled up by a cat or picked off by a hawk.

Had Joyce let him out of the cage on purpose? Was he still in the house somewhere, or had Joyce made sure that she let him go outside? Was she capable of being that vindictive, that downright mean?

Charlotte shook her head and opened her eyes. The answer was *yes*! Yes, Joyce was capable of being that vindictive. At the moment, though, there was nothing that she could do but pray that the little parakeet was safe and sound, hiding somewhere in the house.

Besides, instead of worrying about Sweety Boy, she should be worrying about who murdered Joyce, especially considering that he or she might still have possession of her house key.

But who on earth could have murdered her, and why?

Charlotte frowned. Today was Friday. Wasn't Louis supposed to be back home today? Then, suddenly, a horrible thought crossed her mind. *What if Louis had*—Charlotte shook her head. "No," she whispered. *No way.*

Louis was angry with Joyce and fed up with her lies, but not so angry that he would commit murder. If anything, Charlotte feared that she just might end up as the number one suspect, especially once the police found out about the argument she'd had with Joyce. And they would find out—especially when they canvassed the neighbors. She and Joyce had been shouting at each other loud enough for the entire neighborhood to hear them.

Outside the van, the police sirens grew louder, and within minutes, two police cars skidded to a halt in front of her house. As the sound of sirens died, Charlotte took a deep breath and dug her driver's license out of her purse for identification, readying herself for the ordeal to come.

Driver's license in hand, she unlocked the van and climbed out. Across the street, and on either side of her house, porch lights came on. Neighbors walked out into their yards to see what was going on.

"Ms. LaRue?" a gruff voice called out. "Ms. Charlotte LaRue?"

"Yes," Charlotte answered as a baby-faced young patrolman approached her. Though she held out her license for identification, she thought about demanding to see *his* license, just to check and make sure he was old enough to even be a cop.

The officer glanced at the license, then gave a curt nod. "So where's the dead body?"

Charlotte pointed at her front door. "She's in there on the living room floor. Her name is Joyce Thibodeaux."

Again he nodded curtly. "Wait here, ma'am."

When he turned away, Charlotte called out, "Ah, Officer? Excuse me. Could I have a word with you?" When he stopped and pivoted to face her, she said, "I hate to even bring this up, considering the circumstances, but my parakeet is missing. His cage is in the living room and the door was open. I just wanted to warn you that he might still be loose inside. So don't—ah—don't—"

"Ma'am, I promise, we won't shoot your bird."

Stunned, Charlotte quickly shook her head. "That's not what I meant." The fact that he might accidentally shoot Sweety had never even entered her mind. "I just meant that if he is still loose inside, don't let him get outside."

"I'll watch out for him, ma'am."

She was sure that his words were meant to be comforting, but the little smirk on his face sent a wave of heat up her neck, and she suddenly felt as if her face were on fire with embarrassment . . . and shame. There poor Joyce was lying dead on the living room floor, murdered, and here she was, worrying about a bird getting loose.

"I know it's silly," Charlotte told the officer, "but—but . . ." Unable to offer an excuse good enough to explain her request without seeming even more ridiculous, Charlotte simply shrugged.

With a curt nod, the policeman climbed the porch steps.

Way to go, Charlotte. Now he thinks you're a nutcase.

"Does not," she whispered, her gaze following the young officer as he entered her house.

"What was that, lady?"

Mortified that she'd been overheard talking to herself, Charlotte whirled around to find yet another policeman standing a few feet behind her. At least this one looked old enough to shave.

Charlotte made a show of clearing her throat in hopes he'd think that was what he'd heard. "Nothing," she lied. Then, for good measure, she cleared it again. "I didn't say anything."

Out of the corner of her eye, Charlotte saw a familiar car pull in behind her van, and relief, like a warm spring shower, washed over her. But her relief was short-lived when a van sporting the familiar logo of a local television station drove by slowly, then parked in front of her neighbor's house.

Charlotte groaned. She'd had dealings with the media before, ugly dealings where a nosy reporter had chased her down. The last thing Maid–for–a–Day needed was this kind of publicity. Maybe if she ignored them, they would go away.

"Boy, am I glad to see you," she called out to her niece as Judith climbed out of the driver's seat. Now that Judith was there, she wouldn't have to worry so much about doing or saying the wrong thing to the police or the reporters.

At first, Judith totally ignored Charlotte. "I've got this one, Mitch," she told the patrolman. "And thanks for the quick response." She pointed toward the TV van. "If you can, get rid of them. If they refuse to leave, at least keep them off the property."

"No problem," the older patrolman responded, and with a nod, he walked over to the edge of Charlotte's property line.

As soon as Mitch was out of hearing range, Judith pointed to the van, and in a voice that brooked no argument, she said, "Inside, now!"

While Charlotte climbed into the driver's side, Judith got into the passenger side.

"Close the door, please," Judith told her as she slammed her own door. Judith turned sideways in the bucket seat. "Now start from the beginning, and don't you dare leave *anything* out."

"Well, you don't have to be so—so mean about it."

"I'm sorry that's what you think, Aunt Charlie, but this is serious. If I'm going to help you, I have to know everything. And you have to be completely honest with me."

Charlotte supposed that she should have been insulted, especially at the implication that she wouldn't be "completely honest," but she trusted Judith, trusted her with her life. Even so, at the same time, she didn't want Judith to get into trouble because of her. "Hon, given the circumstances, maybe it would be best if you had another detective take this case."

"Don't I wish?" Judith retorted, her voice rising. "What you, and everyone else in the city, don't seem to understand is that since Katrina . . ." Judith broke off in midsentence with a shake of her head. "Never mind that," she said wearily. "I'm just tired and not in the mood to put up with any bull . . ." Judith sighed. "Sorry, make that baloney."

But Charlotte could easily fill in the blanks. She reached over and squeezed her niece's hand in a brief comforting gesture. For months, Madeline had been complaining and worrying about Judith working such long hours. A large number of the NOPD had left during Katrina and afterward. Many of those who had left had never returned. Though the powers that be were actively trying to recruit more police personnel, they still weren't up to even a pre-Katrina level yet. But then, the city wasn't back up to pre-Katrina residents' level yet either.

"Please, Auntie, just start at the beginning," Judith said.

"Okay, hon. I guess the beginning would be on Tuesday afternoon."

Judith reached up and switched on the overhead light, then withdrew a pad and pen to take notes.

With only a few interruptions from Judith, Charlotte told her everything she could remember, including her suspicions about Joyce stealing from her and her own visits to the pawnshop.

"I know things look bad, but I swear to you, Joyce left my house last night, and that's the last time I saw her until I found her dead on my living room floor."

Inside the van, the silence was deafening, in spite of the activity going on outside. Slowly and with seemingly great care, Judith put away her pen and pad, and just sat staring straight ahead. When she finally broke the silence, Charlotte wished she hadn't.

Judith turned sideways in the seat. "Where were you today, Auntie?"

"Why, working, of course. And then I went to the hospital."

"And your client can vouch for you the entire time you were there?"

Charlotte hesitated. Then, with a sigh, she said, "No, not the entire time. She left right before lunch."

Judith grimaced. "I don't guess I have to tell you that this looks bad, Auntie, for you and for Louis. But mostly for you." Suddenly, Judith's brows drew down into a frown. "And speaking of Louis, where is he?"

Charlotte swallowed hard. "He's out of town on a job. I guess I should have tried to contact him or at least call Stephen. It's just that everything happened so fast, and—"

"It's okay, Auntie. Don't worry about it."

Having once been partners with Louis before he retired, Judith still kept in touch with him and already knew about the troubles he'd had with Joyce and about Joyce's lies.

Judith cleared her throat. "When was he due back home?"

Still trying to digest the possibility that she and Louis might be accused of murdering Joyce, Charlotte ignored the question and glanced down at her lap. "Do I need a lawyer? Should I call Daniel?"

Daniel was Charlotte's nephew and Judith's brother, and he was also a lawyer who was part of a very prestigious New Orleans law firm.

"Only if calling him will make you feel better," Judith said. "Now, about Louis. When is he due back home?"

Calling Daniel would make her feel better, but maybe she should wait and talk to Louis first. "He's due home today," she said, "but sometimes he doesn't get in until late," she hastened to add.

"Uh-huh." Judith grimaced and pulled out her cell phone. After tapping in several numbers, she listened, then spoke into the receiver. "Louis, this is Judith. This is a 911." Judith disconnected the call. "That should do it," she said.

"I take it 911 is a code of some kind."

Judith shrugged. "It means the same as any 911 call—just my way of letting him know that the call is important." Judith switched off the overhead light, then opened her door. "I've got to get in there now, but I'd appreciate you hanging around for a little while longer. Why don't you just sit here in the van for now?" Judith stepped down out of the van. "Do you need anything? Bathroom, water?"

Charlotte shook her head. "There is one thing, though. I told that young police officer, but you need to know too. Sweety Boy is missing. He might be loose in the house somewhere."

"I'll keep an eye out for him. What about something to eat? Have you had anything to eat this evening?"

Charlotte nodded. "I ate at the hospital before I left. I'm fine."

At the mention of the hospital again, and for the first time since she'd arrived, Judith smiled. "And just how are the newest members of the family? Mom says they're gorgeous."

"They're just beautiful," Charlotte answered. "The most beautiful babies in the nursery."

Not long after Judith went inside, the crime lab team arrived, and for well over an hour, Charlotte sat in the van and watched people coming and going from inside her house. She shuddered to think about the mess they were making on top of the mess that Joyce had already made. Though she didn't like to think about it, Charlotte had some experience cleaning up after a crime lab team and knew the kind of mess they could make just dusting for fingerprints.

Suddenly, the heat of shame crawled up her neck. How could she even be thinking about the mess being made while Joyce was lying dead on her living room floor?

Charlotte rolled down both front windows and savored the feel of the cooler outside air on her face. It was hard to believe that just last week, she'd had to run the air conditioner, and mosquitoes had been out in droves . . . and Joyce had still been alive.

Don't think about it, not now. . . .

Charlotte closed her eyes and wished for the blessed oblivion of sleep. Maybe she could catch a nap. Suddenly, she remembered the TV crew, and her lids fluttered open again.

Sure enough, she spotted a cameraman and a reporter standing behind the TV van. Though she couldn't tell for sure, she figured there was a good chance that the cameraman could have the camera pointed directly at her. Why, with all of those zoom lenses they have nowadays, he could even be filming just her face at this very moment.

Charlotte immediately turned her head away and rolled the driver's side window back up. Though the window tinting wasn't all that dark, it was better than nothing. Her gaze settled on the open window on the passenger side. Should she raise it as well?

After a moment, during which time she adjusted her seat to a reclining position, then turned sideways so that her back faced the TV van, she finally decided that as long as that cameraman stayed where he was, leaving the passenger window down for now should be okay. Even though it was cool enough outside, the van would get stuffy fast with both windows up.

Her gaze strayed to the front door of her house. Yet another reason to be thankful for the cooler temperatures. With the cooler night, there would also be fewer mosquitoes getting inside her house, what with the front door opening and shutting every time someone came or went.

With a heavy sigh, Charlotte leaned her head back against the seat and closed her eyes. Even a short nap was better than nothing, and might help her relax.

But sleep, nap or otherwise, proved elusive, and only made her long for her nice soft bed where she could stretch out between cool sheets, instead of being cramped in the van.

"Ms. LaRue?"

Charlotte jumped at the sound of the deep voice and her eyes flew open.

"Sorry, ma'am, I didn't mean to startle you."

"That's okay, just a sec." She quickly adjusted her seat, then turned her attention to the baby-faced police officer standing near the open window.

"Just wanted to let you know that we didn't find your bird inside."

Charlotte's heart sank. "Guess she let him out, after all," she mumbled.

" 'She'?"

"Joyce—the dead woman."

"Oh, yeah. Well, anyway, he's not in there. He'll probably show up, though. Sometimes, even though they get out, they still hang around close to home."

"I hope so. I . . ." Charlotte's voice trailed away when she detected movement and turned her head in time to see a gurney being wheeled out her front door. On top of the gurney was a zippered black bag.

Joyce Thibodeaux's body.

Charlotte blinked back tears. Yes, Joyce was a liar, a drunk, and probably a thief, but she wasn't a monster. She was simply a flawed human being who also just happened to be a mother and a grandmother. . . .

As Charlotte reached up and brushed the tears away, she thought about Joyce's son, Stephen, and her granddaughter, Amy, Stephen's daughter . . . and she thought about Louis. Though none of them were really close to Joyce, and in spite of Louis being so angry with her, Joyce was still part of their family.

"Are you okay, ma'am?"

Charlotte nodded as she turned to watch the gurney being loaded into the ambulance. She was okay—not great, but okay. Then she saw the cameraman and reporter get inside the TV van. Just moments later, the van drove away, and she immediately felt even better.

Tearing her gaze away from the ambulance and the TV van, she asked, "When will I be able to get back inside my house?"

"That's up to the crime lab team," he said.

"But it would be safe to assume that I need to find somewhere else to stay for tonight?" Though Charlotte would have preferred her own home, there was no way she could stay there until it was spic-and-span clean again, and no way was that going to happen tonight.

"Yes, ma'am, I think that's a pretty safe assumption."

"One more question. Now that the media has left, would it be okay if I walked around my yard? I'd like to check it out, just in case my parakeet is still around."

"Hmm, don't know about that, but I can find out for you."

While the young patrolman was gone, Charlotte phoned her sister. When Madeline finally answered on the fifth ring, Charlotte said, "Maddie, I need a place to stay tonight."

"Ah—sure, but what's going on?"

As quickly as possible, Charlotte gave her sister an abbreviated version of what had happened. Then she spotted the young policeman heading her way. "Got to go, Maddie, but I'll see you after a while, and thanks."

"Ms. LaRue, they said it's okay for you to walk around the front, as long as you stay on the sidewalk, but it would be best if you wait till tomorrow to walk around back."

"Thanks."

"You're welcome, ma'am. Anything else?"

"Ah, well, now that you mention it, I hate to bother you again, but could you please find out if it's possible for me to get some clothes out of my bedroom?"

The young officer leaned down until his head was even with the window. He crossed his arms and rested them on the window edge. "I hate to tell you, but the bedrooms are as messed up as the living room, so the answer is probably no—not until the crime lab people finish up."

Charlotte groaned. "Oh, for Pete's sake." She shook her head in disbelief. "That's great," she muttered, her tone dripping with sarcasm. "Just great!"

"Could be it's so messed up because the killer was looking for something."

Charlotte opened her mouth to refute the young officer's assumption. Then Joyce's last angry words echoed in her ears, and she closed her mouth. *"You're going to be sorry for this!"* Joyce had threatened. More than likely, the mess was Joyce's way of "making her sorry," but saying so at the moment wouldn't be a wise thing to do.

"And things could have been worse," the young officer continued.

"Yeah, I guess," she halfheartedly agreed.

"There could have been two body bags—instead of just one."

Charlotte swallowed hard. Up until that second, the possibility that she could have been murdered as well hadn't occurred to her. If she had arrived just a few minutes earlier . . . She cleared her throat. "Guess you're right."

"Tell you what." He straightened up and stepped back. "Why don't I go talk to Judith—I mean, Detective Monroe? She might be able to help you out with the clothes thing."

"Thanks, I'd appreciate it." Charlotte opened the van door. "While you do that, I think I'll take a look around for my parakeet." She climbed down.

"Just remember to stay on the sidewalk," he called out over his shoulder.

It didn't take long for Charlotte to realize that searching for Sweety Boy by streetlight wasn't going to do a whole lot of good. What she really needed was one of those big spotlight-type flashlights. Louis probably had one, but Louis wasn't home yet.

Glaring at Louis's half of the double, she wondered where in the devil he could be.

Chapter 8

In spite of what Charlotte had told Judith, most of the time when Louis returned after being out of town, he tried to take a flight that would guarantee that he was home by dark. He should have been home by now.

And where in the devil was that bird?

After only a few minutes of craning her neck first one way, then another, and peering into the darkness, she spotted the young officer crossing the front porch to the steps. Recognizing the small suitcase that he was toting as her own, Charlotte headed back toward her van.

"Detective Monroe put some things together for you." He opened the back door of the van and placed the suitcase inside. "She said to tell you she'd be in touch, but that you could leave." He slammed the back door closed. "I'll move her car out from behind your van."

"Thanks," she called out as he headed for Judith's car. "But could you wait up a second?" When the officer paused and turned to face her, she said, "If you don't mind, when you see her again, just tell her that I'm spending the night with her mother."

He nodded. "Will do, ma'am."

"Once again, thanks so much," Charlotte told him. "I really do appreciate your help."

"My pleasure, ma'am." He pivoted and stepped over to Judith's car. "Now, you have a good night, you hear?" he called out.

By the time Charlotte knocked on her sister's door, it was almost ten o'clock.

"It's about time you got here," Madeline told her as she let her in, then locked and bolted the door. "I was beginning to get worried."

"Sorry to worry you, Maddie. Things just took longer than I'd expected."

Nodding, Madeline picked up the TV remote and hit the mute button. Then, with a frown, she turned to face Charlotte. "You look like something the cat dragged in."

Charlotte stuck out her tongue at her sister. "Thanks a lot." She could always depend on Madeline to speak her mind. When Madeline grinned, Charlotte sighed. "Truth be told," she said, "I feel like something the cat dragged in. If you don't mind, I think I'll get a shower and put my pajamas on—at least I hope Judith packed pajamas."

"Why would Judith pack—oh, yeah, duh, right. It's a crime scene, so of course you can't go inside." Madeline motioned toward the hallway. "You can sleep in the spare bedroom. The sheets are clean. I just changed them last weekend after Davy spent the night with me."

Charlotte walked toward the bedroom and Madeline followed. Davy was the son of Madeline's daughter-in-law, Nadia, a young woman who had once worked for Charlotte. It had taken a while, but Madeline had finally come to terms with the fact that her son Daniel had chosen to marry Nadia and adopt Davy as his own. And with the addition of Davy's baby sister, Danielle, to hear Madeline tell it, the whole thing was her idea all along.

"And how are my grand niece and nephew?" Charlotte asked.

"Growing like little weeds, but sweeter than honeysuckle. And just think, with the newest additions to the family, now Davy will have a male cousin to grow up with, and Danielle will have a female cousin."

Charlotte laughed. "Yeah, I just hope they don't squabble as much as Judith, Daniel, and Hank did."

The jarring ring of the telephone wiped the smile off Charlotte's face. "That's probably Judith," she explained. "She said that she'd be in touch."

Madeline hurried back toward the living room and Charlotte followed. After a few words into the receiver, Madeline held out the phone to Charlotte. "You were right."

Charlotte took the phone. "Yes, Judith?"

"Bad news, Auntie. Louis's flight landed earlier today, but he's disappeared."

A sick feeling settled in the pit of Charlotte's stomach and her brow creased with worry. Judith was right about the "bad news." Being Joyce's ex put Louis right at the top of the suspect list, and the fact that he was missing made his innocence even more questionable.

Charlotte narrowed her eyes thoughtfully and her grip tightened on the phone receiver. There had to be a logical explanation. "What exactly do you mean 'he's disappeared'?" she asked Judith.

Frowning and unable to stem her curiosity, Madeline stepped in front of Charlotte. "Who's disappeared?"

Charlotte shook her head and threw up her hand in a gesture for Madeline to be quiet. To Judith, she said, "Disappeared, meaning he wasn't on the plane, or disappeared, meaning he was on the plane, but has vanished since it landed? What?"

"I talked to his boss, Joe Sharp," Judith explained, "and he said that Louis's flight arrived this morning. Louis checked in at the office, but no one has seen him since."

Charlotte's nerves tensed even more. "There could still be a logical explanation," she insisted. "Have you tried calling Stephen—"

"Must be talking about Louis," Madeline interrupted, her frown deepening.

Charlotte's lips tightened with aggravation, but she nodded yes to her sister. Then, hoping that Madeline would take the hint, Charlotte turned her back on her sister.

"Yeah, I called Stephen," Judith said in her ear. "He hasn't heard from Louis either, or if he has, he isn't saying so."

"But why would Stephen lie—"

"Duh—why do you think, Aunt Charlie?"

"Uh-uh. No way."

"What else am I supposed to think? Louis won't answer his phone. He hasn't returned any of my calls. He hasn't been home, and he's nowhere to be found."

"Judith Monroe, you know good and well that Louis would never do such a thing. Sounds to me more like he could be in some kind of trouble—other than this, of course. Maybe he was in an accident or something."

"I've thought about that, and we are checking into that possibility, but until we find out differently, I have to go with the facts and the evidence. And speaking of facts, after we got through canvassing all of your neighbors, Brian—you remember him, don't you? He's my partner."

Charlotte nodded. Of course she remembered her niece's Tom Cruise look-alike partner. Everyone who met him remembered him.

"Anyway," Judith continued, "Brian insisted on adding your name to the list of suspects, as well as Louis's name. Brian has a theory that there might have been some kind of conspiracy between the two of you, since you and Louis are so 'close'—his word choice, not mine. And for now, there's not a whole lot I can do about it, not if I want to stay on this case, not that there's anyone to relieve me. . . . Sorry, I'm tired and I'm rambling. What I wouldn't give for a good eight hours of sleep without interruption."

But Charlotte's thoughts were still on Brian's so-called conspiracy theory. She'd known this was coming, but knowing it was possible and having it actually happening were two different things. Charlotte squeezed her eyes closed. Time to call Daniel, she decided, and time to get serious about finding Louis.

"Aunt Charlie? You still there?"

Charlotte opened her eyes. "Yes, I'm still here."

"Well? Aren't you going to say anything?"

Charlotte swallowed hard. No more "Ms. Nicey, Nicey." Time to get tough. Past time. "For now, all that I'm going to say is I love you, hon—love you like my own daughter. But if you want me to answer any more questions, then you'll have to talk to my attorney."

Madeline stepped in front of Charlotte, her frown now a scowl of disapproval. For the moment, though, Charlotte ignored her.

"Aw, come on, Auntie," Judith pleaded over the phone. "Don't be like that. Hey, I'm just doing my job."

"Whining doesn't suit you, Judith, and I realize that you're just doing your job, but I've said all I'm going to say for now." Tired of talking and worried about Louis, Charlotte said, "We'll talk again tomorrow. Try to get some rest. Good night now." Without waiting for a response, she quickly hung up the phone.

"Okay"—Madeline rounded on Charlotte and got in her

face—"what was all of that about? And why were you talking like that to Judith?"

"Talking like what?" Charlotte leveled a no-nonsense look at her sister and stepped back from her. Maybe staying with Madeline wasn't such a good idea, after all. The last thing she felt like doing was defending herself to her sister, but there was no getting around it now, and no backing down.

"You know exactly what I mean," Madeline retorted.

Charlotte sighed wearily. "Yeah, I do." She sighed again. "Listen, Maddie, you, of all people, know that I love Judith and would never intentionally do anything to hurt her. But at the same time, I have no choice but to protect myself. Judith and her partner have put Louis and me at the top of their suspect list. They think we conspired to kill Joyce."

Madeline's eyes grew wide with disbelief. "You've got to be kidding!"

Charlotte slowly shook her head. "Afraid not."

"Why—why—that's just about the most ridiculous thing I've ever heard of!" Madeline sputtered, shaking her head.

Relief washed through Charlotte. She didn't want her sister to have to choose sides, but right now she needed all of the allies she could get.

Charlotte reached out and squeezed her sister's arm. "To be honest and to give her credit, I don't think this whole theory is Judith's idea, and I also don't think that she's comfortable with it."

"Probably that partner of hers," Madeline retorted, eager to blame anyone but her daughter. "Judith knows better. Want me to call her back and talk to her?"

Charlotte shook her head. "No, don't do that. But thanks, I appreciate the offer."

"What about Daniel? Want me to call him about finding you a good attorney?"

Charlotte chewed on her bottom lip thoughtfully, then said, "Maybe later, but not just yet. Right now, I need to find out what happened to Louis."

"How about a cup of hot tea? I think I have some decaf."

Charlotte gave her sister a tired smile. "Thanks, that sounds good. Now, where's your telephone directory?"

While Madeline searched for the telephone directory, Charlotte called Louis's cell phone number. When the answering service kicked in, she left him a message. "Louis, I need you to call me ASAP. It's extremely important that I get in touch with you immediately."

"Here's the directory," Madeline told her as she placed it beside the phone.

Nodding, Charlotte said, "Thanks" as she depressed the switch hook, then tapped out Louis's home phone and left the exact same message.

As Charlotte thumbed through the Greater New Orleans telephone directory, she noted that there were several Sharps listed, but only one Joseph Sharp. "Has to be him," she muttered, and quickly tapped out the number.

Four rings later, a sleepy male voice answered, "Yeah, hello."

"Mr. Sharp—Mr. Joe Sharp, with Lagniappe Security?"

"Yeah, who wants to know?"

"My name is Charlotte LaRue. I'm a friend of Louis Thibodeaux."

"Yeah, yeah, you're the woman he rents from."

"Yes, well, sorry to call so late, but I'm worried about Louis and thought you might be able to help me find him."

"Like I told that police detective, Louis checked in with me about noon today, and that's the last time I saw him. So what the devil is going on? Is Louis in some kind of trouble?"

Charlotte chose to ignore his questions for the time being.

85

"When you saw him, was he okay? Did you notice anything unusual? Anything . . ." Her voice trailed away.

For several long seconds, there was silence, and then Joe cleared his throat. "You know, come to think of it, he didn't look too good. And he complained about having indigestion—said it must have been something he ate." He paused. "That's all that I can think of, though. Other than that, the only other thing he said was that he was going home."

Charlotte's mind raced with possibilities. "Thanks," she said. "Sorry again for calling so late, but I appreciate the information." Charlotte hung up the receiver. What if Louis's so-called indigestion had gotten worse?

Suddenly, she froze. Didn't people sometimes mistake indigestion for the beginnings of a heart attack? What if he didn't have indigestion at all? What if he'd had a heart attack?

Charlotte snatched up the receiver and punched out Stephen's home phone number. Six rings later, the answering machine kicked in, and a wave of apprehension swept through her. Where the heck was everybody?

"Good grief, Charlotte, you look like you've just seen a ghost. What on earth is wrong?" Madeline held out a steaming cup to Charlotte.

Charlotte hung up the receiver and took the tea. "I'm really worried about Louis." After she'd explained about her call to Joe Sharp, she said, "And Stephen isn't answering his phone either."

"Now, Charlotte, you know better than to go jumping to conclusions. There are all kinds of reasons Stephen might not be answering his phone. If Judith has already called him, he might have decided he didn't want to talk to the cops again."

"But he'd see from his caller ID that the caller wasn't Judith again."

86

"Yes, but he wouldn't recognize my phone number—thus the reason he's not answering the phone."

"Yeah, you're right. I forgot about that. I should have left him a message to return my call."

Madeline nodded in agreement. "As for Louis, he's probably just fine."

"Maybe," Charlotte said, mostly to appease her sister. Knowing Louis, though, Charlotte couldn't imagine him simply disappearing off the face of the planet, not without letting someone know. "But just to be on the safe side, I think I'll call around to some of the hospitals."

Madeline shrugged. "Whatever." Then she yawned and stretched her arms above her head. "Sorry," she said, rubbing the back of her neck. "It's been a long day."

"Tell me about it," Charlotte quipped. Then, unable to help herself, she yawned too. Motioning toward the doorway, she said, "Why don't you go on to bed, Maddie? No sense in both of us burning the candle at both ends. Besides, after I make a few more calls, I intend to hit the sack."

Nodding, Madeline headed for her bedroom, and Charlotte turned her attention to the phone. Ochsner Hospital was the third hospital on her list. "Could you connect me with Mr. Louis Thibodeaux's room, please?"

When the switchboard operator said, "One moment, please," Charlotte's breath caught in her lungs as she automatically counted the rings. Part of her hoped she'd finally located him, while part of her dreaded finding out that he was in the hospital because something terrible had happened to him.

"Yeah, hello."

Though the gruff voice was a bit slurred and groggy-sounding, Charlotte recognized it immediately. "Louis Thibodeaux, what in the devil is going on?"

"Charlotte?"

"Yes, it's me. Now, what's wrong? Why are you in the hospital?"

"I tried to call you," he said. "I couldn't remember your cell number, so I was going to leave you a message on your home phone, but I kept getting a busy signal."

Charlotte winced. Now what? She couldn't just blurt out that her home had been trashed and was now a crime scene because someone had murdered his ex-wife. "Ah, well, guess the phone is out of order, and I haven't been home this evening," she hedged. "I've been trying to call you too. So, why are you in the hospital?"

"It's no big deal."

Charlotte rolled her eyes. Just like a man. "Ah, excuse me, but they don't admit people to the hospital for 'no big deal.'"

"Okay, okay. When I first got off the plane, I thought I was having indigestion. But after I checked in with Joe at the office, the pains got worse, so I decided to drop by my doctor's clinic. The doc ordered some tests, but he thinks it's just stress—all the traveling I've been doing lately, and this last job was no picnic. Anyway, to be on the safe side, he put me in here overnight for observation."

"So how are you feeling now?"

"Kind of loopy, but better. The doc ordered something to make me relax."

"That's good." Too bad that feeling wasn't going to last, she added silently. "Does Stephen know?"

"I left a message on both his home phone and cell, letting him know I was checking into the hospital, but I haven't heard back from him yet." Louis paused a moment. Then he said, "He could be at the art gallery, though. Seems to me I remember something about a show he was sponsoring for a new artist.

I didn't think about calling there. Doesn't matter, though. He probably won't bother to check his messages until the morning, and by then I should be home."

So why didn't he get Judith's 911 message? "Speaking of checking messages, have you checked your cell messages?"

"No, once I was admitted to the hospital, I turned off the cell. Why?"

"Ah, no reason." *Liar.* "When you didn't show up at home, I tried to call you and left a message."

Half-lie, half-truth, she consoled herself. If he didn't check his messages, then there was no way he could know about Joyce. Should she tell him now, tonight, or should she wait until tomorrow?

Charlotte swallowed hard. She didn't like the idea of giving him the news about Joyce over the telephone. Something like that should be a face-to-face thing. Besides, since stress was the reason for him being in the hospital to begin with, she didn't want to be the one who added to that stress, not tonight. Tomorrow morning would be plenty of time for him to learn about Joyce and learn that he was a suspect for the murder of his ex-wife. She took a deep breath. "You get a good night's rest, then, and I'll talk to you tomorrow."

"Is something wrong? I mean, why were you trying to get in touch with me to begin with?"

"Well, for one thing, like I said, I was worried. It's just not like you to come back from a job without letting someone know that you're in town."

"And for another thing?"

"What?"

"You said 'for one thing,' so it follows that there has to be another thing, another reason."

Charlotte rolled her eyes. Leave it to Louis to pick up on

the least little blunder. "Slip of the tongue," she retorted. "It's been a rough day and I'm pretty tired." Then inspiration struck. "Oh, yeah, and I'm now officially a grandmother."

"That's great! Boy or girl?"

Charlotte waited a heartbeat, and then said, "One of each." And because she couldn't help herself, she giggled.

"One of each . . . as in twins?"

"Yep, you got it."

"Guess that's a double congratulations then."

"Thanks, and like I said before, I'm pretty tired. I'll see you tomorrow." Before he could ask any more questions, she added, "Good night, then," and hung up the phone.

For several seconds, Charlotte stared at the phone. She hadn't lied to him. Everything she'd told him was the truth.

Yeah, right, Charlotte. A lie is a lie is a lie. And especially a lie of omission, and you omitted a lot.

"Too late now," she argued. What was done was done.

With the intention of shutting off the television, she reached for the TV remote. With her finger poised over the power switch, she hesitated. How cold was it supposed to get tonight? she wondered. But the bigger question was how much cold could a tame parakeet who had never been outside during his whole life stand?

Instead of turning the TV off, she switched to the weather channel. "Great!" she muttered. "Just in time for commercials." Seating herself on the sofa, she waited. If Sweety Boy was still alive, he might have a chance of surviving as long as the nighttime temperature didn't get too cold.

The commercials finally ended, and a segment played showing the local weather, including the radar for the Greater New Orleans area and the forecast. According to the forecast, the night would be mild, with temperatures in the upper 60s to lower 70s. No rain was predicted until the end of the following week; then, an Arctic cold front would be pushing south, bringing with it freezing temperatures.

With a sigh of relief, Charlotte turned off the TV and the living room lights and walked into the guest room. Surely, she'd find Sweety Boy within the next day or two.

If he's still alive.

Ignoring the voice of doom and gloom, Charlotte inspected the contents of the small suitcase, which Judith had packed.

As she rifled through the items, she thought about calling her niece to let her know that she'd located Louis. She glanced at the clock on the bedside table and changed her mind. Judith had seemed really tired, and on the chance that she'd gone home and gone to bed, Charlotte didn't want to disturb her. Besides, she really wanted to talk to Louis, one on one, before the police got to him.

Charlotte was both pleased and grateful for the items Judith had packed. The suitcase contained pajamas, a pair of jeans, a pair of slacks, and a couple of T-shirts, along with underwear and a few toiletries. Charlotte took out the pajamas and headed for the bathroom.

After washing her face and brushing her teeth, she climbed into the bed and turned off the bedside lamp. Now, all that she had to do was pray that neither the police nor Judith found Louis before morning, before she had a chance to talk to him.

Charlotte shifted beneath the covers and turned on her side. With everything that had happened, she'd hardly had a chance to even think about the babies. With two instead of one, and Hank's already busy schedule as a doctor, Hank and Carol were going to need a lot of help, at least in the beginning.

"Grandma," Charlotte whispered, trying out the sound of the word, and liking it.

* * *

Even though Charlotte had gone to bed later than usual, then spent part of the night tossing and turning because of a couple of really strange nightmares about Joyce and Sweety Boy, she still awoke early, just before daylight.

For several minutes, she simply lay there, staring up at the dark ceiling. As she thought about having to face Louis, the heavy feeling in her chest grew even heavier with dread. She'd much rather go back to sleep, or clean a hundred bathrooms, or even eat worms, anything but tell him about Joyce and about Brian Lee's conspiracy theory.

Charlotte groaned. And if Louis wasn't enough to worry about, thanks to Joyce again, she also had Sweety Boy to worry about too . . . if the little bird was still alive.

Charlotte shook her head. *Don't even think it*, she scolded silently. Why, even now he could be perched on her porch swing, just waiting for her to show up and rescue him.

With that though spurring her on, Charlotte threw back the covers and climbed out of the bed. Though there was the possibility that the little bird had not survived the night, Charlotte wasn't quite ready to give up hope yet, and there was only one way to find out for sure.

It was early enough that she had plenty of time to drive by her house before going to the hospital, and by the time she dressed, there would be daylight enough to see, and hopefully find Sweety Boy.

Not wanting to disturb Madeline, Charlotte dressed as quickly and quietly as possible. Then she wrote her sister a quick note of explanation and left it on the cabinet by the coffeepot, where Madeline would be sure to find it. By the time she climbed into her van, daylight was just beginning to creep over the horizon.

Ten minutes later, when Charlotte parked her van in her driveway, the first thing she noticed was the absence of black-

and-yellow crime scene tape on the porch. Last night, her entire porch had been cordoned off with the stuff.

Wondering if that meant she could go back inside, she climbed out of the van and closed the door. Her gaze zeroed in on the porch swing. Though she truly hadn't expected to see the little parakeet perched on the swing, waiting for her, she couldn't help the acute sense of loss that stabbed her when she saw that he wasn't there.

A half hour later, Charlotte finally gave up her search. Blinking back tears of disappointment, she headed back to her van. Though the backyard still had crime scene tape around it, and she hadn't been able to search it, she'd thoroughly searched every nook and cranny of her front yard, as well as on either side of her house.

"Where are you, Sweety Boy?" she murmured, her imagination wild with thoughts of the little bird's tragic demise.

As if doing so would make the thoughts disappear, Charlotte shook her head. "First things first," she muttered as she climbed into her van. Just because she didn't find him in the front yard didn't mean that something terrible had happened to him, or that he was dead. It just meant that he was still missing. At least that's what she kept telling herself, even as she promised herself that she would expand her search later to include her neighbors' yards and the entire block if she had to.

Swallowing hard, she shoved the gear into reverse and backed out of her driveway. For now, though, she needed to talk to Louis before the police found him. And she also needed to figure out how to tell him the bad news about Joyce.

Too bad he and the twins weren't in the same hospital, she thought. Then she could sneak in a quick visit to the twins and Carol as well.

Chapter 9

When Charlotte walked into Louis's hospital room, she was surprised to see him already dressed and sitting in a chair next to the window. When Louis glanced her way, a curious look crossed his face.

"Why aren't you in bed?" Charlotte asked.

Louis shrugged. "Any minute now I expect the doctor to walk through that door and discharge me."

"Even if he does discharge you, you won't be able to simply walk out right then and there. It could take up to an hour or more before the paperwork gets done and the hospital actually releases you."

"I know that, Charlotte, but I figured I can wait just as good sitting here dressed as I can in the bed. So why are you here?"

She was briefly taken aback by his bluntness, and she had to remind herself that along with being a chauvinist at times, Louis was also a proud man, the kind of man who would equate being in the hospital with being weak. He was also the type of man who wouldn't want a big fuss made over him.

Without waiting for a response, he said, "I told you last night that I'd be going home this morning."

Charlotte sighed. Time to do what she came to do. Unable to maintain eye contact with him, she seated herself in the only other chair in the small room and stared down at her tightly clasped hands. "There's no way to sugarcoat this," she said, "but one of the reasons that I'm here is because I have some bad news to tell you."

"Not Stephen? Amy—"

At the alarmed tone in his voice, Charlotte jerked her head up. "No!" she quickly assured him. "As far as I know, they're just fine. It's Joyce, Louis." She stared deeply into his eyes, as if by doing so she could will him to stay calm. "Joyce was found murdered yesterday."

For several seconds, Louis stared at her as if she'd just grown two heads. Finally, he slowly shook his head from side to side, then sighed heavily. "Guess she finally got her wish," he said, his voice steady and even.

"What!" Charlotte sputtered. "That—that's a horrible thing to say. Nobody *wants* to be murdered."

"Maybe not in your world, Charlotte. In your world, the glass is half full all the time. Unfortunately, your world isn't the norm anymore. Your world is the exception to the rule."

Joyce's words came back to her: *"Not in my reality. Maybe in yours, but not in mine."* Though Joyce had chosen a different way to say it, the meaning was the same as what Louis had said. Charlotte didn't consider herself a Pollyanna by any means, but neither was she a pessimist.

Charlotte shook her head. "I don't believe that. I still believe there's more good in this world than there is evil. It's just that we hear more about the evil from the media than we hear about the good."

Louis shrugged. "Maybe—maybe not. All I know is what I saw happen to Joyce. It seems that ever since Stephen was born, nothing was ever the same again. *She* was never the same again. Nowadays, they call it postpartum depression, but back then, I guess, women just coped the best way they knew how. . . ." His voice faded and he bowed his head to stare at the floor. "First there was the depression," he continued. "There were some days she wouldn't even get out of bed. Later, when Stephen was older and got into trouble, she started in with the booze and the drugs. Then, one day, she just walked out, disappeared."

"If it makes you feel any better, Joyce told me that leaving you and Stephen was the worst mistake that she ever made, and she never quite got over it."

Louis's only response was a shrug, before he turned his head to stare out the window again.

After a moment, Charlotte cleared her throat and sighed deeply. "I really hate to tell you this," she said, her voice barely above a whisper, "but there's more."

Louis jerked his head around and narrowed his eyes. "More?"

Charlotte nodded. "To make a long story short, I was the one who found Joyce. She was in my living room. And now, Judith's partner, Brian Lee, thinks that you and I conspired to murder Joyce."

A look of cold fury passed over Louis's face, but before he had a chance to say anything, the door to his hospital room swung open. Judith, accompanied by her partner, Brian Lee, walked into the room.

Judith's eyes narrowed the second that she saw Charlotte. "I should have known you were lying to me last night," she said, glaring at Charlotte. "I ought to run you in for obstruction of justice, and I still might if you don't start telling the truth."

Louis suddenly stood, then stepped between Judith and Charlotte. "Don't talk to your aunt like that. Show some respect, little girl."

Charlotte winced. Most of the time, Louis called Judith

"little girl" to tease her, but this time he wasn't teasing and it was clearly an insult.

"Hey—"Brian took a menacing step toward Louis.

"Back off, Brian." Judith threw up a silencing hand. "I can handle this," she told him, her tone brisk.

"Yeah, junior," Louis drawled, "take a hike."

Though Brian backed away, his expression grew hard with resentment.

Judith glared at Louis. "Stop trying to intimidate my partner. And just where do you get off trying to tell me how to do my job, *old man*."

Louis gave her a pitying look. "You let a woman—a civilian, no less—twice your age get the drop on you."

Judith rolled her eyes. "What, pray tell, is that supposed to mean?"

"You figure it out, and then you might be able to call yourself a real detective."

Judith narrowed her eyes. "Hey, I am a detective, Thibodeaux. Just because you hung up your shield, you don't get to take it out on me. Or my partner," she added.

"Enough!" Charlotte all but shouted as she stomped her foot, and glared first at Judith, then at Louis. "I swear, y'all are acting worse than a couple of two-year-olds fighting over the sandbox."

"Couldn't have said it better myself," Brian Lee grumbled. "Only thing worse than former partners butting heads is a divorced couple fighting over custody of the kids."

Charlotte ignored Brian's remarks and stared first at Judith, then at Louis. "Instead of fighting amongst ourselves, shouldn't we be trying to find out who murdered Joyce?"

"No '*we*' shouldn't," Judith retorted, rounding on Charlotte. "Brian and I are the only detectives in this room, the only ones qualified to work this case. *And*, if you recall, you and Louis are considered prime suspects."

"Oh, I 'recall,' all right," Charlotte shot back. "Never mind that the *real* killer is getting away with murder—pun intended—while you and your partner sit around on your duffs and do nothing."

"That's enough, Aunt Charlie!"

"Not by a long shot," Charlotte shot back. "You've known me all your life, Judith Monroe, and Louis"—she motioned toward him—"for Pete's sake, he was your partner for what . . . at least five years, wasn't it? Do you actually believe that we would conspire together to kill someone, especially Joyce? I mean, come on now, how obvious would that be?"

After staring at Charlotte for what seemed like forever, Judith finally sighed and said, "Aunt Charlie, could you please wait outside for a few minutes? I have some questions for Louis."

Charlotte could have argued, but she figured she'd said all there was to say, and she knew it was standard procedure to question suspects separately. "I could use a cup of coffee, anyway." She picked up her purse and slipped the strap over her shoulder. At the door leading into the hallway, she paused. "Anyone else want coffee?" When no one responded, she shrugged and left the room.

When Charlotte entered the hospital cafeteria, the smell of bacon and eggs reminded her that she hadn't eaten breakfast that morning. "No time like the present," she muttered, and picked up a tray, along with a fork, spoon, and knife. She figured that by the time she finished eating, surely Judith would be finished questioning Louis.

Half an hour later, when Charlotte returned to Louis's hospital room, he was still sitting in the same chair, his gaze fixed on the window. And he was alone.

"Has the doctor come by yet?" Charlotte asked, seating herself in the other chair.

Louis turned to face her. "Yeah, he came by for all of about five minutes. I'm just waiting on the paperwork now."

"So? What did he say?"

"Same thing he said yesterday—stress."

Charlotte wanted to ask more about Louis's condition, but she could tell just by looking at him that he had something else on his mind, and that something, more than likely, had to do with Joyce's murder.

In spite of the problems that Louis and Joyce had over the years, the fact remained that they had been married and had shared a son. Her death alone would have been disturbing enough, but her murder even more so, especially since there were allegations that he could be responsible.

Yeah, and don't forget that they think you're responsible too.

Choosing to ignore the irritating voice in her head, she asked, "What did Judith and Brian want to know?"

"The usual—where I was yesterday around the time that Joyce was murdered."

"That's all?"

Louis shook his head. "Not quite. I have orders not to leave the city."

For several moments, he stared at Charlotte, as if trying to make up his mind about something. Finally, he sighed deeply. "First, I need to thank you for covering for me last night. I'm not so sure I could have handled all of this on top of worrying about having a heart attack. And second, the only way we're going to get your niece and her partner off our backs is if I find out who killed Joyce." He grimaced, then reached up and rubbed the back of his neck. "Right now, though, I feel like a blind man without a cane."

He shifted in his chair, leaned forward, and rested his forearms on his thighs. "I need you to start from the beginning and tell me what happened. And I don't mean the short version. I need details—all of the details. Even those that you don't think are important."

Charlotte slowly nodded. In her heart of hearts, she knew that Judith didn't really think that she or Louis had anything to do with Joyce's murder. But Louis was right. Considering the circumstances, things looked bad. Finding the real killer was the only thing that would set things straight, and if anyone could find Joyce's killer, she'd bet her last penny on Louis.

"As far as I know, it all started this past Tuesday," she told him. "When I drove into my driveway, Joyce was waiting for me on the front-porch swing. She claimed that she'd been released by the hospital."

Louis shook his head. "That was probably a lie. More than likely, she either found some way to check herself out or she sneaked out."

"All I know is what she told me," Charlotte said.

Over the following hour, while they waited for his hospital paperwork, Charlotte told Louis everything that she could remember. Starting with Joyce's fears about relapsing because of her so-called release from the hospital and her claim that she just needed a couple of days to find her own apartment, Charlotte also talked about Joyce's wild story of being an undercover snitch for a detective out in California.

"She claimed that some really bad dudes were after her and she needed to disappear. That's the reason she lied to you about dying—she figured that was the only way that you would bring her back to New Orleans."

Charlotte suddenly frowned. "You know, at the time, I didn't connect the dots, so to speak, but now I'm wondering if the two thing were related."

"What two things?" Louis asked.

Lost in her thoughts, Charlotte ignored his question. "In fact, it does make sense—a lot of sense," she murmured.

"What are you talking about?" Louis demanded.

Startled by the tone of his voice, Charlotte jumped. "Oh—yeah—sorry—guess I need to back up a bit. You see, there was this detective named Aubrey Hamilton." As quickly as she could, Charlotte described the events leading up to the discussion she'd had with the detective about Joyce.

"You know those gut instincts you get about things or about people?" she continued. "Well, when I mentioned that detective to Joyce and told her his name, I could have sworn that just for a second I saw fear in her eyes. Of course she denied knowing the man or anything about him, but now that I'm thinking about it, she had to be lying. If what Joyce told me about working as a snitch was true, what if Aubrey Hamilton was the detective she'd worked for? I didn't put two and two together at the time, but now it makes sense. And another thing, though he claimed to be a detective—even flashed a badge—I called every district station in town, and nobody had ever heard of him. But then, of course, they wouldn't have heard of him if he was a detective in San Francisco."

"Inspector," Louis retorted.

"What?"

"In San Francisco, they call their detectives 'inspectors.' "

Though Charlotte nodded, something about the whole thing nagged her. Then, suddenly, it came to her. Aubrey Hamilton hadn't referred to himself as an inspector. He'd called himself a detective. Of course that could have been because he knew that they were called detectives in Louisiana.

Either that or he was purposely trying to pass himself off as a local detective.

Just as she was about to point out the discrepancy to Louis, the door leading into the hallway swung open and a nurse entered.

"You're all set to go, Mr. Thibodeaux." She held out a packet of papers. "These are your discharge papers and a couple of prescriptions that you need to have filled. You'll also need to call your doctor's office and make a follow-up appointment. Now, if you will just wait here for a few moments longer, someone will be along to escort you to the parking garage."

"I don't need an escort," he replied as he took the papers and stood.

"Hospital policy," the nurse said firmly, wagging her forefinger at him. "You have to leave in a wheelchair."

Without further comment and giving Louis a saccharine smile, the nurse turned and headed for the door.

Louis glared at her back until she left the room. Then he faced Charlotte. "How about if you meet me back at the house and we finish this conversation there?"

Charlotte nodded. "That's fine. I need to see if the police are finished and check on Sweety Boy again, anyway."

"What's wrong with the bird?"

Charlotte shook her head. "I'll explain later."

Louis shrugged. "Okay." He motioned for Charlotte to walk ahead of him.

Charlotte shook her head. "You have to wait for the wheelchair."

His lips twisted into a cynical smile. "You wait for the wheelchair." Stepping around her, he headed for the door. "See you at home," he called over his shoulder, then disappeared through the doorway.

Charlotte rolled her eyes toward the ceiling. "Lord, save me from a stubborn man," she complained. Grabbing her purse, she hurried out of the room. No way did she want to be around when the nurse came back with the wheelchair.

Charlotte fully expected Louis to beat her home, but instead of his car, there was a lone police car parked in front of her house. When she pulled into the driveway, a policeman got out of the car.

Recognizing the baby-faced officer from the night before, Charlotte nodded. "Good morning," she said.

"Morning, ma'am." He walked over to her. "Just wanted to let you know that we're all done here."

"Thanks, I appreciate that."

"The place is kind of a mess, especially the living room, but there are professional crime-scene cleanup crews that you can hire. If you want to hire one, I can give you a referral."

Charlotte figured that he was trying to be tactful about the blood on the floor. But she also had to wonder if it was possible that he got some kind of fee on the side for referrals. "I won't need anyone," she said. "But thanks, anyway."

"Crime scenes can be kind of gruesome," he warned.

"Yes, I know," Charlotte said. "I own a cleaning service myself, Maid-for-a-Day, and I've cleaned up after the police more than once."

"Oh, I see," he said, looking a bit chagrined. "Then I guess you already know what to expect."

"Unfortunately, yes, I do."

The young officer stared at her for a moment. Then he suddenly frowned; "Say, did you ever find your bird?"

Charlotte shook her head. "Thanks for asking, but no, not yet. I'm still hoping that he'll show up, though."

The young officer shrugged. "Hey, it's possible. Stranger things have happened." Then, giving her a two-fingered salute, he said, "Good luck, ma'am, and you take care now."

Filled with dread about what was ahead of her, and not especially looking forward to it, Charlotte watched the officer get into his car and drive away before she turned to face her house. Behind her, she heard a car approaching. When she glanced over her shoulder and saw Louis pulling into his driveway, she breathed a sigh of relief that she had an excuse to procrastinate a little longer.

"A policeman just left," she told him as he climbed out of his car and walked over to where she was standing.

"What did he want?"

"Nothing important. He was just letting me know that the crime lab team is finished with my house."

"For now, why don't we go into my house. I'll fix us some coffee and you can finish telling me what you know."

"Sounds good to me," Charlotte responded. "To tell the truth, I'm not looking forward to cleaning up my side yet." She followed Louis up the steps and onto the porch.

Once inside, Charlotte followed Louis back to the kitchen. While he prepared the coffeepot and turned it on, she explained about searching the guest room, where Joyce had stayed, and she told him about the strange words she'd found etched into the top of the bedside table.

"Do the words *bughouse*, *bluebird*, or *daisy* mean anything to you?" she asked.

A thoughtful frown on his face, Louis grabbed two mugs out of the cabinet and placed them beside the gurgling coffeepot. After a moment more, he faced her and shook his head. "Don't know about *bluebird* or *daisy*," he said, "but *bughouse* is what Joyce called the hospital ward she was staying in." Giving her a shrewd, knowing look, he said, "Mind telling me why you were searching her room?"

"I wasn't so much searching her room as I was checking the few valuables I have to make sure I still had them." Charlotte dropped her gaze to stare into her steaming coffee mug. "She stole my father's gold watch, Louis. Then she hocked it at a pawnshop down in the Quarter."

"Does Judith know about this?"

Charlotte nodded.

"So how did you know that Joyce was stealing from you?"

"That's the strange part. Thing is, I probably never would have missed the watch or suspected anything—at least not for a while, anyway—but I happened to see Joyce coming out of a pawnshop in the Quarter. Then, later that night, when I confronted her about it, she denied even being in the Quarter—"

"Let me guess," Louis interrupted. "You decided to check out the pawnshop for yourself."

Charlotte narrowed her eyes. "Yes, I did, and don't take that tone with me, Louis Thibodeaux. Besides, I was right. She did steal the watch and she hocked it." Recalling her confrontation with the pawnshop manager, Charlotte shuddered. "I'm here to tell you, the man that manages that place is one creepy, scary dude." She shuddered again. Then she told Louis about her encounters with Roy Price and about her conversation with the young woman who had accosted her outside the pawnshop.

"Don't you think that's kind of strange?" she asked.

Louis nodded slowly, his gaze fixed on a point just beyond Charlotte's shoulder. "Yeah, strange, all right. Is there anything else I need to know?"

"Yeah, I guess I should tell you about the fight we had. Not a fight exactly. Argument is probably a better description. Anyway, there was a lot of shouting, and that's when I told Joyce to get her stuff and get out. Then, the next afternoon, I found her dead."

Louis reached up and rubbed the back of his neck. "Everyone has arguments once in a while. Right now, though, I'm more interested in this man who claimed to be a detective. Did you mention him to Judith?"

"I think I did," she said. "I remember that I tried to call her about him, but had to leave a voice mail." She shook her head. "I honestly don't remember, though, for sure."

"That's okay. I'll find out. But first, before you clean your house, if it's okay with you, I'd like to take a look around—see if I can find anything that the crime lab bunch might have missed."

Charlotte nodded. "That's fine. And while you do that, I'm going to look around again outside for Sweety Boy." And later maybe she'd see if she could find out anything more about Joyce's stay at the hospital, she added silently. Since Joyce was in the hospital for several weeks, she just might have confided in someone there.

Louis frowned. "You never did tell me what's wrong with the bird. And what do you mean, 'look around again outside'?"

Louis's question jerked Charlotte's thoughts back to the present. "Ah—oh, yeah. Well, Sweety is missing. I don't want to think that Joyce did it on purpose," she hastened to explain, "and I don't like speaking ill of the dead, but I'm afraid that she let him loose out of spite, because I kicked her out."

Louis tilted his head downward and sighed deeply. "Sorry about that, Charlotte."

"Hey, it's not *your* fault, and I could be wrong. The good Lord knows I want to be wrong." She shrugged. "Besides, it's always possible that the person who killed Joyce let him out." Charlotte didn't really think so, and from the expression on Louis's face, she could tell that he didn't think so either. In fact, she was pretty certain that Joyce was the one who had let Sweety out into the harsh world, but she felt sorry for Louis and didn't want him to feel any worse about the matter than he already felt.

* * *

While Louis looked around inside Charlotte's half of the house, she took her time searching not only her yard, but also her neighbors' properties as well.

It was a gorgeous day with the sun shining and the temperature in the low 70s. Charlotte figured if the weather held and Sweety could evade the neighborhood cats, the hawk she'd seen, and any other possible predators, he might survive . . . unless . . .

"But what if he's already dead?" she whispered.

As she squinted against the light and stretched her neck first one way, then another, peering into her neighbor's oak tree, her heart lurched at even the thought of the little bird being dead.

Charlotte didn't really want to think of that possibility, so she headed back to her house. Surely by now, Louis had had enough time to see what he'd needed to see.

She was almost to her house when she noticed a car backing out of the driveway of one of her neighbors, who lived two houses down across the street. On the side of the car was a small magnetic sign advertising a local real estate company.

Seeing the sign suddenly reminded her about the visit she'd had from Flora Jennings. With everything that had happened, she'd completely forgotten about the real estate woman giving her a free price analysis of her property.

Making a mental note to contact Flora Jennings, she continued on to her house.

At the front door, Charlotte hesitated. She dreaded going inside, dreaded the thought of the task ahead of her.

Don't think about it. Don't dwell on it. Just do it.

After a moment more, she straightened her shoulders, lifted her chin, and then reached for the doorknob. As soon as she opened the door, she immediately detected the scent of pine cleanser and another scent that smelled like bleach.

Pine cleanser? Bleach? That's strange.

Just then, Louis walked into the living room from the kitchen. "Any luck finding the bird?" he asked.

Charlotte shook her head as she stepped farther into the living room. "Afraid not."

"It's just been since yesterday. He could still show up."

Though Charlotte heard what Louis said and nodded a response, her eyes were focused on the spot where she'd found Joyce on the floor in her living room. The oak floor appeared to be damp, but damp with water, not with blood.

Pulling her gaze away from the floor, Charlotte turned to face Louis. "You didn't have to do that, you know," she said, her voice shaky with emotion.

"Yes, I did have to do it," he said gently. "You shouldn't have to clean up Joyce's blood. You'll have enough to do cleaning up the mess she made when she ransacked your house and the mess the police made. Bad enough that she took advantage of your generosity and stole from you, and then got herself murdered in your house. . . ." His voice trailed away.

Charlotte was touched beyond belief and grateful more than words could express. On impulse, she stepped over to where Louis was standing and wrapped her arms around his waist and hugged him. She couldn't begin to imagine what kind of effect cleaning up the blood of someone you'd once loved would have on a person. "Thanks," she whispered against his shoulder; then, she released him and stepped back.

"No problem," he said, his voice gruff with emotion. Clearing his throat, he also stepped back. "Right now, though," he continued, "I've got some calls to make—funeral arrangements and such—so I'll see you later." He walked past her to the door.

"If there's anything I can do, just let me know," she called out. "I'm here if you need me."

He paused at the door, and though he smiled at her, his eyes were full of sadness. "I know you are," he told her. "And you'll never know how much I appreciate that. Thanks." With a somber nod, he stepped through the doorway, but then paused again. "I don't want to scare you or anything, but until they catch whoever did this, you might want to be even more careful about keeping your doors locked. And you probably need to check your answering machine. It looks like your phone is working again. You've received a whole bunch of calls." Then he pulled the door closed.

Hearing the door click shut, along with Louis's warning, was a sudden, unpleasant reminder that she still didn't know what had happened to her extra house key. Just to be on the safe side, Charlotte walked over to the door and slipped the dead bolt into place; then she went to her desk to make a call to her niece. Since the phone and the answering machine were back on her desk, she figured that the police probably placed it there before they left.

Just as Louis had said, the message light was blinking like crazy. Ignoring it, she tapped out Judith's cell phone number.

"Monroe here," Judith answered on the second ring.

"Judith, Aunt Charlotte. I won't keep you but a moment. Did anyone happen to find the key to my front door during the search of my house? That extra key that I keep beneath the ceramic frog is missing," she explained. "I meant to tell you about the key last night, but forgot."

"Hmm, that would explain how Joyce or the killer got inside, but no, no one mentioned finding a key, Auntie. I'll check it out, though, and let you know for sure. Oh, and by the way, in case you haven't been told yet, we finished up at your house, so you can get back inside now. And another thing, I set up your phone and answering machine before I left."

"Yes, I know. And thanks. That nice young officer from last

110

night was waiting when I got home from the hospital this morning."

"Good. Well, I've got to run now, Auntie, but I'll check about that key. In the meantime, you might want to think about having your locks changed—either that or make sure you use the dead bolts."

"Does this mean that you no longer consider me a suspect?"

Over the phone, Charlotte could hear her niece sigh deeply. After a pregnant moment, Judith said, "I'm not at liberty to discuss this with you, Auntie, and you know it. And more than you could know, I'm sorry that we're at odds about this thing. You do know that I love you very much, don't you?"

"Of course I know, hon. Same goes for me."

"Then please just trust me, and let me do my job."

A smile pulled at Charlotte's lips when she heard the disconnect click in her ear, and she hung up the receiver.

Charlotte's smile faded as she stared at the blinking light on her answering machine. With a deep sigh, she tapped the play button.

"You have six messages," the machine's robotic voice announced. "Six messages." Then, the machine beeped.

"Charlotte, I just heard what happened at your house. Are you okay? Call me."

Bitsy Duhe. Charlotte rolled her eyes. She should have known that Bitsy would know about the murder. There was little that went on in the city that the old lady didn't know about.

The machine beeped again.

"Where are you, Charlotte? They didn't arrest you, did they? Call me."

Bitsy, again. Charlotte groaned, and the machine beeped for the third message.

"Are you ignoring me? Or are you in jail?"

"Oh, for Pete's sake," Charlotte grumbled when yet another message from Bitsy finished playing.

As Charlotte listened to the fourth and fifth messages, she was relieved that neither were from Bitsy. One was from Dale Brown, her employee, and the other one was from her nephew, Daniel, both calling just to make sure she was okay.

Then she listened to the last message.

"Mom, are you okay? Why didn't you call me?"

"Because I—" Charlotte shook her head as the message continued.

"You should have called me. Instead, I had to find out about Joyce from Judith when she dropped in to see the twins. I love you, Mom."

Charlotte closed her eyes for a moment and sighed. Yes, she should have called him. He should have been the first person she'd called. And she would phone him, she decided. But after she returned Bitsy's call. Knowing how the old lady could be, Charlotte wouldn't put it past her to show up on her doorstep.

Charlotte dialed Bitsy's number. Maybe she'd luck out and the old lady wouldn't be home. Then she could simply leave a message.

No such luck.

"Hello?" the old lady said in her squeaky voice.

"Bitsy, this is Charlotte."

"Well, finally. For a while, I thought I'd have to go bail you out of jail."

Though Bitsy's willingness to "bail her out" was a truly generous gesture, Charlotte shuddered at just the thought of being locked up in jail.

"But then I found out from my neighbor's son that you were okay," Bitsy continued.

Her neighbor's son?

"He works down at the jail," Bitsy explained. "So what happened? I heard that the woman who was murdered was your boyfriend's ex-wife."

Charlotte smothered a groan. "Bitsy, first of all, Louis is not my boyfriend, and second, I really can't talk about it, not until the investigation is finished." It was a half-lie at best, but giving Bitsy more fodder for her gossip mill was not an option.

"Well, if you're going to be that way, then just rot in jail."

Now she'd gone and hurt the old woman's feelings. "Aw, come on, Bitsy. You know how these things work. And rest assured, that as soon as I can, I'll tell you everything."

Several moments passed, and Charlotte could just picture the old lady's face screwed up in a pout. Then, finally, Bitsy relented. "Okay," she said in a petulant tone. "I was just worried about you."

"That's really sweet of you and I truly appreciate your concern. Now, you have a good evening, and I'll talk to you again really soon. Bye now."

Charlotte depressed the switch hook, then immediately dialed her son's cell phone. After the sixth ring, the cell phone switched to his answering service.

Once the beep finally sounded, Charlotte said, "Son, I'm sorry I didn't call you right away about Joyce, but just wanted to let you know that I'm okay. I spent the night with your aunt Maddie, but I'm back home now. I hope Carol and the babies are okay. Love you."

Once again, depressing the switch hook, she spent the following twenty minutes reassuring first Dale Brown, and then her nephew, that she was okay.

When she finally hung up the phone from her last call, she headed for the bedroom. A few minutes later, dressed in a set of work scrubs, she began the job of cleaning up the mess that Joyce and the police had left.

As she cleaned, she worried about whether to have her locks changed, and finally decided that she'd wait until she heard from Judith. Besides, there was always the possibility that she might find the key while cleaning. She was pretty sure that Joyce had probably used the spare key to get inside the house in the first place. And typical of Joyce, she probably hadn't bothered to lock the door behind her once she was inside.

Unfortunately for Joyce, her carelessness more than likely had gotten her killed, plus there was no telling what she'd done with the key once she was inside.

Charlotte narrowed her eyes as she surveyed the extent of the damage. Judging by the level of vandalism, Joyce had to have been there a while before the killer showed up.

By lunchtime, Charlotte had finished cleaning and reorganizing the living room; then, she'd started on her bedroom by changing the sheets on her bed. Thanking the good Lord above that Joyce hadn't gotten around to destroying her kitchen, Charlotte searched the refrigerator for something to eat.

She finally settled for soup and a sandwich, and while she mindlessly watched the midday news on TV, her thoughts were on ways she could check out the hospital ward where Joyce had stayed. With the new privacy laws, not just anyone off the street could come in and expect to get answers about a patient. Even so, there had to be a way to find out what she needed to know.

By the time that Charlotte had taken the last bite of her turkey sandwich, a plan had begun to formulate, a plan that she was pretty certain would work.

Chapter 10

After church on Sunday morning, Charlotte hurried back home. There she picked up the pot roast, potatoes, and carrots, which she'd cooked earlier that morning, then drove to Hank's house. Hank and Carol's maid, Julie Harper, met her at the door.

Of all Charlotte's professional accomplishments, pairing Julie with Hank and Carol rated at the top of her list. Charlotte had met Julie while working at a temporary job at the Jazzy Hotel. At the time, Julie, a single mother who had worked as a maid at the hotel, had been wrongfully fired and was having a hard time getting another job. It was due to Julie's cooperation that Charlotte had been able to figure out a valuable clue that helped solve a double murder. After meeting Julie and knowing about her dilemma, Charlotte had known that Julie was the perfect person to work for Hank and Carol.

"Nice to see you again, Julie," Charlotte said.

"Nice to see you too, Ms. LaRue. Carol is napping in the bedroom, and Doctor Hank is in the nursery with the babies. Here, let me take that." She reached for the covered dish in Charlotte's hands.

Charlotte nodded and smiled. "Be careful, it's still pretty warm," she said as she handed over the dish of food.

A few minutes later, when Charlotte approached the nursery, she paused at the doorway and had to blink back tears of joy.

Hank, unaware that she was standing there, was seated in an oversized rocking chair. His head was leaning back against the chair, his eyes were closed, he had a baby in each arm, and he was humming one of the old nursery lullabies that she had once sung to him.

Not wanting to startle him or wake the babies, Charlotte quietly cleared her throat. "I wish I had a camera," she said softly. "Seeing you holding your babies is something I've waited a long time for."

Hank opened his eyes and smiled at her. "Hey, Mom. Come on in." Then he winked at her. "And there's a camera over on the changing table. I think Carol had Julie buy several of those throwaways, and she put one in every room in the house."

Charlotte grinned. "What a great idea." She hurried over to the changing table and picked up the small camera. "Smile," she told him. After taking two more pictures, she finally set the camera down.

Hank leaned forward, then sat back again. "Ah, I think I might need a little help here."

Charlotte stepped over beside him and gently lifted the baby wrapped in blue out of Hank's arms. "Oh, son, he's just beautiful," she whispered as she cradled the bundle close and stared down into his perfectly formed little face.

Hank grinned. "And the loudest and most demanding." He stood and lowered his pink bundle down into one of two bassinets. "And if we're lucky, maybe they'll both sleep long enough for us to have lunch. You did say you were bringing lunch, didn't you?"

"I sure did," Charlotte answered as she lowered her bundle down into the other bassinet. With one last adoring look at each baby, Charlotte followed Hank out of the nursery.

"Do they have names yet?" she asked as they walked down the hallway.

"How about Pete and Repeat?"

Charlotte rolled her eyes. "Come on, get serious."

Hank laughed. "After a lot of haggling, Carol and I both finally agreed on Samantha and Samuel."

"Hmm, Mandy and Sammy."

"No, Mom. We also agreed that there would be no nicknames."

"Well, y'all might have agreed, but nobody asked me."

This time, Hank rolled his eyes.

By midafternoon, Charlotte was back home again. After changing into her work scrubs, she headed for the hospital where Joyce had stayed. Her plan was simple and was a ploy that she'd used one other time when trying to find out information. She would pretend to be part of the maintenance personnel, and hopefully, she would be able to work her way into the ward that Joyce had been assigned to. She figured that even if her presence there was questioned, she could always claim that she had received a call from someone who said they represented the hospital, so the mistake wasn't her fault.

Once inside the hospital, Charlotte took her time and, as unobtrusively as possible, she simply observed the inner workings of the staff until she located a member of the maintenance crew who appeared to have a kind face.

The middle-aged woman was African-American, with beautiful skin the color of café au lait and a head full of curly salt-and-pepper hair. Charlotte was relieved to see that she was

117

dressed in scrubs, instead of an official-type cleaning uniform. Though the woman appeared to be strong enough, the poor thing was so skinny that a good stiff breeze could blow her over. The woman had just finished mopping one of the empty hospital rooms when Charlotte finally gathered enough courage to approach her.

"Ah, excuse me, but I seem to be lost."

The woman placed her mop inside the mop bucket and gave Charlotte a brief smile, then waited expectantly.

"I'm supposed to be filling in for someone who called in sick today," Charlotte explained, the lie tasting bitter on her lips. "But no one told me where to go." She shrugged. "Or who to report to, or what to do."

The woman nodded knowingly. "That sounds about right. What you need to do is take that elevator over there to the basement." She motioned toward a bank of elevators. "In the basement is where you clock in and where they keep all the cleaning supplies. There's also a break room for employees down there too. Do you know what floor you're supposed to be working on?"

"It's the floor where they treat the mental patients and the alcohol and drug abusers."

The woman nodded. "That's the psychiatric ward up on the tenth floor. Tell you what, I'm heading down to the basement now. If you want, you can come along with me and I'll get you hooked up with the right person. And by the way, my name's Mira. What's yours?"

"Nice to meet you, Mira. My name's Charlotte, and thanks so much for your help."

Half an hour later, Charlotte had her own mop and mop bucket, a wringer-combo type, as well as her own temporary name tag, thanks to Mira. Mira had also loaded her up with a cleaning kit that hooked onto the side of the mop bucket. In the kit were window cleaner, disinfectant, sponges, and various other cleaning items she might need.

As Charlotte stepped off the elevator onto the tenth floor, the first thing she saw was a large octagon-shaped counter area, which she assumed was the nurse's station. To the right of the nurse's station was a long hallway, and to the left was a wall; in the middle of the wall was a set of large double doors.

According to what Mira had told her, Charlotte was fairly certain that the place she needed to go was behind the closed double doors.

There were two nurses seated behind the large counter, one male and one female. Both were busy entering data into computers, and except for a brief glance her way, neither paid her any attention. Over the years, Charlotte had learned that no one paid any attention to the maid, and for once, she was glad.

Using the wringer attached to the mop bucket, she wrung out the mop and began mopping the large open area of medium-gray-tiled floor that was directly in front of the nurse's station.

When she'd finished, she set out a couple of the bright yellow CAUTION WET FLOOR signs, and then pulled her mop bucket over to the double doors. Unsure just exactly what the procedure was for getting beyond the doors, she studied what appeared to be a call box of some type on the right-hand side of the wall beside the doors. Below it was a small electronic button.

"Just press the button," the male nurse called out. "State your business, and someone will buzz you in."

Guess they were paying attention, after all, Charlotte thought as she glanced over at the nurse. "Thanks."

Charlotte pressed the button. "Maintenance. I've come to mop."

A minute or so later, the doors swung open to reveal another open area, with yet another nurse's station. Beyond the small open area was a long hallway. Two nurses were seated at the nurse's station, and another one was standing nearby going over a chart. All glanced briefly at her, then went back to what they were doing.

Since she'd never been in a psychiatric ward before, she wasn't quite sure what she'd expected, but what she hadn't expected was how quiet the ward seemed to be. As she studied the layout, she suppressed the urge to smile as thoughts of a couple of old movies she'd seen that were set in mental institutions came to mind. Unlike in the movies, there were no tortured cries or hysterical laughter here.

On the left side of the hallway, just beyond the nurse's station, was a partition that was half wall, half glass. The door leading into that area had a sign that read RECREATION ROOM. It was just a feeling, but Charlotte figured that the recreation room might be a good place to ask questions.

On the opposite side of the hallway was another similar partition, but on the door was a sign that read GROUP SESSIONS. The rest of the hallway was made up of rows of numbered doors spaced evenly apart on both sides. More than likely, those were the patients' rooms, she decided. At the very end of the hallway, daylight streamed through a large window.

So what now? she wondered as she stood staring down the hallway.

"Is there a problem?" one of the nurses asked.

Charlotte shook her head. "No—no problem." Grabbing the mop, she pushed the mop bucket toward the window end of the hallway.

Whatever she did, she needed to look legitimate or risk getting caught, and looking legitimate meant mopping. She figured that she'd start at the end and work her way back down the hall, but her main goal was the recreation room.

She was halfway down the hall when a door on her left opened, and a nurse carrying a chart emerged from the room into the hallway.

When Charlotte walked past the nurse, the woman looked up briefly from the chart she was reading. "Ah, excuse me," the nurse said. "As soon as you can, the walls in 1005 need to be wiped down." With her head, she motioned toward the room she'd just come out of. "The patient in there decided that her lunch would look better smeared on the walls. I've just given her a sedative. So, if I were you, I'd get in there and get out before the sedative wears off."

Charlotte nodded and smiled. "No time like the present," she quipped.

Though the nurse smiled back and stepped out of the way of the door entry, she resumed studying her chart without further comment.

The tiny room was just barely large enough for the single hospital-style bed, a lone chair, and an overbed table. And it was semidark, lit up by only the pale light that leaked through the closed slats of the blinds, which covered the small window. The attached bathroom was also really small, with only room for the shower, a toilet, a sink, and nothing else.

On the bed, curled into a fetal position and covered by a sheet, was a young woman, who was softly snoring. She looked to be in her early twenties.

A good half hour had passed by the time that Charlotte had finished cleaning all the food off the walls. Over the years, she'd cleaned up lots of messes, but that particular room rated right up at the top of her list as one of the most unique messes that she'd ever cleaned.

Though Charlotte had never been claustrophobic, by the time she'd finished, she felt like she was going to suffocate if she didn't get out of there.

When she finally did get out, she figured it was high time to get on with the reason she was really there. Keeping her fingers crossed that she wouldn't run into anyone else who needed her to clean up another mess, she made a beeline for the recreation room.

In two opposite corners of the recreation room were large-screened televisions, with several padded chairs arranged in a group setting around each TV. She counted no less than five of the patients seated in the chairs and watching, of all things, cartoons on one of the TVs, and four patients seated around the other one. A smile pulled at her lips when she realized that the cartoon they were watching on one of the TVs was *Woody Woodpecker;* on the other, *The Simpsons* played. Maybe laughter was the best medicine, after all.

In the middle of the room were several round tables, and seated around each table were more patients. The group at one of the tables was playing Monopoly. A group at another table was painting. At another table, several patients were playing cards.

Along one side were several chairs against the wall, and in one of the corners was a group of patients talking or reading books.

Unlike the hallway, the recreation room was noisy with the buzz of voices, occasionally punctuated by laughter.

While Charlotte mopped her way around the room, she studied the different patients in an attempt to figure out which one she should pick to question about Joyce.

At first, she didn't think that any of the patients were paying her any attention, but after only a few minutes, she got a prickly feeling that she was being watched. Thinking she was imagining things, she ignored the feeling for several minutes. But ignoring it didn't make it go away. Then one of the patients in particular caught her eye.

The sharp-looking little man was sitting in the corner that didn't have a TV, reading a book, but something about him made her suspicious. Though Charlotte couldn't put her finger on the reason, she was pretty sure that he was the one who had been watching her.

Charlotte had noted that some of the patients were dressed in pajamas and housecoats, while others were dressed in regular everyday clothes. The little man was neatly dressed in khaki pants and a pullover knit shirt. Charlotte figured he was in his late sixties or early seventies. Except for a thin white fringe of hair, he was bald, and the pointy features of his face reminded her of a leprechaun.

By the time she worked her way over to where the little man was sitting, she'd made up her mind to try and question him first.

Charlotte stopped mopping, and with her hands wrapped around the mop handle, she said, "Hi, there. How's it going?"

He narrowed his eyes suspiciously. "Who wants to know?"

Smiling at him, she said, "My name is Charlotte. What's your name?"

He tilted his head to one side and grinned. "Are you flirting with me?"

Taken aback, Charlotte was momentarily at a loss for words.

" 'Cause if you are," he continued, "you should know up front that I've already had the love of my life, and I'm not looking for another, at least not today."

Unsure whether to laugh or be insulted, she said, "Guess that makes two of us." Then she realized that he'd said "had," as in past tense. Taking a chance, Charlotte asked, "How long has it been since your wife died?"

"What's today?"

"Sunday," she answered.

"What month?"

"November."

"It's been a year ago this month."

"I'm so sorry for your loss. The man I loved died in Vietnam."

He nodded knowingly. "You still miss him?"

"Yes, at times. And I'm guessing that you miss your wife very much."

He shrugged. "That's why I'm in here. My daughter put me in here a couple of months ago. They say I'm depressed—can't manage on my own. Said that I wasn't taking care of myself—you know—eating, keeping clean, that kind of stuff."

"Yes, I do know," Charlotte told him. She could well sympathize with him about grieving. After the death of Hank senior, and then later, the death of her parents, she had been a basket case for a while. If it hadn't been for the responsibility of caring for her son, who was an infant at the time, she probably would have ended up in a mental institution.

Charlotte frowned thoughtfully. Still, if depression was all that was wrong with the little man, why was he still in a hospital ward? Shouldn't he have been transferred to another type of long-term-care facility, like a nursing home? Then again, since Hurricane Katrina, not everything was back to normal. There were all kinds of problems with the medical care in the city, including not enough hospital beds for the number of patients, especially the psychiatric patients. According to what she'd heard and read, beds for psychiatric patients were few and far between, which made the length of the little man's stay even more puzzling.

"Haven't seen you before," the little man said.

Charlotte shook her head. "No, I'm not a regular. I'm just working today to fill in for someone who's sick."

"You'd better watch it, then."

"Pardon me?"

The little man crooked his finger for Charlotte to come closer. Though a bit wary, she did lean down a little bit, but she still kept a healthy distance.

The little man's eyes darted nervously from side to side, as if checking to make sure that he wasn't being watched or over-heard; then he whispered, "Watch out for Nurse Ratched. You never know when she's going to show up, and if you make her mad at you, you'll end up getting shock treatment. Or worse," he added, tapping his forehead with the tips of his fingers. "Lobotomy, you know." Then he wiggled his craggy eye-brows, à la Groucho Marx.

Charlotte slowly straightened and eased back a step. *Great! Just my luck. The one person I pick is loony tunes and thinks he's star-ring in* One Flew Over the Cuckoo's Nest. She swallowed hard and forced a smile. Now all she had to do was figure out a way to get away from him without seeming too obvious.

Suddenly, the little man threw back his head, and clapping his hands with glee, he howled with laughter. "Gotcha," he cried. "I gotcha good."

Realizing that she'd been had, Charlotte narrowed her eyes, tilted her head, and glared down at the little man. "That wasn't very nice."

The little man chuckled. "Nope, it wasn't, but it was funny as all get-out." He grinned. "You should have seen your face." When Charlotte didn't smile, he said, "Aw, come on, lighten up. I was just fooling with you."

After a moment, she allowed the beginnings of a smile to pull at her lips. "Just don't do it again," she told him sternly.

He shrugged. "Hey, except for when they bring in those so-ciety dame whackos or discover another theft, this place can be pretty boring."

Theft? Aha, finally. Now she was getting somewhere. Pre-tending she didn't know what he meant, and praying that he would elaborate, she frowned as if confused.

Just as she'd hoped, when he saw her frown, he explained. "Some of the really ill patients are society women who think they're still at home, or think they're throwing a party or some such. They've brought 'em in here wearing those fancy-type evening gowns that women wear for Mardi Gras balls and dripping with diamonds and jewels. And I'm talking the real stuff here."

The ploy had worked once, so maybe it would work a sec-ond time. Playing dumb, Charlotte frowned again like she didn't understand. "And the thefts?"

He crooked his finger at her like he'd done before, and she leaned down closer.

"While I've been here, all kinds of valuable stuff has gone missing," he told her in a low, secretive voice. "If you know what I mean," he added, waggling his eyebrows. "Especially the gold and diamond jewelry, like those ladies wear. All of the valuables are supposed to be catalogued, then put in a vault for safekeeping. But you can't put away what's already gone by the time the patient reaches the admissions office."

Charlotte hated that a mental picture of Joyce immediately popped into her head, hated that she now equated Joyce with thievery.

She also hated having to lie to the little man. "Believe it or not, I've heard about that," she told him. "A friend of mine was in here for a while. You might remember her. Her name was Joyce." She waited a heartbeat to see if he showed any sign of recognizing Joyce's name.

He frowned thoughtfully. "Seems I remember that a woman named Joyce was here for a while."

"She was a skinny woman about my age, with red hair."

The little old man shrugged. "Could be the one I'm thinking about, but so many come and go in here."

Though Charlotte was disappointed that he didn't remember Joyce, she figured he might if she kept him talking. "Anyway," she continued, "Joyce mentioned something that I didn't understand in connection to the thefts, and I didn't get a chance to ask her about it. Do the words 'bluebird' or 'daisy' mean anything to you?"

Again he frowned thoughtfully. "You know." He paused. "Bluebird could be a brooch that was stolen. See that woman over there, the one with black hair and wearing the red blouse?" He pointed at a woman who was playing cards. "When she was first brought in, she claimed that her brooch was stolen. I heard her describing it to one of the nurses. She said the brooch was shaped like a bird. Said it was made of diamonds, and in the center, representing the bird's body, was a big blue diamond. Reason I remember is because I'd never heard of *blue* diamonds. Supposed to be worth a ton of money."

Charlotte had heard of blue diamonds. They were very rare and very expensive.

"Anyway," the little man continued, "nothing was ever done about—"

"Just what do you think you're doing?"

Startled by the harsh sound of the woman's voice, Charlotte jumped. *Uh-oh, caught red-handed.* She'd heard that voice before, but couldn't immediately place where. Without looking up, Charlotte slid her eyes sideways. White clogs and white pants. A nurse?

"I said, what do you think you're doing?"

127

"Ah, nothing," Charlotte replied, hoping the woman would move on. "Just mopping."

When the nurse didn't move on, but continued to stand where she was, Charlotte straightened up and slowly turned to face her. Then she gasped.

Chapter 11

Immediately recognizing the nurse as the same young woman who had flagged her down outside the pawnshop and complained about Roy Price, Charlotte could hardly believe her eyes. Unlike many of the nurses nowadays, who chose to wear multicolored scrubs, this one was wearing a standard white uniform, complete with nurse's cap.

Charlotte figured that she was in trouble for sure now, caught red-handed, especially if the knowing gleam in the woman's eyes was any gauge to measure by.

The woman gave her a sly smile. "I didn't expect to see *you* here."

Charlotte shrugged. "I didn't expect to see *you* either."

The woman's mouth took on an unpleasant twist. "So, just what are you doing here?"

"I'm a maid by trade," Charlotte explained; then, motioning toward the mop bucket, she said, "I'm working temporarily, filling in for someone who called in sick." She placed the mop back inside the mop bucket. "Now, if you'll excuse me, I have work to do."

A warning cloud settled over the woman's features and suspicion darkened her eyes. "Then do it, and no talking to the patients," she said, her voice suddenly hard and cold. When the woman didn't immediately step aside, Charlotte figured it was just her way of posturing to show her authority.

"Ah, excuse me," Charlotte repeated.

The woman remained standing in Charlotte's way a moment more before she finally relented and stepped aside.

As Charlotte wheeled the mop bucket toward the door, she chanced one last look at the little old man.

The nurse was still there and it appeared that she was grilling him. But the little man seemed to be ignoring her and was staring down at his book. Then, just as Charlotte was about to turn her head, he looked up and winked at her.

Smiling and winking back at him, Charlotte left the room. Deciding that she could use a cup of coffee and a break, she headed straight for the bank of elevators. Inside one of the elevators, she pressed the basement floor button.

When the elevator reached the basement, she headed straight for the room that Mira had showed her earlier. Leaving her mop and mop bucket outside the door, and praying that no one else would be inside, she went inside the break room.

To her delight, someone had just made a fresh pot of coffee. After pouring herself a cup, she sat down at one of the tables, and as she sipped her coffee, she thought about everything that she'd learned.

Other than the fact that there was evidently a theft ring of sorts going on at the hospital, and she now knew what the word "bluebird" meant, she hadn't learned a whole lot. And what she still didn't know was what, if anything, any of it had to do with Joyce's murder.

Too bad her conversation with the little old man had been so rudely interrupted, or she might have learned even more.

Charlotte closed her eyes and sighed. Though stranger things had happened, she still couldn't believe that she'd run into the woman who had flagged her down outside the pawnshop, especially at the hospital *and* particularly in the psychiatric ward, of all places—the same ward that Joyce had been in. It just seemed like too much of a coincidence to be believable.

But was it a coincidence? Charlotte drummed her fingers against the tabletop. Or was it all somehow connected? Outside the pawnshop, the woman had been eager for Charlotte's help and she'd seemed really knowledgeable about Roy Price and the workings of the pawnshop. So why would a nurse know so much about the pawnshop, and why the hostility, unless . . .

Charlotte sighed deeply. Unless what? Without more information, everything was speculation for now. And why hadn't she simply come right out and asked the woman what was going on, instead of running like a scalded dog?

A slight noise outside the door interrupted Charlotte's reverie. Thinking that someone was coming, she opened her eyes, tilted her head, and listened, waiting for someone to walk in.

After several moments, she decided that she must be hearing things, and she also decided that she had a decision to make. Should she stay and keep pretending to be part of the maintenance crew, in hopes that she might learn something more, or should she leave now and go home? If she stayed, she ran the risk of getting caught. And she ran the risk of running into that woman again.

For now, maybe she needed to go home.

Coward. No guts, no glory.

Yeah, well, who needs glory, she silently answered the irritating voice in her head.

Charlotte took one last swallow of coffee, then tossed it in the trash bin. First she needed to return the mop and mop bucket to the supply room.

The time card. Don't forget the time card.

Charlotte grimaced. Mira had insisted on fixing her up with a time card, and unless she really wanted to get caught, she'd have to remember to retrieve it and get rid of it.

Outside the break room, Charlotte grabbed the handle of the mop and used it to push the mop bucket toward the narrow, smelly corridor that led to the supply room. She was just a few feet into the corridor when a door suddenly slammed behind her, effectively cutting off that particular exit.

For several moments, Charlotte stared at the door as the hairs on the back of her neck stood on end and an uneasy feeling crawled up her spine. Then, without warning, the door to the corridor in front of her slammed shut, cutting off the only other exit and trapping her in the small hallway.

"What on earth?" Leaving the mop bucket, she hurried to the first door and tried to open it. Locked? But why would it be locked? Turning, she hurried to the other door and found that it was also locked.

With the palm of her hand, she banged on the door. "Hey!" she yelled. "Anybody out there? I'm locked in! Somebody let me out!" When there was no response, panic welled in her throat, and she had to fight the urge to scream her head off.

Just stay calm. You're okay. Just stay calm.

Charlotte took a deep breath, then let it out slowly. Standing on tiptoe, she peered through the small glass window near the top of the door. At first, she saw nothing. Then, suddenly, a face appeared. With a shriek, she jumped.

On the other side of the small window was the woman from the pawnshop. Charlotte glared at her. "Let me out of here," she demanded.

For a long moment, the woman simply stared back at her. Then, with a brief malevolent smile, her face disappeared.

"Not good," Charlotte murmured, her uneasy feeling returning full force. "Not good at all." For whatever reason, the woman was trying to scare her, to intimidate her. And doing a fine job of it too.

But why?

Without warning, the lock on the door clicked. Charlotte gulped. "Uh-oh." Not knowing what to expect, she quickly backed away from the door. What she needed was a weapon of some kind, just in case the woman truly intended on doing her harm.

Except for the mop bucket, the small corridor was completely empty. She glanced down at the bucket in hopes that a weapon of some kind would magically appear. The window cleaner had ammonia in it; nothing like a shot of ammonia in the eyes to slow a person down. Just as Charlotte wrapped her hand around the bottle of window cleaner, the door opened and the woman slipped inside.

"You should have minded your own business," the woman said as she quickly locked the door again, then slipped the keys into her pants pocket.

"I don't know what you're talking about," Charlotte retorted as she tried to remember if she'd turned the little doodad on the sprayer part of the bottle closed or left it open. More than likely, she'd closed it, she decided, and without taking her eyes off the younger woman, she quickly twisted it to what she hoped was open.

The action didn't go unnoticed by the young woman, and she laughed. "What?" She pointed at the window cleaner bottle. "Are you going to spray me to death?"

Charlotte chose to ignore the woman's taunt. She figured that in size she and the younger woman were about equal, but strength was another matter altogether. The woman was at least thirty years younger and bound to be stronger.

Buy time. Keep her talking. Maybe someone will come.

"Just what is it that you want?" Charlotte demanded.

The woman glanced down at the window cleaner in Charlotte's hand once again, then raised her gaze to glare at Charlotte as she took a step closer. "Like I said, you should have minded your own business."

"Mind my business about what?" Charlotte cried.

"You know what," the woman snapped, "so stop playing dumb." She slid her hand inside her pants pocket and pulled out a hypodermic syringe.

Charlotte eyed the syringe and her heart began pounding in her chest. It had to be one of the biggest needles she'd ever seen. "W-what's that?"

Giving Charlotte another of her malevolent smiles, the woman slipped the sheath off the needle. "We can do this the hard way or the easy way," she said. "Your choice."

Trapped. She was trapped and she was in big trouble.

Buy time. Keep her talking. Surely, someone will come along who can help.

Charlotte wanted to still believe that someone would come, but in her heart of hearts, she knew she was on her own.

Stop being such a wuss and get mad. She's nothing but a bully, and she's just bluffing, so call her bluff.

As silent pep talks went, it was a good one, but Charlotte didn't believe it. The woman was almost within touching distance, and wasn't bluffing. She meant business and was out to get her, whatever it took.

Spray her in the face. Do it now!

But Charlotte held back, and in one last-ditch effort to avoid the nasty confrontation she feared was about to happen, she threw up her free hand, palm up. And in her very best, most stern tone, she said, "Stop! Just wait a minute. I told you before that I don't even know what you're talking about. Whatever it is that you think I know, I don't, so back off.

Leave now and we can both forget this little confrontation ever happened."

Suddenly, without warning, the woman stepped forward and, at the same time, drew her hand back. Then she struck out with the syringe, aiming for Charlotte's neck.

Charlotte reflexively jerked backward, avoiding the woman's first attempt, and like two boxers in a sparring match, they danced around the mop bucket. While Charlotte feinted from left to right in an attempt to keep the woman off-balance, she pointed the window cleaner bottle at her and pulled the trigger. When nothing happened, she kept pulling the trigger, and still nothing happened.

Abruptly, the woman stopped and stood stone still. Then, with a scream of frustration, she viciously kicked the mop bucket aside and lunged at Charlotte.

Instinctively, Charlotte swung the window cleaner upward to block the woman's attack. The bottle connected with the woman's wrist, and the syringe flew out of her hand. When the syringe hit the floor, it skidded toward the first locked door.

Screaming obscenities, the woman scrambled to get the syringe.

Her fingers shaking, Charlotte twisted the end of the spray bottle, squeezed again, and still nothing happened.

Trembling, she saw the woman bend over to grab the syringe off the floor. Going on pure instinct, Charlotte drew back, and using every bit of strength she had, she threw the bottle at her, aiming for her head.

Caught off-balance and by surprise, the woman was unable to duck in time, and the bottle hit her in the face. Blood spurted from her nose, and when the woman reached to grab her nose with her free hand, Charlotte seized the mop handle.

Flipping the mop, and with a growl of fury, Charlotte used

the handle end like a battering ram, and she slammed it into the woman's stomach.

The woman cried out and dropped the syringe again. Gasping for breath, she grabbed her stomach and fell to her knees.

The voice in Charlotte's head screamed, *Get the keys! They're in her pocket. Get them now!*

With her foot, Charlotte kicked the syringe out of the woman's reach. Flipping the mop again, she gripped the handle with both hands and raised the mop up, just above the woman's head. Using the woman's head for a target, she rammed the mop head downward. The force of the blow vibrated through her arms and dazed the woman. She groaned, her eyes fluttered shut, and she fell to the floor.

Charlotte dropped the mop, and while the woman was still stunned, Charlotte bent over her and quickly filched the keys from her pants pocket.

Wasting only enough time to snatch up the syringe, Charlotte ran over to the door, unlocked it, then slammed it closed behind her, locking it again.

With the syringe in one hand, and the keys in her other hand, she leaned back against the locked door. At first, she was still so shocked by the attack that all she could do was shiver and try to catch her breath.

What if she'd killed the woman?

It was kill or be killed . . . self-defense.

Charlotte shook her head. "No, no, no," she moaned. Besides, she was pretty sure that she hadn't killed her. Then again, she hadn't taken the time to check and make sure that the woman was still breathing and still had a heartbeat.

On shaky feet, Charlotte turned and peered on tiptoes through the window at the top of the door, but from where she was standing, all she could see were the woman's feet. And they weren't moving.

Charlotte turned her back to the door again. Without warning, her legs suddenly went weak. She slid down the door to the floor and burst into tears.

Charlotte wasn't sure how long she sat there, alternately shivering and crying, but it was the sudden sound of screams coming from within the locked corridor and the banging on the door that finally spurred her to her feet again.

At least now she knew that the woman was alive. Time to get out of there, and time to go home.

Later, when she pulled into her driveway, Charlotte didn't quite recall how she got out of the hospital, and she barely remembered the drive home. It was like her brain had shut down and she was running on automatic pilot.

Once at home, though, she went straight to the bathroom, stripped, and took a long, hot shower. By the time she shut off the shower and dried off, it was almost dark outside, so she dressed in her pajamas.

In the living room, she eyed the hospital name tag and the syringe that she'd left on her desktop. Before she'd left the hospital, she'd still had sense enough to drop the keys, which she'd taken from the nurse, in the trash on her way out. She'd also had enough of her wits that she'd found her time card, ripped it into several pieces, then thrown it in the trash too.

Wondering why she had brought the name tag and syringe home with her, instead of simply throwing both in the trash, she slipped the name tag into a drawer. Then she stared at the syringe.

Curiosity, she decided. She was curious as to what kind of lethal drug was in the syringe, and she'd figured that there had to be some way of finding out. Charlotte shivered. The woman had intended on killing her, but with what? And just as important, what did the woman think she knew that warranted murder?

Suddenly startled by another thought that flashed through her mind, Charlotte's breath caught in her throat, and she went stone still. Why hadn't she seen it before? Why was she just now making the connection?

Because you were fighting for your life, but now you're safe, came the answer.

It all made a weird kind of sense. The evil nurse worked at the hospital and had tried to kill her because she'd seen her talking to the little old man. Joyce had been a patient at the hospital. Joyce was murdered. Both Joyce and the nurse had some kind of connection to the pawnshop.

Taking a deep breath, then letting it out slowly, Charlotte gingerly picked up the syringe, then headed for the kitchen. Though she wasn't quite sure why she felt the need to hang on to it, she did know that she shouldn't get rid of it. Not just yet, anyway.

She also suspected that the little old man knew more than he'd had time to tell her. Just thinking about the old man made her all jittery inside, and she swallowed hard as she pulled a package of foil out of a drawer in the kitchen. She somehow needed to talk to him again and find out what else he knew. But how in the world could she do so without running into that awful nurse again?

Just as she tore off a strip of foil, she suddenly had a horrible thought. If the nurse was afraid of what the old man might have told her, what would she be willing to do in order to shut him up? Could he, even now, be in danger for his life?

Don't think about it.

The last thing she wanted was to think about someone else getting murdered, especially if they were murdered because of talking to her. And over what? Surely not just a theft ring.

People have been killed for a lot less.

Charlotte shuddered, remembering an incident that she'd

read about where one teenager had killed another teenager for his tennis shoes.

Dear Lord, what was the world coming to, she thought as she wrapped the syringe carefully in foil and placed it in a bottom drawer of her refrigerator for safekeeping. Later, she'd figure out exactly what she was going to do with it.

Just as she closed the refrigerator, the phone rang, and Charlotte hurried to the living room to answer it.

"Hello?"

"Charlotte, this is Louis. Are you busy?"

"No, not really."

"Would it be okay if I came over for a while? I thought I would share a few things I've learned this afternoon about Joyce and see if you have anything to add to it."

Oh, boy, do I. Images of her battle with the evil nurse flashed through her mind. "Yeah, fine. Come on over."

"Have you had supper yet?"

Charlotte frowned. With everything that had happened, she'd completely forgotten about eating. "No, I haven't eaten yet."

"Is KFC okay?"

"You don't have to do that."

"It's not a problem. I'm hungry, and you haven't eaten, so why not? How about one of those two-piece meals?"

Charlotte's mouth watered at the thought of fried chicken. "Well, if you put it that way. And a two-piece meal would be just fine. Make my side items coleslaw and green beans." The coleslaw probably contained a little more sugar than she needed, but it was oh so good.

"Great. I'll be there in about fifteen minutes or so."

By the time Louis arrived, Charlotte had decided to change into a jogging suit, rather than explain why she was wearing her pajamas so early in the evening. Of course she would eventually tell him about what had happened at the hospital. She'd have to. But this way she could tell him when she was ready and avoid getting the third degree right away.

When Charlotte took the plastic bag of food from Louis, the smell of fried chicken was heavenly. "It's been a long time since I had the Colonel's chicken," she said as she pulled the covered disposable plates out of the bag and set them out on the table. "I went ahead and poured us both a glass of iced tea, but I can get you something different if you don't want the tea."

"Tea is fine, Charlotte."

Once they were both seated, Charlotte asked, "Would you say the blessing?"

Louis shook his head. "Why don't you do it?"

With a nod, Charlotte bowed her head and offered up a brief prayer of thanksgiving for the food. When she closed with "Amen," they were both silent for several minutes while they uncovered the plastic disposable plates, then began eating.

"Joyce told the truth about that California business," Louis said once he'd devoured the chicken leg that came with his meal. "She was a snitch, and the detective she worked for was named Aubrey Hamilton. Funny thing, though, my contact in San Francisco said that not long after Joyce left the city, Aubrey Hamilton came up missing and hasn't been heard from since. Seems Hamilton had been working on a particular case involving a certain member of the Russian mob."

Louis shook his head. "Too bad Joyce didn't trust me enough to tell me the truth, instead of making up that stupid story about being terminally ill. I figure something or someone scared her pretty badly and she had to be desperate. When I showed up looking for her, she grabbed at the opportunity to disappear. If only she'd trusted me more and told me the truth, I could have tried to help her, and just maybe, she might still be alive."

"You can't blame yourself, Louis. If she didn't feel like she could tell you in the beginning, she had ample opportunity to tell you later."

"Yeah, well, maybe. Maybe not."

While Louis continued talking, Charlotte simply listened. Joyce had already told her most of what Louis was saying, but since she couldn't recall if she'd shared all of it with him when they'd talked before at the hospital, keeping quiet seemed the best solution.

"I figure that whoever scared her off to begin with must have finally caught up with her," he continued.

Charlotte slowly nodded as she stabbed several green beans with her fork. "Makes sense," she agreed. And it did make sense, but it still didn't explain the Joyce/evil nurse/pawnshop connection.

"What I haven't figured out yet, though, is who killed her, whether it was the Russian mob or Aubrey Hamilton? Of course there's another possibility too. The mob could have hired a professional hit man. The SFPD is looking into it more from their end. I also told Judith what I'd found out, so she'll be checking that angle as well."

When Louis said, "hit man," a mental image of the nurse popped into Charlotte's head. "Could have been a hit woman," she muttered.

"What was that?"

Charlotte sighed heavily. No time like the present, she decided. She might as well come clean now. "I have some news too," she told him. "Remember I said I'd check out the hospital where Joyce stayed?"

Louis's brows drew together in obvious displeasure, and he

slowly shook his head. "Nooo." He drew the word out ominously. "I don't seem to recall that particular conversation. But why doesn't that surprise me?"

Uh-oh.

Charlotte could have sworn that she'd told him about her idea of paying a visit to the hospital. Judging from his sourprune expression, evidently she hadn't. Well, too bad. She glared at him defiantly. "Well, I checked it out," she told him.

"And?"

"And I found out a couple of things. I talked to this little old man who's a patient in the psych ward, and he turned out to be a font of information."

"Uh-huh. And why would you believe some loony tunes guy in the psych ward?"

"He wasn't in there because he was loony tunes," she retorted. "If you must know, he had a depression problem. Anyway . . ." Charlotte went on to tell Louis what the man had said about the thefts that had occurred, specifically the bluebird brooch.

"So what you're saying is that Joyce might have been mixed up with some kind of theft ring in the hospital?"

Charlotte shrugged. "Not necessarily mixed up in it or even taking part in it, but maybe she found out about it by accident, and someone wanted to keep her quiet."

" 'Someone'? Sounds like you've got '*someone*' in particular in mind?"

Charlotte lowered her gaze to stare at the congealing gravy on her plate. "Yeah, I do. There was this nurse, and when she saw that I was talking to the old man, she got upset. Well, not exactly upset in the normal sense of the word. But upset as in it was obvious that she didn't want me talking to him."

"And it didn't enter your mind that maybe she didn't want you talking to him because he was a patient and you . . ." He suddenly frowned. "Come to think of it, just how did you get in there to begin with?"

Knowing that Louis wasn't going to like or approve of what she'd done, Charlotte squirmed in her seat. "I was a maid, mopping floors. What else?"

Comprehension suddenly dawned in his eyes, and shaking his head with disbelief, he groaned. "Don't tell me. Let me guess. You went in there and pretended to be part of the maintenance crew?"

Charlotte shrugged. "Well, it worked." She paused. "At least it worked until that nurse showed up. Turns out she just also happened to be the woman who flagged me down outside the pawnshop, and she recognized me. But that's not even the good part." Charlotte winced. "Not exactly good, I guess, especially since she tried to kill me later, but—"

"She did what?" Louis shouted. "What do you mean, she tried to kill you?"

"If you'll stop yelling and let me finish, I'll tell you."

When Louis finally gave her a tight-lipped nod, Charlotte gave him a blow-by-blow account of her basement confrontation with the nurse. "Which reminds me, you don't happen to know someone who could tell me what kind of drugs were in that syringe, do you?"

"Not without the syringe."

"Well, yeah, I realize that, but I have it. I brought it home with me." She got up from the chair and went to the refrigerator, where she removed the foil packet containing the syringe. Back at the table, she carefully unfolded the foil and showed the syringe to Louis.

He nodded. "Yeah, I do know someone who could tell us what's in that thing. Give it to me."

Charlotte wrapped the syringe up in the foil again and handed it to Louis.

He gave her a long, steady look. "So why didn't you call the police?"

Charlotte shrugged. "And tell them what? Tell them that I was in the hospital under false pretenses? Besides, even if they didn't cart me off to jail, it would have been her word against mine. And she could have claimed that I stole the syringe."

Nodding, Louis said, "Yeah, you're right." He paused for a moment of thoughtful silence. "You could be right about there being a theft ring, but I don't think that had anything to do with Joyce's murder. Besides, I'd rather believe my contact in the SFPD than some loony old man."

"I told you, he's not loony. Besides, what about the attack on me?"

Louis stared down at the foil packet, and then said, "Are you sure she didn't just mistake you for a wayward patient?"

Chapter 12

Charlotte could hardly believe her ears, and shock yielded quickly to fury. That he could so easily dismiss her dangerous encounter made her want to slap him silly.

" 'Wayward patient'?" she retorted. "Down in the basement? And me with a mop and mop bucket? You've got to be kidding! Besides which, not just anyone can come and go in that psych ward. There *are* locked doors, you know."

"Yeah, but you said yourself that you pretended to be part of the maintenance crew. For all she knew, you could have stolen the mop and mop bucket from a real maintenance person and used it to escape."

"Then she would be one stupid nurse. I think the reason she attacked me was because she recognized that I wasn't one of her patients."

"Maybe, maybe not," he retorted. "I doubt that the nurses remember every patient."

Seething with indignation, Charlotte glared at him. "I'm not believing this." She quickly shoved back her chair, stood, then snatched up the disposable plates and threw them in the trash can.

When she reached across the table and grabbed Louis's glass, he slid his chair back. "Are you mad?"

Charlotte was actually so angry, she couldn't have answered if her life depended on it.

"What the deuce are you mad about?"

When Charlotte snatched up her glass as well and marched over to the sink, Louis stood. "Guess that means we've finished eating, huh?"

Still too angry to do anything more than glare at him, she loaded the glasses in the dishwasher, then slammed the door shut. Grabbing a dish towel, she stepped back over to the table, and with jerky motions, she began wiping it off.

For several moments, Louis silently watched her. When she still didn't say anything, he finally said, "I don't see what's got you so all-fired angry."

Charlotte stopped long enough to scowl at him, then resumed wiping the table.

"Okay, then, guess it's time to go. I'll let myself out." With one last baffled glance at her, he finally turned and headed toward the doorway leading to the living room. "Don't forget to use the dead bolt," he called out over his shoulder.

The second she heard the front door close and knew he was gone, Charlotte threw the dish towel on the counter, flipped off the kitchen light, and went into the living room.

Still fuming over his callous dismissal of what she'd found out at the hospital, and his lame explanation for her dangerous encounter with the nurse, she stood glaring at the dead bolt on her front door.

" 'Don't forget to use the dead bolt,' " she mimicked in a singsong voice. "As if I would," she retorted indignantly as she threw the dead bolt. Considering his attitude, there was only one thing she could do. Like it or not, she was going to have to find out who murdered Joyce. "That'll show him," she muttered between clenched teeth. Regardless of what he'd said about the Russian mob, she still believed that Joyce's murder had something to do with the theft ring at the hospital.

Out of habit, she turned from the door and reached out to cover Sweety Boy's cage for the night. Her hand froze in midair. "Old habits die hard," she murmured as she stared at the empty cage. Seeing the empty birdcage was a stark reminder that the little bird was still missing.

Or was he dead?

Like a puff of smoke, her anger disappeared, leaving her feeling sad and weepy. And really drained and tired. Placing her hands on her hips and bending backward, she stretched. Time to go to bed. She glanced over at the cuckoo clock, and wondered if it was too late to call and check on Carol and the twins.

You just saw them a few hours ago.

"So what," she muttered, tempted to call in spite of the silly voice of reason in her head. After a moment, however, she finally decided that given her own present mood, it might be best to wait until tomorrow, after all.

On Monday morning, Charlotte hurriedly dressed and rushed through her normal routine in order to give herself a little extra time to look around outside for Sweety Boy before it was time to leave for work. But on her way out the door, she stopped long enough to phone Carol.

"How are you?" Charlotte asked.

"Tired and sleepy," Carol told her. "With the twins wanting to eat every two hours or so, I didn't get a lot of sleep last night."

"Is that son of mine helping out?"

"Oh, Charlotte, Hank has been wonderful. It's just that two babies are a handful."

Though it had been over forty years, Charlotte still remembered how it had been taking care of one newborn baby. She couldn't begin to imagine two. "How about supper tonight? I'd be more than happy to bring over something."

"Oh, Charlotte, that's so sweet. I really appreciate the offer, but we still have enough roast left over for tonight. Maybe tomorrow evening, instead? If it's not too much trouble," she added.

"Tell you what," Charlotte said. "I know you like my homemade chicken potpie. That and a green salad make a pretty good meal. I'll make one of those for you for tomorrow night."

"That sounds great. And if you can, would you mind planning on staying for a while? Hank has a late surgery tomorrow that he can't get out of, and Julie has an appointment with her little girl's kindergarten teacher after school."

After assuring Carol that she would help her out, Charlotte said good-bye. Gathering her sweater and purse, she hurried out the door.

Outside, the sky was overcast and she shivered from the slight chill in the air. Wondering what the weather forecast held for the next few days, she checked her own yard first, and then she checked the trees along the sidewalk on either side of her house, all to no avail. The little bird was nowhere to be found.

Her heart heavy, and knowing that with each day that passed, her chances of finding the little bird grew slimmer, she finally climbed inside her van and headed for work. For now, all she could do was keep searching and praying that the weather didn't turn colder. Then she thought of something else. Madeline was really good with computers. Maybe she should have her make up some flyers and offer a reward. If she could persuade Maddie to do it today, then first thing in the morning, she could begin passing them out to her neighbors.

* * *

Charlotte's Monday client was Sally Lawson, an attractive, middle-aged blonde who owned a lovely old cottage-style house.

Built in the 1840s, with its broad galleries, high ceilings, floor-length windows, and louvered shutters, the old home had survived Hurricane Katrina with flying colors, sustaining only minimal wind damage. Sally and her husband had meticulously and lovingly renovated the old house, then decorated and furnished it to reflect the historical period that it represented. Though modest in size by comparison to many of the other homes in the Garden District, the old house was one of the favorites to be listed each year for the annual Christmas tour parade of homes sponsored by the Preservation Resource Center.

From the sympathetic look on Sally's face when she greeted Charlotte at the front door, Charlotte knew immediately that she'd heard about Joyce's murder. But how? The newspaper? The news on television? Maybe even both, she decided, remembering the TV van that had showed up at her house.

Charlotte swallowed hard. All she could do now was hope that no one connected her house to her maid service. Having her name connected with a murder and plastered on TV or in the newspaper wasn't exactly good advertisement for Maid-for-a-Day.

"Are you okay?" Sally asked.

Charlotte forced a little smile and nodded.

"That had to have been a horrible experience for you, discovering someone murdered in your home. Did you know the woman?"

Charlotte nodded again. "She'd been staying with me a couple of days, until she could find an apartment of her own," she explained as she set down her supply carrier and vacuum cleaner on the floor in the entrance hallway. "How did you find out about it, if you don't mind me asking?"

"I ran into Bitsy Duhe at the Garden District Book Shop on Saturday," Sally said, "and she told me."

"Now, why am I not surprised?" Charlotte murmured.

Sally laughed. "Oh, Charlotte, you know how Bitsy is. Nothing goes on in this town that she doesn't hear about, one way or another."

Truer words were never spoken, Charlotte thought.

Of all of Charlotte's clients, Sally was the least messy. Charlotte's job consisted mostly of dusting, vacuuming, changing the bed linens, and keeping up with the laundry. All morning long, as Charlotte cleaned and dusted her way through Sally's home, her thoughts kept going back to what had happened at the hospital on Sunday afternoon. By lunchtime, she'd decided that somehow she had to find a way to talk to the little old man again. By quitting time, it had warmed up a bit outside and the sun had come out, and she'd come up with a plan for getting back inside the hospital to talk to the old man without running into the same nurse.

As she parked the van, Charlotte was relieved to see that Louis's car wasn't in his driveway. Once inside her house, she hurried back to her bedroom and took down a small hatbox from the top shelf in the closet. Inside the box was a medium-length wig of curly black hair.

Charlotte frowned as she fluffed out the wig. Today wouldn't be the first time that she'd used it for a disguise. In front of the bathroom mirror, she fitted the wig over her head. As she tucked her own hair under the wig, she couldn't help remembering the last time she'd worn it, and the reason why.

Then, like now, she'd used it for a disguise in hopes of

150

catching a murderer. The murderer was caught, and afterward, she'd intended on pitching the wig in the garbage. Now she was glad she'd kept it, after all. Maybe this time it would help her catch yet another killer.

Once the wig was firmly in place, she applied a darker shade of makeup than she normally wore. Using a black eyebrow pencil, she darkened her eyebrows.

Charlotte searched a dresser drawer until she finally found the old pair of reading glasses that she'd meant to donate to one of the many charity groups that collected them. After slipping the glasses on, she took a critical look at herself in the mirror, then smiled at the results. She doubted if even Louis would recognize her in this getup.

On her way out the door, at the last minute, she remembered to retrieve the hospital name tag from the desk drawer.

Afternoon work traffic was a bit heavier than normal, so the drive to the hospital took a little longer than usual. Once inside the hospital, Charlotte caught an elevator and went straight to the basement.

In the utility room, as she quickly picked out a mop and mop bucket, she listened carefully for the least sound that might indicate that someone was coming. No way did she want to get caught again or trapped by the evil nurse.

Stop being such a ninny. No one, not even that awful nurse, is going to recognize you in this getup.

"Yeah, yeah," she mumbled, wishing there were a switch of some kind that she could throw to shut off the aggravating voice in her head. Still, the voice was right, and now she needed to find the little old man.

As she rode the elevator up to the tenth floor, she prayed that the old man was still there and that he was okay. It gave her shivers to even think about what the nurse might have done to him.

Like she'd done the day before, Charlotte mopped the main area between the bank of elevators and the nurse's station. And like before, she walked to the double doors and pressed the call button.

Once inside the psychiatric ward, she went straight to the recreation room. The room was full of patients, and, both TVs were playing cartoons again. As she mopped and searched the room, she felt a wave of momentary panic when she didn't see the old man.

Just because you don't see him in here doesn't mean that something happened to him. He could be in his room or in therapy.

What now? she wondered. Should she search every room? Or maybe she could ask some of the other patients.

No, just mop slower and hope he shows up before you finish.

Charlotte figured a good twenty minutes had passed by the time she'd mopped the entire room, and she'd just about decided to start asking the patients about the old man when the entry door to the room opened, and a small group of patients meandered inside.

Charlotte spotted him almost immediately, and once again, he had a book in his hands. She was so relieved to see that he was okay, she had to restrain herself from running over to give him a hug. She waited, though, until he'd settled in the same corner chair he'd been in the first time she'd seen him, before she approached him.

"Hi," she said.

He peered up at her and his craggy eyebrows drew downward into a frown. After a moment, he suddenly grinned. "It's you again."

Uh-oh, maybe her disguise wasn't as good as she'd thought it was. "How did you know?" she asked.

"I know all the pretty women around here," he retorted with a wink.

Charlotte laughed, and repeating what he'd said to her the first time that they had talked, she asked, "Are you flirting with me?"

For an answer, he winked and then grinned.

"Seriously, how did you know?" she asked, still worried about her disguise.

His grin turned into a frown. " 'Cause I've been expecting you to come back. At least I was hoping you'd come back. I wanted to warn you to watch out for Daisy. Besides, you're wearing the same name tag."

Duh, of course. The name tag. Then she frowned. "Daisy?"

"Yeah, I was gonna warn you yesterday when you asked about her, but then she showed up and ran you off."

"That nurse—her name was Daisy?"

"Yeah, that's her."

"Daisy," she murmured, repeating the name. At least now she knew what all of the words meant: "daisy" for the nurse, "bluebird" for the brooch, and "bughouse" for the hospital. And she also knew now that all of them were connected to Joyce and connected to the hospital.

"Like I said, you need to watch out for her," he warned again.

"Yeah, well, you're just a little late. Yesterday after I left, I went down to the basement to take a short break. To make a long story short, Daisy showed up, and let's just say the meeting got nasty."

The little man shook his head. "That's too bad. I was afraid of something like that. She's a mean one."

Recalling just how mean she had been, Charlotte shuddered. "You've got that right."

"Yeah, a mean one, all right," he repeated again. "Why, after you left, she grilled me like a drill sergeant—wanted to know everything you said to me." He gave Charlotte a smug smile. "Don't worry, though. I'm no snitch. I just played dumb and made out like I didn't know what she was talking about."

"So what's her problem?"

His eyes darted around the room nervously. Then he crooked his finger at her, and she leaned down closer. "I've got some information for you," he said, "but I want to make a deal."

Deal? With a frown, Charlotte glanced to the left, then to the right, to make sure that no one was paying attention to her or to the old man. Three chairs down on the right, a woman who looked to be in her mid-twenties, was reading a book, and to the old man's left, another woman was simply sitting and staring into space, a blank look on her face.

With a final glance over her shoulder, Charlotte sat down in the empty chair beside the old man. "What kind of deal?" she asked him.

He shifted sideways to face her. "Let me explain something first," he told her. "I don't trust that Daisy as far as I can throw her. We're in luck today, though. Today is her day off. Anyway, yesterday, I bluffed my way through her asking me questions, but if she finds out I'm even talking to you again, she could cause me all kinds of trouble. And you can be sure she'll find out," he added. Then he lowered his voice to almost a whisper. "She's got spies everywhere."

Unsure whether to take him seriously, and wondering if Louis might have been right when he'd called the old man "loony tunes," Charlotte hesitated. After a moment, though, she decided that she should probably hear what he had to say before passing judgment. "Okay," she finally said. "What kind of deal are we talking about?"

"I'll tell you everything I know—and I know a lot—but you've got to get me out of here."

"Get you out of here?"

"Shush," he whispered, his eyes darting around the room. "Lower your voice. Somebody might hear you."

"Okay, okay, I'll lower my voice, but why do you need me to get you out of here? I'm pretty sure that with seventy-two hours' notice, you can check yourself out without anyone's permission."

He shook his head. "That's true most of the time, but not in my case. I was committed by the court."

"Then how on earth do you expect *me* to get you out of here?"

"You could call my daughter for me and tell her I'm in danger in here. Tell her that she needs to move me somewhere else—another hospital. I'd call her and tell her, but she'd come closer to believing you than she would me."

Mollified somewhat that he hadn't asked her to actually help him escape or anything like that, Charlotte studied the old man. He knew he still needed to be in treatment, but he was scared. And after her own experience with Nurse Daisy, she could hardly blame him for being scared. Unlike her, he was trapped and at Daisy's mercy. Even if he did complain to hospital staff, there was a good chance that no one would pay any attention to what he said. They'd just figure that he was trying to get out, period.

A moment more passed, and Charlotte finally made up her mind. Even if he wasn't able to tell her anything useful, she owed it to him to try and help him. After all, if it weren't for her, he wouldn't be on Daisy's radar to begin with.

"I'm so sorry that I've involved you in all this," she finally said. "That was not my intention. Tell you what, all I can do is promise to call your daughter and tell her what I know. But unfortunately, I can't guarantee that she'll listen or get you out of here."

"But you will call her?"

"Yes, I'll call her."

"Then we've got a deal."

The relieved look on the old man's face would have been comical if it hadn't been so pathetic, and Charlotte nodded. "Yes, we've got a deal." She pulled out a mini spiral notebook and a pen from her pocket. "Now tell me your name, your daughter's name, and give me her phone number."

"My name is Delbert O'Banion—my friends call me 'Bert'—and my daughter's name is Linda Harris."

Charlotte smiled and stuck out her right hand. "And I'm Charlotte LaRue. Nice to meet you, Bert."

The old man grinned and briefly shook her hand. Then Charlotte jotted down his name, his daughter's name, and his daughter's phone number. After she'd tucked the notebook and pen back inside her pocket, she looked up expectantly. "Okay, Bert, what have you got?"

Keeping his voice low, Bert said, "Remember me telling you about all the jewelry going missing?"

Charlotte nodded.

"Between you, me, and the fence post, I think Daisy is the one behind it all," he said. "Or at least she was until that other woman showed up."

"Are you talking about a woman named Joyce? Remember me asking you yesterday if you knew her?"

He nodded. "Yeah, yeah, come to think of it, that was her name. I just couldn't remember it yesterday. She's gone now, though." He suddenly frowned. "At least I think she's gone. I haven't seen her around here in a while. I wondered what happened to her. You know her?"

"Yeah, I knew her. That's the reason I'm here asking questions. Someone murdered her."

"Oh, man." He gave a low whistle. "That's too bad—hard to believe. Did they catch who did it?"

Charlotte shook her head. "No, not yet, but there have been some things that have happened that made me think someone here might know something."

"All I know is that if it is the same woman, when she first showed up, everything changed. Daisy didn't like her from the get-go. She and this Joyce woman were always sniping at each other, like two alley cats." He nodded several times. "Yep, tied up more than once, I tell you. Word is, Joyce wanted in on Daisy's action, and Daisy didn't like it one bit. Didn't want to share. So Joyce decided to work on her own. I say on her own, but she had someone on the outside helping her. Joyce would steal the stuff, and then, on visiting days, her outside person would show up, pretending to be family, and Joyce would slip the stuff to her."

Her? "You know for a fact that whoever was helping Joyce on the outside was a woman?"

He nodded. "Yep, saw her myself a time or two."

Charlotte was about to ask him to describe the so-called accomplice, but he spoke first.

"Word is, the outside woman took the stuff to a fence, a guy named Price, who runs a pawnshop down in the Quarter."

Charlotte went stone still. *Bingo!* Now she was finally getting somewhere.

"Y'all must be talking about that crazy Nurse Daisy?"

In unison, Charlotte's and Bert's heads snapped to the right to where the young woman who'd been reading was seated.

Though the woman had dark circles beneath her eyes, and her shoulder-length blond hair looked as if it could use a good shampooing, she was still an attractive woman.

"Yeah." The woman nodded and grinned. "I heard y'all whispering over there about Miss Joyce and 'Crazy Daisy'." She snickered. "That's what I call her—Crazy Daisy. If you ask me, she's the one who should be a patient in here."

Charlotte and Bert looked at each other. Then, with an oh-well shrug, Charlotte said, "So just how much have you heard?"

The woman glanced around the room, then moved over to the empty chair beside Charlotte, and sat again. "Enough to know that you're both in over your heads," she said with a meaningful look, first at Charlotte, then at Bert.

"How so?" Charlotte asked, purposely stalling, since she was unsure whether the woman could be trusted. For all they knew, she could be working with Daisy. "And why do you care?" Charlotte asked bluntly.

"I care because that witch with a capital *B*—my other name for Crazy Daisy—tried to recruit me. For me, this place is my last chance, and I don't intend to screw it up. It's either get through the program here or go straight to jail. Humph! Been there and done that once before—jail, that is—and don't intend to do it again. So when she tried to recruit me, as they say, I just said no." The younger woman narrowed her eyes. "Evidently, Crazy Daisy isn't used to anyone telling her no. Ever since, she's made my time in here a living hell. Anyway, I've got one more week, and then I'm out of here. So I figure, what the heck? If I can help in some way bring Daisy down, then why not?"

Charlotte glanced at Bert. "Good enough for you?"

Bert shrugged. Then after a moment, he nodded. "Why not?"

Charlotte turned back to the other woman. "Okay, so what do you know?"

With a satisfied grin, the young woman said, "That bird brooch y'all been talking about? Well, it's not just any old brooch. That big blue diamond in the middle is worth over a million dollars."

Charlotte's mouth dropped open and she shot the woman a look of disbelief.

The woman threw up her hand. "If I'm lying, I'm dying. I swear. Well, Joyce beat Daisy to it and lifted it from the old woman it belonged to when the old woman was first brought in."

"How?" Charlotte asked before finally closing her mouth.

"I don't know exactly how she got it, but she did, because I overheard Crazy Daisy talking about it on the phone to one of her contacts on the outside. She didn't know I was listening, of course. I made sure of that. Anyway, once Joyce had the brooch, she conned her way out of here. Then she took it to that pawnbroker in the Quarter—that guy named Price."

Charlotte frowned. If Joyce had a brooch worth that much, then why on earth would she have needed to steal the gold watch?

"Seems he refused to give her the amount she wanted for it," the woman continued. "Said it was too hot to handle."

That's why, thought Charlotte. She probably needed some money to tide her over until she could find someone to buy the brooch. Then another thought struck her. "So that means that Joyce had to have had the brooch in her possession when she was murdered. And, as far as I know, the police didn't find anything like that when they went over the crime scene. And that means that whoever murdered her was really after the brooch."

Charlotte stared down at the floor, but in her mind's eye, she could still see the awful mess that Joyce had made at her house before she was murdered. Charlotte had automatically assumed that Joyce had made the mess out of spite because she'd kicked her out. But had Joyce really made the mess? What if someone else had followed Joyce to the house and confronted her about the brooch? Then, when Joyce had refused to hand it over, the killer had murdered her, and the killer was the one who made the mess while searching for the brooch?

Charlotte slowly shook her head. Did that mean that Joyce had hidden the brooch somewhere in her house? Charlotte shivered. If so, and if the killer wanted it badly enough to kill Joyce, would he come after it again?

But who? Who could the killer be? Suddenly, she remembered something that Bert had said earlier. She turned to Bert. "Remember that you mentioned Joyce had an accomplice on the outside?" When Bert nodded, she said, "Do you know who her accomplice was?"

Bert gave her a sly grin, then nodded again.

"Who, Bert? Who was Joyce's accomplice?"

Bert's grin faded, and his rheumy eyes glazed over as he stared past her into space. "Woody Woodpecker," he told her, his voice raspy. "Good old Woody Woodpecker did it."

The young woman next to Charlotte burst into laughter, and Charlotte jerked her head around to stare at her. Still laughing, the woman abruptly stood, and in between fits of giggles, she said, "I've got to go now—time for my group session. Y'all take it easy." Still laughing, she hurried toward the entry door.

For a moment, Charlotte was too stunned to do anything but watch until the young woman disappeared into the hallway. When she finally turned back to Bert, her heart plummeted.

Chapter 13

Bert had slumped down in the chair. His head was tilted to one side, his eyes were closed, and soft snores whistled through his nose.

Woody Woodpecker?

Charlotte's face clouded with bewilderment as she stared at Bert. One minute, he had been perfectly lucid, and now . . .

Was Louis right about the old man, after all? Was Bert "loony tunes"? Maybe the poor man had been brainwashed from watching too many cartoons? But even more disturbing, did she dare believe anything he'd told her?

And what about the young woman who had suddenly beat such a hasty retreat? Had she been telling the truth?

Charlotte frowned thoughtfully. There was another possibility. What was it Bert had said when they'd first met? *"This place can be pretty boring."*

Suddenly, Charlotte's face grew hot with humiliation. What if, out of boredom, Bert and the woman had been pulling her leg all along? What if they'd made up the whole theft ring story?

Surely not, she thought, still staring at the old man. Right now, he didn't look capable of anything, much less a ruse like that. Of course anything was possible, but both Bert and the woman had seemed truly sincere.

Charlotte groaned softly. Just thinking about it made her head hurt. Maybe it was time to go home.

Past time. Just leave, Charlotte. Take the mop and mop bucket back to the basement and leave.

"Good idea," she murmured. Maybe once she was home, she could sort it all out.

With one last puzzled look at Bert, and with the sounds of cartoons blaring from the two televisions, Charlotte grabbed the mop and mop bucket and left.

Once back in her van, Charlotte pulled off the eyeglasses and itchy wig. Too bad she hadn't thought to bring a brush along, she thought as she pushed her fingers through her own flattened hair in an attempt to fluff it up a bit. Fluffing it helped some, but when she peered into the visor mirror, she grimaced at the face staring back at her. There was nothing she could do about the garish makeup. Removing the makeup required face cleanser and water and would have to wait until she got home.

Charlotte savored the blessed quietness of the inside of the van after the noisy psych ward recreation room, and by the time that she turned onto Milan Street, she'd more or less sorted everything out. Though Bert and the woman might have embellished some of the story about the theft ring, Daisy, and Joyce, she didn't believe that all of what they said had been fabricated out of boredom.

For one thing, how would either of them have known about Roy Price and the Quarter pawnshop? And for another thing, they certainly hadn't orchestrated Daisy's attack on her. That had been real. She'd been there and had to fight for her life.

When Charlotte pulled into her driveway, she spotted

Louis on the porch. "Oh, great. Just what I need," she grumbled. Though it was possible that Louis could simply be sitting on the porch swing to enjoy the beautiful late-afternoon weather, she doubted it. More than likely, he was sitting there waiting for her to get home.

Grabbing her purse, Charlotte climbed out of the van and headed for the porch. When she neared the steps, Louis's eyebrows drew together into a frown. "What's wrong with your face? And what happened to your hair?"

Charlotte figured she had two, maybe three, choices. She could either fess up to where she'd been and what she'd been doing, she could outright lie, or she could bluff her way through it. Since she didn't feel like getting a lecture from Louis about minding her own business, and she hated having to lie to anyone, she decided that bluffing was her best bet. Besides, a real gentleman would never ask a lady such a thing to begin with. Not that Louis could ever be accused of being a real gentleman most of the time.

Shame on you, Charlotte LaRue. You know good and well that Louis is a good man and has been there for you on more than one occasion.

Yeah, yeah, she silently answered the irritating voice of her conscience. *He's also been a real pain at times too.* But to Louis, she said, "It's just been one of those days."

At least that wasn't a lie—a bit of an understatement, but not an outright lie. And maybe, if she were lucky, it would appease his curiosity. Just in case it didn't, changing the subject was probably a good idea.

"So what's happening?" she asked as she climbed the steps.

"A lot," he answered, still eyeing her suspiciously. "If you'll invite me in for a cup of coffee, I'll tell you."

Though company was the last thing she wanted, after a brief hesitation, Charlotte's curiosity won out. Forcing a smile, she said, "I'd like a cup myself. Tell you what, it's turned out to be such a nice day, why don't I fix the coffee and bring it out here." That way, she'd have a chance to freshen up a bit. If Louis went inside with her, there would be no way she could clean her face and brush her hair without him making a big deal over it. Besides, after being cooped up in the recreation room on the psych ward, she was ready for some fresh air and space.

"Out here is fine," Louis said. "Still hoping the bird will show up, huh?"

Though Sweety Boy wasn't her real reason for opting to sit on the porch, and she was ashamed to admit that she hadn't even been thinking about the little parakeet, she did still have hope, so she nodded. "Hope springs eternal," she quipped. "Be back in a few minutes."

Once inside, Charlotte hurried to the kitchen and quickly prepared the coffeepot. After turning it on to brew, she made a beeline for the bathroom, where she washed her face and applied a light dusting of powder, mascara, and lipstick. Though there wasn't a whole lot she could do about her hair, she gave it a good brushing, anyway.

A few minutes later, armed with a mug of coffee in each hand, Charlotte went back out onto the porch. Louis took one of the mugs and scooted over to make room for Charlotte on the swing.

"Feel better?" he asked, shifting slightly in the swing to face her.

"What?"

He pointed at her face and hair.

"Oh, that." Unsure exactly what to say, Charlotte decided to ignore the question. "Earlier you said a lot was happening. What's that about?"

"You do look better," he told her with a knowing grin, "and, yeah, I got some new information from my source in California."

"What kind of information?" she asked, relieved that he'd let the thing about how she looked slide.

His expression grew serious. "Seems that Joyce wasn't running from the Russian mob, after all. More than likely, she was running from Aubrey Hamilton."

"Running from Hamilton? How come?"

"Hamilton was into all kinds of trouble, including being investigated by Internal Affairs. It's even possible that Joyce might have been a witness to a murder that Hamilton allegedly committed to cover up a money-laundering racket he had going. After I told the San Francisco PD about Joyce's murder, which, by the way, was a similar MO of the alleged murder he's suspected of committing, they contacted the NOPD about him. Now that our guys here know about him, they've put out an APB for Hamilton and consider him their prime suspect for Joyce's murder."

"At least that lets you and me off the hook for the time being."

Louis nodded. "Yeah, it does, but I don't really believe we were serious suspects to begin with, not according to what Judith said when I talked to her. That partner of hers is an eager beaver trying to climb up the ranks and he got sloppy. He's been like that since he was a rookie. Why, I remember one case in particular that he worked. . . ."

As Charlotte listened with half an ear to Louis talk about Brian Lee's shortcomings as a detective, she couldn't shake the feeling that Louis and the NOPD were wrong about Aubrey Hamilton having killed Joyce. While it seemed logical that he could have been looking for her, and might have killed her, in Charlotte's opinion Joyce's murder was more likely to be connected to that whole theft ring business at the hospital.

A mental picture of Bert slumped in his chair popped into her mind. Whether or not Bert was loony didn't really matter when all was said and done, she finally decided. Bert's state of mind had nothing to do with the fact that Daisy had tried to kill her down in the hospital basement. Why would Daisy have done such a thing if she hadn't been afraid that Bert had spilled the beans about something?

Then there was Joyce to consider. After Joyce had stolen Charlotte's father's watch and hocked it, it was easy to believe that Joyce could have been mixed up in a theft ring.

Charlotte sighed. Then she took a sip of her now-cold coffee. Unfortunately, either scenario was possible. Maybe she should just forget about it and be relieved and grateful that neither she nor Louis were suspects now. And she *was* grateful. Problem was, after everything that had happened, she couldn't just forget about it, especially considering the circumstances surrounding Joyce's murder. If the police were mistaken, and she was pretty sure they were, wasting time going after the wrong person would only serve to let the real killer get away. And if Bert was right about the theft ring, and Joyce had taken the bluebird diamond, then the real killer might still think that it was hidden somewhere in her house.

Charlotte shivered at the thought and stared down at her coffee cup. If only there was someone she could talk to, confide in, someone she could tell about what she'd learned from Bert and the young woman at the hospital.

Too bad that Louis was such a chauvinist and so pigheaded. He'd already dismissed her run-in with the nurse and the information she'd gotten from Bert as inconsequential, and once he made up his mind about something, there was no changing it.

What about Judith?

Charlotte grimaced. Judith was just as bad, if not worse than

Louis was. Besides, until Joyce's killer was caught, she preferred to stay away from Judith and Brian's radar as much as possible.

Thinking about Judith, Charlotte suddenly panicked. With everything that had happened, she'd forgotten about trying to buy back her father's watch. Had she even told Judith about it? She'd meant to tell her. Searching her brain, Charlotte recalled that yes, she had told her niece about her suspicions that Joyce had stolen the watch, and she'd told her about her visit to the pawnshop—all on the night that she'd found Joyce dead in her living room. Charlotte's heart sank. For all the good it had done. Even if Judith remembered about the watch, Charlotte was pretty sure that her niece had been too wrapped up in Joyce's murder investigation to do anything about it. And with the overload of murder cases Judith was dealing with, Charlotte figured that the theft of a watch was way low on her priority list.

Charlotte's panic grew even more. What if Roy Price sold it before she got the chance to reclaim it? She swallowed hard and tried to get a grip on her runaway panic. She had to do something. If she didn't do something about the watch, and do it soon, there was a good possibility that she would never see it again.

Louis cleared his throat. "And then he grew horns and a tail."

"What?" Charlotte jerked her head around and stared at Louis.

Louis chuckled. "Just wanted to see if you were paying attention. You looked like you were in another world there for a while."

"Sorry," she told him. "It's been a long day and I'm tired."

"Have you eaten yet?"

Charlotte shook her head.

"How about if we run over to Joey K's and grab a bite?"

Tempted, Charlotte hesitated. Joey K's was a great neighborhood restaurant located on Magazine Street and her mouth watered just thinking about a bowl of their seafood gumbo. After a moment, though, she shook her head. "Thanks, but not tonight. I've got a lot I need to get done tomorrow, and I don't really feel like going out again. Rain check?"

Louis nodded. "Yeah, sure. Another time maybe." He handed her his empty coffee mug, then stood. "I think I'll go, anyway." He walked to the porch steps, then paused. "Can I bring you something back?"

Again she was tempted, but once again she shook her head no. "Thanks, anyway," she said as she pushed out of the swing and stood.

With a two-fingered salute, Louis loped down the steps and headed for his car. As Louis was backing out of the driveway, Charlotte suddenly remembered that he hadn't said anything about what was in the syringe. Probably because he didn't know anything yet, she decided.

In the distance, a mockingbird sang, and Charlotte closed her eyes, enjoying the brief serenade. After a moment, though, she opened them again. "Where are you, Sweety?" she whispered.

Setting both mugs on the floor of the porch near her front door, she walked down the steps. "One quick look around," she murmured. Maybe this time she'd find him.

It was while she was peering up into an oak tree that she remembered she never had called Madeline about making flyers to hand out.

When Charlotte finally decided to climb out of bed on Tuesday morning, she felt like she'd barely slept at all. Every two hours, just like clockwork, she'd wake up, and each time all she could think about was her father's watch.

On her way to the kitchen, Charlotte grabbed a pen and a tablet off her desk. In the kitchen, she poured herself a cup of coffee and sat down at the breakfast table.

Since Dale was finished with his finals and able to clean for Bitsy, she had the day free. And since lately she'd seemed to be forgetting things, she decided to make a list of everything she needed to get done that day while her mind was fresh and uncluttered.

At the top of the list, she wrote, *One: call Madeline about flyers.* Next she added, *Two: make a chicken potpie. Three: go over Maid-for-a-Day payroll. Four: clean house. Five: make hair appointment. Six: sweep the front porch.*

For several seconds, Charlotte stared at the list. Finally, she wrote, *Seven: get Poppa's watch back. Eight: help Carol out with the twins.*

Then she suddenly remembered yet another chore she had to do, and wrote down, *Nine: call Bert's daughter.*

After a final glance at the list, she placed the pen on top of the tablet and got out of the chair. "First things, first," she said, and headed straight for the telephone. Though it was still a bit early, she knew that her sister would be up and about. Madeline was a CPA, and though she worked at home, she tried to keep regular business hours.

After tapping out her sister's phone number, Charlotte waited through five rings, when Madeline finally answered.

"Hey, Maddie. I was just about to hang up."

"Sorry. I'd just stepped out of the shower and couldn't get to it right away. Listen, I'm standing here dripping all over the carpet. Can I call you back later?"

Knowing her sister, Charlotte figured later would never

come. "I won't keep you but a second, so just grab a towel. I need a favor."

"Oh, for pity's sake. Hold on." Even through the phone line, Charlotte could hear her sister grumbling all the way to the bathroom. Barely a minute had passed before Madeline indicated that she had a towel.

"Don't be such a grumpy goat," Charlotte told her. "It's not often I ask you for help." Then, as quickly as she could, Charlotte explained about the flyers. "And I want to offer a reward: fifty dollars."

"Fifty dollars! Charlotte, for fifty dollars, you can go out and buy another bird. I hate to burst your bubble, but that bird is probably either long gone by now or dead."

"Maybe, maybe not," Charlotte told her. "But I have to try. And I don't want another one. I want *my* bird back. Will you do the flyers?"

Hesitating, Madeline finally said, "Yeah, I guess so, but you're just setting yourself up for a big disappointment. I'll make up one flyer and you can take it to Kinko's and run as many copies as you want. But don't ask me to help you pass 'em out."

"Wouldn't dream of it. So when can I pick up the flyer?"

"How about midmorning, say around ten?"

After agreeing on the time to pick up the flyer, Charlotte went in search of the notebook that had the name and phone number for Bert's daughter. She finally found the notebook on her bedside table, exactly where she'd left it when she'd undressed.

With the notebook in hand, she went back into the living room. But as she reached for the telephone receiver, she hesitated. What if Bert was loony, after all, or what if he'd been playing games out of boredom?

Debating, she finally decided to make the call, anyway. If

all else was false, Daisy was real, and so was her attack down in the basement. Besides, she'd promised Bert she would call his daughter, and a promise was a promise.

Taking a deep breath, Charlotte tapped out the phone number from the notepad. After the third ring, a woman answered.

"Hello? Is this Linda Harris?"

"Yes, it is," the woman answered, her tone suspicious. "Who's this?"

"Ms. Harris, my name is Charlotte LaRue. You don't know me, but I know your father, Delbert O'Banion. I promised him that I would call you about a problem going on at the hospital where he's staying."

Over the next few minutes, Charlotte explained about the theft ring at the hospital and about Daisy the nurse. "Your dad is really scared that Daisy might try something, since she saw him talking to me. And he was afraid that you wouldn't believe him if he told you all of this stuff. Ms. Harris, he knows he still needs help, so it's not about him just wanting out of the hospital. He's hoping that you can get him transferred to another facility."

For long moments, all that Charlotte heard was breathing over the phone line, and then she heard something that sounded like someone crying.

"Ms. LaRue, thank you," Linda Harris said with tears in her voice. "I love my dad and had no idea that kind of stuff was going on. I will get him out of there as soon as possible. And just so you know, it wasn't my idea to admit him to that particular hospital in the first place. I had a bad feeling about it from the beginning, but my brother got a lawyer. After that, there was nothing I could do."

Her brother? Funny, Bert didn't mention having a son.

As if Linda had heard Charlotte's silent question, she said,

"My dad has been really upset with my brother ever since he had him admitted to the hospital. Dad knew he needed help, but I think he'd hoped that he could work it out on his own. Ever since, he's refused to see or talk to my brother." She paused a moment, then said, "Again, I do want to thank you for bringing this to my attention."

By a quarter to ten, in addition to calling her sister and calling Linda Harris, Charlotte had crossed off numbers two and four on her list. The chicken potpie was in the refrigerator, ready to bake, and she'd cleaned her house—not cleaned, exactly, more like a good straightening. She still needed to dust and vacuum, but decided to save that for another day.

By ten, Charlotte was knocking on her sister's door. Several minutes passed, then the door swung open.

"Hey, sis, come on in," Madeline said. "I've got your flyer ready, but you need to take a look at it and see if I've included everything."

Charlotte stepped inside her sister's living room, then followed her to the room she used as an office.

Madeline picked up a sheet of paper and handed it to Charlotte. Charlotte scanned it, then smiled at her sister. "Maddie, this is great. It's just what I had in mind." Charlotte laughed. "Where did you get the picture of the parakeet? That's a really nice touch."

"Off the Net," Madeline told her. "You can get just about anything off the Internet."

Charlotte nodded. "Yeah, one of these days I'm going to learn to do all that stuff myself."

A few minutes later, back in her van, Charlotte headed for the nearest Kinko's. Once there, she ran off thirty copies of the flyer. By noon, she'd walked up one side and down the other side of the block she lived on, leaving a flyer at every house.

"Just one more house," she murmured as she walked up the steps to the porch of the house next door, then slipped a flyer through the mail slot in the door. Just as she turned to leave, an unfamiliar car pulled up in front of her house.

"Now, who could that be?" she said aloud, her eyes on the late-model tan Toyota. As she hurried down the neighbor's steps, the car door opened, but no one got out.

Squinting, Charlotte stared at the car as she crossed over to her own yard, but the heavily tinted windows hid whoever was inside. If she remembered right, some years back a law had been passed that prohibited heavily tinted windows.

Charlotte had just reached her steps when the car door slammed shut. Why hadn't the person inside gotten out? She had just about decided to walk over to where the car was parked when, with a roar of the engine and the tires squealing, the car suddenly took off, speeding down the street.

"What on earth?" For several seconds, Charlotte stared at the retreating car as an uneasy feeling crept up her spine. Then the car disappeared from sight.

You should have taken down the license number.

"Shoulda, woulda, coulda," she muttered. "Too late now." Besides, she thought, there could be a perfectly rational explanation. Maybe when the driver had seen her, he'd realized that he had the wrong address.

Though the explanation was plausible, a bad feeling settled deep in her gut. There was still the problem of her missing house key. What if Joyce's killer hadn't found the brooch the first time? What if he'd taken the key so that he could come back and look for it once things calmed down again?

Silently blasting herself for not having the presence of mind to get the Toyota's license number, she grabbed the broom she kept near the end of the porch. As long as she was outside, she might as well sweep the stupid porch. At least then she could cross two more items off her to-do list.

Once the porch was swept clean, she propped the broom against the wall between her front window and the door, then went inside.

Still puzzled and a bit creeped out about the strange car, she debated whether to report the incident to the police. After going over the pros and cons of reporting it, she walked to her desk and called Judith. When Judith's answering service came on the line, Charlotte almost hung up the phone, but at the last second, she decided to leave a message, after all.

"Judith, this is Aunt Charlotte." After she'd quickly explained about the incident and described the car, she said, "I'm not sure it has anything to do with Joyce's murder, but my house key is still missing, and I thought you should know what happened. I'd feel a lot better if a patrol car drove down my street once in a while until Joyce's murderer is found. And yes, my next call is to a locksmith. Love you, hon. Bye."

Once Charlotte put in a call to a locksmith and set up a time for him to come by, she went into the kitchen. While a can of chicken noodle soup warmed on top of the stove, she made herself a turkey sandwich.

Since she'd done all she could do at the moment about the strange car and having her locks changed, while she ate her lunch, she concentrated on her plan to approach Roy Price about her father's watch.

After giving it a lot of thought, Charlotte figured that the only way that Price would even let her look at the watch was if he thought she was someone else. The disguise she'd used to get back inside the hospital had worked pretty well, so she'd decided to try it again.

"No time like the present," she murmured as she stacked her dirty dishes into the dishwasher, then went to the bathroom to put on her disguise.

Half an hour later, dressed in jeans and a sweatshirt, and wearing the darker makeup, glasses, and wig, she drove toward the French Quarter. Along the way, she pulled into the drive-through at her bank, and using her ATM card, she withdrew three hundred dollars. She figured that using cash was the only way she could pay for the watch without giving out her name. She only hoped that three hundred was enough.

Though a little cool, it was once again a beautiful day, and like she'd done before, Charlotte parked in a parking lot near Jackson Brewery.

When she passed by the display window at the Jax Brewery mall, she couldn't help taking a peek to see if the blue sweater and slacks were still there. Sure enough, they were still on display, and Charlotte had to force herself to keep walking.

As she strolled past the easels and the finished canvases hanging on the wrought-iron fence along the side of Jackson Square, she slowed her pace.

Several of the artists specialized in portraits, and as Charlotte stared at one portrait in particular of a little blond-haired girl, she smiled. As soon as the twins were old enough, she'd have to bring them to the Square and have their portrait done. There was a perfect spot on the wall in her living room near the television to hang it.

She was almost past the Cabildo when a raggedly dressed boy, who looked to be in his mid-teens, approached her.

"Hey, lady, I'll betcha a dollar I can tell you where you got them shoes."

The barefoot boy was just a bit taller than her own five foot three inches and as skinny as a rail. Though Charlotte was well familiar with the old shoe con, a trick played mostly on tourists, she also knew that many of the street kids had no other way to earn money. Some were runaways, on the streets because they had fled from abusive home situations or had gotten kicked out because of drugs. But there had been reports of hundreds of teenagers separated from their parents and either living alone, living with older siblings, or living with other relatives. Their parents had evacuated during the Hurricane Katrina disaster and, for one reason or another, weren't able to return yet.

"Why aren't you in school?" she asked.

"It let out early today."

Yeah, right, she thought, *and I'm only thirty-nine years old instead of sixty-two. So tell me another whopper.*

"So how about it, lady? You gonna take my bet?"

Oh, what the heck, she thought, *why not?* Pretending to be puzzled, she said, "Now, what was the question again?"

"I said I betcha a dollar I can tell you where you got them shoes."

Pretending to give it some thought first, she finally said, "Okay, I give up. Where?"

The boy grinned. "You got them shoes on your feet." He thrust out his hand. "You lose, so pay up."

Charlotte chuckled, and reaching inside her purse, she pulled out a twenty-dollar bill. "Afraid, this is all I have."

When she handed him the twenty, his eyes grew wide, and then his face fell. "I don't got no change, lady."

He offered it back to her, but Charlotte smiled and shook her head. "The correct thing to say is, 'I don't *have any* change.'"

The boy shrugged. "Okay, 'I don't have any change.' You want your money back, or don't you?"

"Tell you what, if you'll promise me that you'll go buy yourself a pair of tennis shoes, you can keep it." Charlotte figured that there were enough thrift stores around that twenty should be enough for a pair of tennis shoes. Even if he had to buy used ones, used shoes were better than none.

Suddenly, his face split into a wide grin. "Hey, thanks, lady!"

"But you've got to promise," she warned. "You've got to look me in the eyes and promise."

The boy gave her a solemn nod, and looking her straight in the eyes, he said, "I promise."

As she watched the boy turn and lope down the street, she had no illusions that he would keep his promise. She hoped he would, but more than likely, the first place he'd stop would be somewhere he could get something to eat.

With a shake of her head and a heavy heart, Charlotte turned away and headed up the block again. It was a crying shame that in this world, in this country, and in particular, this city, it was usually the children and the elderly who suffered the most.

Squinting against the afternoon sun, she spotted the pawnshop, not far up the street, a grim reminder of her purpose for being there in the first place. Fighting against the sudden tight knot of tension building in her stomach, she took a deep breath and picked up her pace.

She truly dreaded having another confrontation with Roy Price. If only there was some way he wouldn't be there. Charlotte frowned as she suddenly remembered something that Daisy had told her. When she'd first been accosted by Daisy outside of the pawnshop and hadn't known who she was, Daisy had mentioned that Price had a partner, a woman who worked on Fridays and the weekends. Maybe she'd luck out and the partner would be working today, on Tuesday, instead of Price.

Charlotte's steps slowed as she approached the entrance to

the pawnshop. One look at the CLOSED sign hanging inside the upper glass insert of the entrance door, and her temper flared.

"Aw, come on," she cried in frustration. It was barely midafternoon. Why in the world would it be closed? Besides which, the posted hours read that the shop was open until six, and here it was only two.

For a second, she was sorely tempted to give the door a good swift kick, but common sense finally prevailed. Besides, with her luck, she'd either break her foot or set off a burglar alarm and end up in jail.

"Probably off fencing someone else's stolen property," she sneered. "Or stealing more stuff to sell in the pawnshop."

Finally, glaring at the CLOSED sign one last time, and with a heavy sigh, she did an about-face and trudged back down the street. If there was one thing she hated, it was wasted time, time that could have been better spent going over the Maid-for-a-Day payroll or dusting and vacuuming her house, instead of the half-cleaning she'd had to do.

There's always tomorrow. You can try again then.

"Yeah, yeah," she grumbled. But tomorrow might be too late. The watch was a really nice timepiece, and someone was bound to come along and scoop it up. Price had already claimed it was sold, but she had her doubts. With every day that passed, the chances of the watch still being there grew less.

Not if they're closed.

Okay, okay, she silently relented. There was nothing she could do about it for today, anyway, but trying again another day also meant that she would have to dress up in the silly wig and glasses again.

"Live and learn," she whispered. The next time she came, and she would be back, she'd make sure that she called first.

Chapter 14

Still aggravated that she'd wasted half the afternoon, Charlotte was tempted to treat herself. As long as she was down in the Quarter, anyway, why not stop in at the Café Du Monde and have a cup of café au lait and some beignets? But the closer she got to St. Peter Street, all she really wanted was to go home and get out of the ridiculous disguise. Besides, the beignets were loaded with powdered sugar. The last thing she needed was more sugar in her diet. Anyway, Carol was expecting her to bring dinner and help with the twins, and she still had to drive home, clean up a bit, and actually bake the chicken potpie before going over there.

Once in her van, Charlotte pulled off the glasses and the itchy wig. Fluffing out her hair as best she could, she headed home.

When Charlotte pulled into her driveway, the last person she had expected to see was Louis. Only this time, instead of sitting on the porch swing waiting for her, he was pacing, and if the look on his face was any gauge to measure by, he was fit to be tied.

Unease rippled through her veins as she parked and

stepped out of the van. But Louis didn't even wait until she reached the steps.

"Where have you been?" he called out. "And what in the blue blazes is going on?"

After the aggravation of finding the pawnshop closed, Charlotte was in no mood for the third degree from Louis. As she stomped up the steps, she said, "Though it's none of your business where I've been, I had an errand to run. And what do you mean, what's going on?"

"I've been home less than an hour and your phone hasn't stopped ringing the whole time. At first, I ignored it, but as thin as that wall is between your half and my half, after a while it gets hard to ignore."

All of Charlotte's anger immediately melted into panic. If someone was calling that many times, then there had to be an emergency of some kind. Had something happened to the twins . . . Hank . . . Madeline . . . Judith? . . . *Just calm down and breathe. If there was an emergency, then someone would have called your cell phone when they couldn't reach you at home, wouldn't they?*

The thought helped alleviate her panic somewhat, and Charlotte took a deep breath, then released it slowly. As usual, she had overreacted. Of course they would have called her cell phone, she thought. But no sooner had the thought entered her mind, than panic struck again. *You did remember to turn on the cell phone, didn't you?*

Charlotte yanked open her purse and pulled out her cell phone. Sure enough, it was on, fully charged and plenty of signal bars showing. Even better, according to the display area, there had been no messages either.

"There it goes again," Louis pointed out.

Sure enough, even from outside on the porch, Charlotte could hear her phone ringing. By the time she unlocked her door and rushed inside, the ringing had stopped. Beside the phone, though, the light on the message machine was blinking like a strobe light, so fast that she couldn't even count the calls.

"What on earth?" she murmured, barely aware that Louis had followed her inside. Reaching down, she punched the play button.

"You have ten messages," the machine's robotic voice announced. "Ten messages." Then the machine beeped.

"Ms. LaRue, I'm calling about your bird. I got your flyer and think I may have seen him. My number is . . ."

Sudden realization about the reason for all of the calls hit her, and Charlotte groaned. "The flyers," she muttered. "Of course." She turned to Louis and quickly explained about distributing the flyers, and then continued listening to the rest.

Halfway through the ten messages, Charlotte began giggling. Her mother used to call them the "delirious giggles" and said that when some people were faced with either extreme exhaustion or profound relief about something, inappropriate giggling was their emotional release valve.

By the time the last message played, she was laughing so hard that tears were running down her cheeks. Even Louis was laughing. If the people calling were to be believed, then half the people on her block alone had seen her bird roosting in a tree on their property. With few variations, all of the messages were the same.

Louis was still chuckling when he cleared his throat. "Ah, Charlotte, now don't bite my head off, but where *have* you been?"

His question was a stark reminder of the pawnshop, and she quickly sobered. Though telling Louis about her visit to the pawnshop was probably the prudent thing to do, the safe thing to do—especially if she got into trouble—she already knew that he wouldn't approve. Besides, she was in no mood for one of his lectures. "I had errands to run." And that was the truth. Going to the pawnshop was on her to-do list that she'd made earlier that morning.

"Okay." But his tone indicated that he really didn't believe her. Giving her a strange look, he said, "And what's with your face and hair again?"

The makeup and her flattened hair . . . again.

Not wanting to outright lie to him, she shrugged. "It's just been one of those days."

"Humph! That's the same thing that you said the other night."

"Well, we all have good hair days and bad hair days," she quipped in an attempt to make light of how she looked. From the knowing, suspicious gleam in his eyes, it was evident that he wasn't buying her explanation.

"Lately, you seem to have more bad hair days than good ones."

"Thanks, Louis," she drawled, her tone dripping with sarcasm. "That's just what a woman likes to hear."

Louis shrugged. "The truth's the truth. And on that note, I think it's time for me to go home."

Charlotte gave him a brittle smile. "Sounds like a good idea to me."

At the front door, Louis paused, then turned to face her. "When you're ready to tell me what's going on, I'll be ready to listen."

Yeah, right, she thought. *When pigs fly.*

Louis suddenly did an about-face. "Oh, yeah, I almost forgot. About that syringe, my lab guy says its potassium chloride, a dose big enough to kill a horse."

Or a lone woman. Charlotte shivered.

"It's normally taken in small doses by IV, but too much of that stuff can stop a heart almost immediately," Louis explained. "Unfortunately, it's still your word against hers. And there's no way now to prove she attacked you. Sorry." He paused, then said, "Don't go back there, Charlotte. Next time, you might not be so lucky."

"Don't worry, I have no intentions of going there again."

"Good," he replied. "See you later." Then he left, closing the door behind him.

Still thinking about the hospital and syringe, Charlotte walked over and secured the dead bolt.

While the chicken potpie was baking, Charlotte removed the dark makeup and applied the lighter color she normally used. With a little help from a curling iron, she also freshened up her hair.

While the chicken dish finished baking and then cooled a bit, she used the time to go over the books and payroll for Maid-for-a-Day. When all was said and done, she wasn't getting rich, but she wasn't starving either, she thought with satisfaction once she'd finished. With what Maid-for-a-Day brought in and now her monthly Social Security checks, her finances were fairly stable.

Social Security.

Charlotte winced. Having turned sixty-two in October, she had mixed feelings each time she thought about the Social Security check she would receive at the first of every month from now on. Before, whenever she'd heard someone talking about Social Security, the word "old" immediately came to mind. Only old people drew Social Security checks.

Charlotte grinned as she put away the paperwork for Maid-for-a-Day. Now that she was drawing the checks, she'd changed her opinion. After all, she didn't consider herself as being old. Now, when she got on Medicare in three years, then she'd be old.

"Not likely," she retorted, her grin widening. With each additional birthday, her opinion of what was considered old seemed to change.

Half an hour later, balancing the still very warm chicken potpie in one hand, Charlotte rang the doorbell at Hank's house.

As she waited patiently for Carol to let her in, even from outside, she could hear the babies crying. Poor Carol. She definitely had her hands full.

When Carol did open the door, the look of relief on her face tugged at Charlotte's heartstrings.

Normally of a slim build, Carol looked as if she'd lost even more weight. The large, bruised circles beneath her eyes attested to the sleep she'd lost over the past few days, and her shoulder-length dark hair hung in oily strands.

"Oh, Charlotte, I'm so glad to see you." Carol backed away from the doorway so Charlotte could come inside. After she'd closed the door, she turned to face Charlotte, then suddenly burst into tears. "Sorry," she cried. "Today has been really hard."

Charlotte quickly set down the potpie and wrapped her arms around her daughter-in-law. "There, there," she soothed. "I know it doesn't seem like it, but things will get better."

"I—I know they will," Carol sobbed. "If I could just get some sleep, but with breast-feeding . . ." Her voice trailed away.

Charlotte took Carol by the shoulders and held her at arm's length. "Listen, hon, right up front, I want to say that I'm no expert about these things. I know that most pediatricians push the breast-feeding, and rightly so. It's been proven that it's better for the baby. But sometimes a mother's milk, for whatever reason, doesn't quite satisfy. And that's no reflection on the mother, one way or another. It just happens sometimes.

Why don't you ask your pediatrician if you can switch to formula and see if that satisfies them better? I know of lots of babies who grew up on formula and turned out just fine. Your husband, for one."

"As a nurse, I know that, and I've been thinking about it, but—" She shrugged. "So you wouldn't think that I'm a terrible mother for not breast-feeding my babies?"

"Oh, honey, of course I wouldn't, and if anyone else thinks that, then they can go butt a stump. Besides, if your milk isn't satisfying them, they need something that will both satisfy them and give them the nutrition they should be getting." Charlotte squeezed Carol's shoulders. "Now—you go put that potpie in the kitchen. Spoon yourself out a nice big chunk of it, and sit down and eat, while I see what I can do about those precious angels crying in there. And that's an order."

Carol smiled. "Yes, ma'am. Right away, ma'am."

By the time Hank arrived home, Charlotte wondered if she looked as exhausted as she felt. The only thing she'd found that soothed the babies was rocking them. She'd tried rocking first one, and then the other one, but had finally decided that the best solution was to rock them both at the same time. As a result, her arms ached with numbness.

"Hi, hon," she said quietly when Hank walked into the nursery. Both babies had finally, blessedly, fallen asleep in her arms.

"Hi, yourself," he answered as he leaned down to kiss her cheek. "Need some help getting them into their bassinets?"

Charlotte nodded. "Yeah, about an hour ago, but I didn't want to wake Carol and finally decided I'd just wait for you."

When Hank had settled both babies in their beds, he and Charlotte walked into the living room.

"I really appreciate you helping out tonight."

"It was my pleasure," Charlotte answered, and meant every word as she rubbed her aching arms. "If you're hungry, I brought over a chicken potpie. You can warm it up in the microwave."

"I am hungry, and thanks."

"Son, one thing before I leave. You really need to consider hiring a full-time nanny, just until Carol regains her strength. And it's not that I mind helping out. I don't. But I can only help part-time, and she needs someone who can be here full-time. Like I said, just until she gets her strength back."

Hank's eyes crinkled with amusement and a slow grin pulled at his lips. "You're right," he told her. "Great minds think alike. But I'm one step ahead of you. I have an agency sending someone out first thing tomorrow morning. Of course you could always retire and move in with us, instead."

Charlotte opened her mouth but couldn't utter a sound. First of all, she didn't want to retire. Not just yet. And second . . . Charlotte frowned in thought. Well, there was a second point, but she couldn't think what it was.

Hank laughed. "Just kidding you, Mom. Just kidding. Not about the retirement part, but about the moving-in part."

Aha! Now she remembered the second point.

Wednesdays were Charlotte's day to clean her client Sandra Wellington's house. Sandra was good friends with Bitsy, and had hired Charlotte because of Bitsy's recommendation.

Bitsy had forewarned Charlotte about Sandra. While Sally Lawson might be her least messy client, Sandra Wellington was definitely her messiest. And today was no exception.

Sandra's home was among the largest of the old mansions in the Garden District. Built in the 1850s, Sandra's Italianate-style home was a combination of bricks, marble, iron, and stucco, and somehow Sandra found a way to mess up every room in the old mansion. On Charlotte's most paranoid days, she strongly suspected that Sandra messed up the rooms on purpose, just because she knew that Charlotte was coming to clean.

Sandra, a stout woman with short, tightly permed hair that was supposed to be gray, but always looked purple, was in her late seventies, and she greeted Charlotte at the front double doorway.

Without so much as a greeting, Sandra said, "So what's the news on that murder at your house?"

And good morning to you too, Charlotte thought as she set down her vacuum and cleaning supplies carrier.

"You're just lucky that they didn't throw you in jail. Probably because of your niece being a detective and all."

And probably because I didn't do it, Charlotte wanted to say, but didn't.

"So, have they caught who did it yet?"

Shades of Bitsy, thought Charlotte. "No, ma'am, not yet, but I hear they have some good leads."

"Yeah, I heard that her ex-husband was a good possibility." Sandra paused a heartbeat, then said, "Say, isn't he the one that's your boyfriend?"

Charlotte gritted her teeth. *Definitely shades of Bitsy. Two peas in a pod.* "No, ma'am. I don't have a boyfriend."

"That's too bad, you still being so young and everything."

Young? Charlotte had to bite her tongue to keep from laughing out loud.

"But he is your tenant, isn't he?" Sandra continued, without skipping a beat. When Charlotte grudgingly nodded, Sandra shook her head from side to side and made a clicking noise with her tongue. "Seems mighty convenient if you ask me, him living right next door to you and everything."

And so it went the entire day. While Charlotte cleaned, Sandra peppered her with question after question about Joyce, her murder, and Louis, until Charlotte thought she would scream.

With Sandra following her around and asking questions, it took Charlotte longer than usual to clean. And when she did catch a break from Sandra's eternal questions, all she could think about was getting her father's watch back.

By the time Charlotte got home, it was almost four. Another hour or so, it would be dark, and Charlotte didn't want to be caught walking the streets of the Quarter, or anywhere else, all by herself after dark.

The moment Charlotte entered her house, she went straight to the phone and called the pawnshop. After the fourth ring, a woman answered. Charlotte figured the woman was probably Roy Price's partner. And if she was his partner, that meant that there was a good chance that Roy Price wouldn't be there.

"Ah, hello," Charlotte said. "I was just wondering how late you were going to be open today?"

"We're open until six."

"Thank you. I—" Before Charlotte could finish her sentence, the woman hung up on her. How rude. "Never mind," Charlotte grumbled, and she hung up the receiver.

For several seconds, she stood there staring at the phone. She could be wrong—and granted, their exchange had been brief—but she could swear that the woman's voice sounded familiar. With a puzzled shake of her head, she hurried back to the bedroom to change into her disguise.

When Charlotte pulled into the parking lot near Jackson Brewery, she was surprised that it was so full that time of the day in the middle of the week. But a full parking lot meant that there were people, whether tourists or locals, shopping in the Quarter, and shopping was good for the city's flagging economy.

After driving through a couple of rows, she finally found a parking space between two other vans, near the far end of the lot. Once she'd parked and locked the van, she walked quickly back toward the Jackson Brewery mall building.

When she passed the window where she'd seen the pretty sweater and pants, she glanced at the display. With a pang of regret, she saw that the sweater and pants were gone. In their place was a dress now, and she briefly wondered if the sweater and pants had been sold, or if the store had simply changed out the display to show off something different.

At the traffic light, she waited for the walk signal, and then she crossed Decatur over to St. Peter Street.

The late-afternoon air was chilly, the sky had grown overcast, and daylight was fading fast. In the distance behind her, the sudden blast of a foghorn from one of the riverboats made her jump.

The artists along Jackson Square were packing up their supplies and canvases, calling it a day. From the other side of Jackson Square, she could hear the sound of a lone saxophone wailing out the strains of an old Fats Domino song, "Walking to New Orleans."

She'd better walk, all right, she thought, and walk fast if she wanted to beat the dark. Buttoning up her sweater against the chill, Charlotte picked up her pace.

By the time she reached the pawnshop, she was out of breath. Taking a moment to compose herself and gather her courage, she also said a quick prayer that the rude woman who had answered the phone would still be there, instead of Roy Price.

When Charlotte entered the pawnshop, the bell over the door jingled. The inside of the dimly lit place was just as dirty and yucky as she'd remembered it being. The place still needed a good cleaning, and as before, she did her best to avoid rubbing up against anything.

As she glanced around the dimly lit shop, as far as she could tell, it was empty. Not empty, she decided. They wouldn't go off and leave it without someone being there. More than likely, whoever was running the shop was probably in the back storage room.

With a shrug, she slowly walked toward the counter to the section of the glass case where she'd seen the watch. She had almost reached the spot when she heard a voice call out, "Be with you in a minute."

Charlotte jumped at the unexpected sound of the woman's voice, and again wondered why it seemed so familiar.

At least it's a woman's voice, and not that awful Roy Price character.

"Thank you, Lord," she whispered. While relief washed through her that her prayer had been answered, she still couldn't shake the notion that she'd heard the woman's voice before.

Several moments passed as Charlotte stared down into the case. When she spotted her father's watch, she sent up another prayer of thanks that it was still there and hadn't been purchased.

She was still looking at the watch when she heard the door located near a dark corner at the back of the shop suddenly open.

"Can I help you?" a woman called out.

At first sight of the woman with her arms wrapped around a cardboard box, Charlotte froze, and all she could do was stare in disbelief. At least now she knew why the woman's voice had sounded so familiar.

Chapter 15

Charlotte could hardly believe her eyes as she watched the smiling woman, with the flaming red hair, set the box she was carrying down on the floor, then walk slowly her way.

What on earth was Flora Jennings, the real estate lady, doing here at the pawnshop?

At that moment, the phone on a desk behind the counter rang and Flora stopped in her tracks. "Excuse me," she said as she stepped over to the desk. "I'm expecting a call, so I have to get this. I won't be but a moment."

As Charlotte watched Flora take the call, her mind raced. Was it possible that Flora was the woman that Daisy the evil nurse had told her about when she'd first accosted her outside the pawnshop? Was Flora Roy Price's partner?

The name of the shop is P & J Pawnshop. Price and Jennings?

"So what happened?"

Flora's question to the caller, along with the rest of the conversation, faded amid the speculations racing through Charlotte's head. Most of the time, Charlotte didn't believe in coincidences, and this particular time was no exception. Though it was possible that Flora could be Roy Price's partner, and be moonlighting on the side as a real estate agent, something about the whole thing smelled as fishy as a shrimp boat after a day out in the Gulf.

Coincidence?

Charlotte frowned in thought. The pawnshop . . . the hospital . . . Daisy . . . the bluebird diamond . . . Joyce . . . Joyce's accomplice . . . *Woody Woodpecker!*

Charlotte's frown deepened. Now, why on earth had Woody Woodpecker popped into her head, for Pete's sake? Then, like a million lights exploding in her brain, it hit her. Suddenly weak in the knees, Charlotte grabbed hold of the top of the glass case for support.

Maybe Bert wasn't so loony, after all. What if Flora was Joyce's accomplice on the outside? Bert hadn't known the accomplice's real name—so what if, in his mind, he'd connected her with the cartoons that the patients watched all the time, and because of her flaming red hair, he'd nicknamed her "Woody Woodpecker"?

To Charlotte's horror, it made sense, especially if Flora had just pretended to be a real estate agent in order to gain access to her house, so she could look for the bluebird diamond brooch. For some reason Flora must have thought that Joyce had already moved in.

But surely the woman wouldn't have been so stupid that she would use her own name. How lame was that? Then again, it had been proven time and time again that most crooks were pretty stupid when all was said and done.

Suddenly, warning spasms of alarm erupted within Charlotte as yet another horrible thought ripped through her mind. Assuming that Flora was Joyce's accomplice—*Yeah, and you know what they say about people who assume.* Her thoughts still spinning, Charlotte chose to ignore the irritating voice in her head. What if when Joyce had been released from the hospital, she'd somehow found out about the partnership between Flora and Roy Price.

Probably when she went to hock the watch.

Charlotte nodded just slightly, agreeing, for a change, with the irritating voice. Then, once Joyce had discovered the partnership, it would have been just like her to decide to strike out on her own, instead of splitting the take for the brooch three ways? Charlotte hated to think ill of the dead, but knowing Joyce, it would be just like her to want it all for herself. Flora could have realized what Joyce was doing and then killed her for the brooch.

At that moment, Flora hung up the phone receiver and turned to face Charlotte. "Now," she said as she stepped closer to where Charlotte was standing. "What can I do for you?"

When Flora tilted her head to one side and narrowed her eyes, Charlotte quickly bent her head downward and pretended to be studying a bracelet in the glass case, hoping that doing so would help hide her face. Though she was pretty certain that there was no way that Flora would see through her disguise, she couldn't be certain, especially considering that the disguise hadn't kept Bert from recognizing her. Of course she did have her name tag on then.

"I said, what can I do for you?" Flora repeated, her voice agitated and a strange gleam in her eyes.

Do something! Say something quick!

With a shrug, Charlotte feigned a nonchalance she was far from feeling. And lowering her voice half an octave in an attempt to disguise it, and in an attempt to buy time to sort out her thoughts, she said, "Just looking right now."

If Flora hadn't already recognized her by now, the last thing she needed was for her to see through her disguise at this point. But had that gleam in her eyes been recognition or something else? A cold knot formed in Charlotte's stomach, and she feared the worst.

"Let me know if you see anything you're interested in," Flora said.

The peculiar tone of Flora's voice sent up red warning flags and only helped to confirm Charlotte's suspicions that Flora had indeed recognized her in spite of the disguise.

Charlotte gripped the counter even tighter as the cold knot in her stomach grew even larger, and she pretended to study the various pieces of the jewelry in the glass case. There was nothing she could do now but try and bluff her way through, get the watch, and get out of there as fast as she could.

You could just walk away now.

Not without my father's watch, Charlotte silently argued as the knot of fear tightened.

"Are you okay?" Flora asked. "You look as white as a sheet."

Though the question itself seemed one of concern, the tone of it brought to mind a cat toying with a mouse before he pounced. Charlotte stiffened and swallowed hard.

Oh, for Pete's sake, Charlotte, get a grip.

Charlotte cleared her throat. "I'm fine," she lied, careful to lower the tone of her voice.

"Can I get you a glass of water or anything?"

Again there was that cat-and-mouse tone. Charlotte shook her head. "I said I'm fine," she retorted. She tapped the top of the glass case above her father's watch. "I think I'd like to look at that watch there."

"Sure, just a sec."

As if Flora sensed that all Charlotte wanted was to get the watch and get out, she seemed to take an inordinate amount of time searching first for the keys to the glass case, then unlocking the back of the case.

"This one?" Flora asked, her tone syrupy sweet as she tapped her forefinger against another watch that sat next to the one that Charlotte wanted.

Charlotte ground her teeth in frustration. Either the woman was deaf and blind, or she was purposely dragging her feet. "No, not that one," Charlotte told her. "It's the one next to it that I want to look at."

"Oh, you must mean this one."

When Flora finally tapped the correct watch with her forefinger, Charlotte nodded. "Yes, that's the one."

Flora took out the watch and handed it to Charlotte. For several seconds, Charlotte stared at the watch. It looked like her father's watch, but she wanted to be certain. Turning it over, she examined the bottom of the casing. Sure enough, as obvious as the nose on her face, her father's initials were engraved on the bottom of the casing.

"How much?" Charlotte asked.

"Hmm, if I remember right, the case on that one is real gold—fourteen carats. I guess I could let it go for two-fifty."

Charlotte was sorely tempted to shove the money at her, grab the watch, and run, but on the off chance that Flora wasn't already suspicious, pulling a stunt like that was sure to make her so.

Charlotte shook her head. "Uh-uh. That's too much. It has initials engraved on the back. I wanted it as a gift for a friend, and it's gonna cost me to get those initials polished off. I'll give you one seventy-five."

Could you even get engravings polished off gold? Charlotte didn't know for sure, but it sounded good.

Flora Jennings shook her head. "Sorry, but that's way too low."

"Okay, how about two hundred?"

Flora hesitated. "Hmm." She pursed her lips, then heaved

a big sigh. "Okay, but I hope that you realize you're getting a bargain."

Some bargain, thought Charlotte, especially considering that she was buying back her own stolen property.

"Cash or credit card?"

"Cash," Charlotte told her as she reached inside her purse and pulled out the bank envelope of money that she'd previously withdrawn. "And I'll need a receipt," she added as she counted out two hundred dollars.

Other than hearsay, there was no way she could prove that Flora murdered Joyce, at least not yet, and maybe not ever. She might have to leave that up to the police. At least a receipt would be hard evidence that she could hand over to the police to prove that Flora and her partner, Price, were dealing in stolen goods.

"Did you say you wanted a receipt?" Flora asked.

Charlotte had been pretending to look at the other items in the case, but she managed to see Flora frown.

"Yes, please," Charlotte snapped, her patience at an end. "I want a receipt."

"Okay. You don't have to bite my head off."

Apologize. Be nice. At least for now. "Sorry," Charlotte muttered.

Flora reached under the counter and snatched out a receipt tablet, then slammed it onto the top of the counter. "So who do I make it out to?" she asked, her agitated tone curt.

Great, Charlotte. Just great. Now see what you've done. Not only have you ticked her off, but now you have to give her a name.

Before she'd realized that Price's partner was Flora Jennings, Charlotte had planned to use her own name for the receipt. Using her name now was out of the question. She cleared her throat, stalling for time. A second later, inspiration struck.

"Make it out to Judith Monroe," Charlotte told her. Judith probably wouldn't appreciate her name being used, but that was just too bad. It was the best she could do at present.

Charlotte held on to her money until Flora had scribbled out the receipt. When Flora held out the receipt, the temptation to grab it and run without paying was strong. After all, what would Flora do? Call the cops?

Suddenly, a mental image of the big gun that Roy Price had pulled from beneath the counter the last time that she had been in the shop popped into her head.

No, Flora wouldn't likely call the police on her, but she just might shoot her, and Charlotte knew that there was no way that she could outrun a bullet.

With one hand, Charlotte took the receipt, and ever so carefully, with her other hand, she placed the money on top of the counter. Then, without another word, she turned, and as she walked quickly to the entrance door, she slipped the watch and the receipt into her purse. During the short trek to the door, she could feel Flora's eyes boring a hole into her back. When she opened the door, out of the corner of her eye, she saw Flora head straight for the telephone. When Charlotte closed the door behind her, Flora was talking low into the receiver and gesturing wildly with her free hand. What was that about?

"Who knows and who cares?" she muttered, once outside. Slinging her purse strap over her shoulder, Charlotte wasted no time hotfooting it down the street. Night had fallen swiftly, and for the most part, the block was deserted. Though there were streetlights, there were still too many shadows and alleys for Charlotte's peace of mind.

She was halfway down the block when somewhere nearby brakes squealed, a car door slammed, and then she heard footsteps running.

The sound of running footsteps faded, but just minutes later, the hairs on the back of her neck suddenly stood on end. Still walking, she chanced a quick look behind her. There were a few people strolling along, but she didn't see anyone who looked like they were following her. Still, she couldn't shake the creepy feeling that someone was tailing her.

Probably just your imagination, she told herself, but erring on the side of caution, she picked up her pace. And still the feeling persisted and grew stronger.

By the time she reached the end of the block, every instinct within was sending out warnings. Her heart racing, she went from a fast walk to a slow jog as she hurried past the Cabildo and down the side of Jackson Square. By the time she finally reached Decatur, she was panting worse than a hound dog chasing a deer. Whether she was winded from fear or physical exertion, she didn't know, and didn't care, as she stood on the corner of Decatur and St. Peter for several minutes gasping for breath.

Just to her left, there were a couple of horse-and-buggy teams waiting for tourists' fares. But for the moment, all that she cared about were the people milling around, lots of people.

"Safety in numbers," she whispered as relief slowly seeped into her veins and she could finally take a deep breath. She was safe now. She walked over to the curb, and when the traffic light changed, she headed across the street toward Jackson Brewery.

Once in the nearby parking lot, she fished out her keys from the side pocket of her purse and hurried toward the other end of the large lot, where she'd left her van. She was two cars away from her van when a man suddenly stepped around the end of another van parked beside hers.

Startled, Charlotte yelped. Her instincts were to scream and run, but her legs and voice refused to do her biding. The term "frozen with fear" came to mind as the man grabbed her upper arm and jerked her between the cars. Maintaining a viselike grip on her arm he jammed something hard into her back.

She immediately realized two things: first of all, her suspicions that she was being followed were not just her imagination, and second, somehow, her stalker had gotten ahead of her and had been hiding and waiting for her there between the vehicles. But how did he know which vehicle belonged to her? *He didn't have to know,* came the answer. *All he had to do was wait and watch.*

"This is a gun," he warned menacingly from behind her.

With each word, he jabbed the barrel against her ribs for emphasis, and Charlotte whimpered from pain.

"Don't scream or you're dead," he threatened. "And don't struggle or you're dead," he added, jabbing her again.

Charlotte's knees went weak, and blood pounded in her ears. For the second time that evening, she recognized a voice. Even if she'd wanted to scream, and she wanted to badly, she was too frightened to utter a sound.

Chapter 16

Roy Price, the man from the pawnshop.

Charlotte shivered with fear and repulsion. But how did he know where she would be? And what did he want? Flora, of course. That first phone call Flora received . . . Flora dragging her feet, taking her time waiting on her . . . that last phone call . . .

Charlotte figured that Flora must have recognized her. She also figured that the first phone call was from Roy Price, and Flora had somehow let him know that she had Charlotte there at the shop. He'd probably told Flora to keep her at the shop as long as possible until he could get there.

In her head, she could still hear the squealing brakes, the car door slamming, the running footsteps. That had to have been Roy Price.

"Thought you could fool us with that idiotic disguise, huh?" Price gave a nasty laugh and bent down close to her ear. "Well, the joke's on you."

Charlotte could feel and smell his hot, putrid breath against the side of her face, and she swallowed the bile that rose up in her throat.

What to do? What to do?

Play dumb.

Playing dumb wouldn't be hard—nope, not hard at all. At the moment, she felt like the most ignorant person in the world.

Sudden tears sprang into her eyes, and Charlotte blinked furiously to keep them at bay. She shouldn't have been so stubborn and so independent. Sometimes being stubborn could have dire consequences. Why, oh why, hadn't she just asked Louis or Judith to come with her?

Too late now. Water under the bridge.

Charlotte swallowed hard. "W-what do you want?" she asked Price, hating that her voice sounded so scared even to her own ears.

"I want that bluebird brooch. Now, where is it?"

Oh, dear Lord in Heaven, Charlotte thought. Just minutes ago, she'd been certain that Flora had killed Joyce, but now . . .

"I said where is it!" Price demanded.

It was Price, not Flora, who had murdered Joyce. Of that, she was definitely certain now. "Ah, it—it's in a safe place," she lied. Anything to buy time. "But if you kill me, you'll never get it."

"Oh, I don't intend to kill you," he drawled nastily. "At least not yet. But if you don't give me that brooch, you'll wish you were dead by the time I get through with you. One way or another, I intend to have that brooch."

Stark terror turned her blood to ice. No matter what she did, he intended to kill her. It was either fight now or buy time and fight later. Both had their advantages and disadvantages. If she fought now, all he had to do was pull the trigger, and *bam!* It was over. If she waited until later to make her move, there was always the possibility that she might figure some way out of this mess, some way to keep him from killing her.

"Now!" Price jabbed her with the gun barrel. "Take me to it or I'll shoot you where you stand."

Moving only her eyes, Charlotte searched for help, but as far as she could see without being obvious, there was no help to be had.

"Okay," she finally answered, her voice barely a whisper.

Price laughed. "Somehow I knew you would see it my way. This is what we're gonna do. First, you're gonna hand over your keys. Second, we're gonna walk to your van, and then we're both going to climb in on the passenger side—you first. One wrong move," he warned, "and I'll shoot you on the spot."

It was déjà vu, and as Charlotte handed over her keys and walked the few steps to the passenger side of the van, she couldn't help remembering another time that she'd been forced to drive an unwelcome passenger in her van. In order to get out of the situation that time, she'd crashed her van on purpose.

Price unlocked the van's doors and shoved Charlotte into the passenger side. "Now move over to the driver's side," he ordered.

Feeling like a pretzel, Charlotte turned backward toward the center console. Folding herself almost double, she wiggled up and over the console. It was almost an impossible feat, but with only a few grunts and groans, she did it.

After she was seated in the driver's seat, Price climbed inside on the passenger side, and only then did he hand over the keys.

At first, she was trembling so badly that she wasn't sure that she could drive. By a miracle, she backed out of the tight spot without hitting or scraping the vehicles around her, then she had to weave her way through the parking lot.

Within a couple of minutes, the small booth where she had to pay for parking came into sight, and her mind raced. If only there were some way of alerting the parking attendant that she was in trouble.

As if Price had heard her thoughts, he said, "Be careful. If you try anything, I'll shoot you and the woman in the booth."

Charlotte had no doubt that Price meant what he said, and there was no way that she wanted to be responsible for someone else getting killed.

Careful to keep her expression as neutral as possible, she pulled up to the booth. After retrieving the correct amount of money from inside her purse, she handed over the parking fee, and then drove out of the lot onto the street.

Normally, the drive to her house from the Quarter didn't take over ten or fifteen minutes at the most, depending on traffic. Charlotte purposely drove as slowly as possible to give herself time to think of some way to get out of the mess she was in. Though several ideas came to mind, none of them really appealed to her.

You could always crash the van again.

No way, she thought. She'd been lucky that other time. She'd come out of the accident with a few bumps and bruises, and the driver in the vehicle that she'd rammed had walked away with only minor scrapes and cuts, but her unwelcome passenger had truly been injured. Trying the same stunt again was just asking for trouble.

After discarding several more ideas, she'd almost given up when the solution finally came to her. If, and that was a big fat *if,* but if Louis was home, and she could figure out some way to alert him about her situation, he'd take Price out in a heart-beat.

By the time Charlotte turned onto Milan Street, she was feeling somewhat better about her situation. But as she drove down Milan, the breath of a memory flitted in and out of her mind. She frowned in concentration. Though she couldn't quite remember, she knew that it was something important. But what?

After a moment, it came to her. It was something about the strange incident involving the tan Toyota when she'd been passing out the flyers.

Of course, she thought, suddenly remembering why the incident was important. She'd be willing to bet her last dollar that the driver of the Toyota had been Price.

Charlotte frowned. Price had to have known that she was home, though. Her van had been parked in the driveway. So why would he have risked going to her house in broad daylight, knowing that she was there?

Only one reason, she decided. As long as Price held the gun, there was no risk, in his mind, especially from a mere woman—a mere woman who happened to be a senior citizen at that. She figured that at first he had assumed that she was inside, but when he saw her outside, he'd gotten cold feet. Inside, he would have been safe when he pulled out his gun. Outside, in broad daylight, he would have been taking a chance that any one of her neighbors might see him.

Not so at night, she thought.

"Men loved darkness rather than light, because their deeds were evil."

Oh, so true, she thought as the Bible verse from John 3:19 popped into her head. Though her application was a broad interpretation of the verse, it fit. One thing for sure, Price was evil.

Charlotte was almost to her house when a horrible thought hit her. What if Louis wasn't at home, then what?

In spite of her sister accusing her of being superstitious, Charlotte didn't think of herself that way. But when she neared her house, all hope she had died an instant death. Louis's driveway was empty.

If you hadn't thought it, it wouldn't have happened.

Superstitious nonsense, she silently countered, and chewing on her bottom lip, she pulled into her driveway. But was it superstitious nonsense? Sometimes, especially in times like this, she had to wonder.

"Turn off the engine and give me the keys."

The sound of Price's voice jerked her back to her present dilemma.

Think of something, but think fast.

Her mind spinning, she took her time as she slowly shoved the gear into park, then reached up and switched off the engine.

Talk to him and keep him talking. Maybe Louis will show up.

Her fingers still on the keys, Charlotte turned her head and stared at Price. "You don't have to do this, you know," she told him. Again, taking her time, she pulled the keys from the ignition. "My niece is a police detective and my boyfriend is an ex-cop. If you kill me, they will hunt you down like a dog."

Boyfriend? Since when did you decide that Louis was your boyfriend?

Charlotte blinked several times as if doing so would silence the voice in her head.

"Just give me the keys and shut your mouth." Price reached over and wrenched the keys out of her hand. Then he laughed. "Your niece and boyfriend will have to catch me first. With the money I can get out of that brooch, I can live in Mexico very nicely for a long time. Enough talk."

Opening his door, he got out. "Now you." He motioned with the gun for her to get out on the passenger side.

Climbing back over the center console wasn't any easier the second time. Once she was out of the van, he grabbed her arm and force-marched her across to the steps. During the climb up the steps, Charlotte spied the broom she'd left leaning against the wall. If she could somehow get her hands on that broom . . .

"Here"—Price held out the keys—"you open the door."

Dear Lord, I need help here, she silently prayed as she found the house key on the ring and unlocked her front door. Just as she shoved the door open and reached inside to flip on the living room light, she heard a familiar squawk.

"Missed you. *Squawk*. Missed you."

"What the—" Price whirled around and let out a yelp just as Sweety Boy dive-bombed him, then flew straight into the living room.

When Price ducked, Charlotte threw the keys into the living room and snatched up the broom. Using it like a bat and aiming for Price's gun hand, she swung with all of her might.

Home run!

Price howled with pain as the gun flew off the porch into the hedge. Charlotte immediately whipped the broom back and swung again, this time striking Price smack in the face.

Price let out a scream, whether of pain or fury, she couldn't tell. When he grabbed his face, Charlotte jumped through the doorway, slammed the door shut, locked it, and threw the dead bolt.

Breathing hard, she ran to the phone. Outside, Price was cussing a blue streak. Locked inside, her hands were shaking so badly that she had to try three times before she was able to dial 911.

"This is Charlotte LaRue," she told the 911 operator, and quickly gave the woman her address. "A man is trying to break into my house."

While Charlotte tried to listen to the operator's instructions, the sudden silence from the porch sent chills of terror chasing

207

down her spine. Where was Price? What was he doing? Had he given up, or even now was he scrounging in the bushes for his gun?

Then she heard it, the distinct sound of a key sliding into the front door's keyhole, and the click of the lock on the door. Then the doorknob turned. But the dead bolt held. Muffled curses poured from Price's mouth, and he banged on the door, probably with his fist, Charlotte figured.

"He's still trying to get in," she cried into the receiver.

"Ma'am, help is on the way."

Sending up a prayer of thanks for the dead bolt, Charlotte's gaze flew to the key ring on the floor, where she'd tossed it. How had he unlocked the door without a key?

"My missing house key," she whispered. All along, Price had the missing key, which proved, at least in Charlotte's mind, that he was definitely the one who had murdered Joyce.

Charlotte suddenly went stone still and tilted her head. Was that a police siren? Yes, a police siren, growing louder with each second.

Thu-wack! Charlotte jumped at the loud noise at the door. The door shuddered, but held. Price wasn't a big man and she couldn't imagine him slamming his shoulder to the door and expecting it to break open, but she could imagine him trying to kick the door down. A couple more kicks like the first one, and the door might not hold.

The siren grew to an earsplitting scream. Within moments, she saw revolving lights reflecting through the front window and the siren abruptly died. She sagged against the desk with relief. Finally, help had arrived.

Charlotte closed her eyes. "Thank you, Lord," she whispered.

"Missed you, missed you."

"Sweety?" Charlotte opened her eyes and quickly scanned

the room. Right away, she spotted him perched on the cuckoo clock hanging on the wall behind the sofa. "Good boy," she crooned. "My hero."

The loud knock at her door made her jump.

"Ms. LaRue? Ms. Charlotte LaRue? I'm an officer with the New Orleans police. Open up, ma'am."

"Just stay there, Sweety," Charlotte told the little bird as she rushed over to the door. Her impulse was to throw open the door immediately, but common sense screamed caution. Since impulse was one of the emotions that had gotten her into this predicament to begin with, she decided to go with caution.

Sliding along the wall to the side of the window, she called out, "I'm here, but show me your badge. Hold it up to the front window."

Once she saw the badge, she threw the dead bolt and opened the door. She immediately recognized the officer as the older of the two that showed up right after she'd reported Joyce's murder. If she remembered right, his name was Mitch. Right behind him, near the bottom of the steps, his gun drawn, was his partner, the younger officer who had accompanied him before.

"He was here, just a moment ago," she cried, careful to pull the door closed behind her. Then, as quickly as she could, she told both officers about her ordeal, giving them Price's name and a description of him.

"He's on foot, so he can't have gotten very far," she said. "Oh, and another thing. Unless he found his gun, it's somewhere in my front hedge."

"How did it end up in the hedge?" Mitch asked.

Charlotte shook her head. "That's not important right now." She figured that he probably wouldn't believe her, anyway. "The important thing is the gun. If it's still there, I think you'll find that it's the same gun that was used to murder Joyce Thibodeaux."

While Charlotte was talking, she heard the younger officer radio in the information to the dispatcher and ask for backup to hunt down Price.

Suddenly, without warning, Charlotte's eyes blurred, and her mind drifted into a foggy haze. It was that kind of sinking, nauseating feeling she only got when her blood sugar level dropped. She needed to sit down—sit down immediately. If she didn't sit down soon, she knew from experience that she'd pass out.

"Excuse me," she choked out. "N-need to sit down." She pushed the door back open, and weaving like a drunk and gasping, she tried to make it to the sofa.

"Whoa, here, let me help you." Mitch stepped inside and grabbed her around the waist. Once he'd eased her over to the sofa, he said, "Are you injured?"

Charlotte shook her head. "No, not injured. Diabetic—I'm a diabetic—low blood sugar. And please shut the front door. My bird is loose."

Though Mitch gave her an odd look, he stepped over and closed the door. "Are you sure you don't need an ambulance?"

"I'm sure. No ambulance."

"Can I get you something, a glass of water, pills?"

Charlotte nodded. "A glass of orange juice—in the refrigerator."

"Okay, ma'am. You just stay right there."

Nodding again, Charlotte closed her eyes and leaned her head back against the sofa. Even if she'd wanted to move, she would have had to crawl. Too much stress, she thought, and nothing to eat since lunch.

Within minutes, the officer was back with a glass of juice,

and Charlotte eagerly drank every drop of it. "Just give me a moment," she said when she'd finished.

The officer hesitated a moment more, then went to the front door. "I'd better keep an eye on her," he called out to his partner. "See if you can find that gun. She said it was in the hedge."

Though she was still weak, the sinking feeling was easing up somewhat. "He could see better if you turn on the porch light," Charlotte pointed out.

With a nod, he flipped on the light switch.

"And please shut the door so my bird won't get out."

Though he closed the door, once again he gave her an odd look. *Probably thinks I'm some loony old woman,* she thought. At that moment, though, Sweety Boy, bless his little heart, let out a squawk.

Startled, the officer snapped his head toward the noise. "Oh, I see," he murmured. "That bird."

Charlotte felt a smile tug at her lips. At least now he wouldn't think she was crazy . . . that is, unless she told him about Sweety Boy saving her.

Within what seemed like only minutes, Charlotte heard a caterwaul of sirens. If the sound was any gauge to measure by, her neighborhood would soon be crawling with police. She only hoped that they could find Price before he got away and before he hurt someone.

A few minutes later, the younger police officer knocked on the front door, then opened it. "Found the gun," he told his partner. "Just where she said it would be."

Good, she thought. At least now they could prove that Price murdered Joyce. Charlotte shivered. She sure hoped they found him soon. For all she knew, he could still have her key in his pocket, and he could—

Stop it! Stop it right now! They will find him.

Mitch turned to Charlotte. "Ma'am, I need to be out there. Will you be okay for a while by yourself?"

"Yes, of course."

With a glance at Sweety Boy, he carefully pulled the door closed behind him.

Once he was gone, Charlotte sighed. Time to put Sweety back inside his cage. Though she still felt a little weak, she got to her feet. Turning around, she reached up with her forefinger extended to the little parakeet's feet. "Come on, Boy," she coaxed. "Time to get back in your cage."

To her surprise, he hopped right onto her finger. "You're such a good boy," she soothed. As she slowly walked toward his cage, she examined him as best she could. Though he looked a bit roughed-up, he seemed to be okay.

"Just as soon as possible, I'm taking you to the vet and get you checked out," she said as she opened the cage door and eased him inside. "Good boy," she murmured when he hopped onto the perch inside the cage. Since there was still plenty of birdseed in the small feeder, she closed the cage door and latched it.

Feeling drained by the small exertion, she went back to the sofa and sat. Leaning her head back, she closed her eyes and tried to relax. And for a moment, she suspected that she dozed off. It was the sound of loud, familiar voices out on the porch that jerked her back awake.

"What's going on here?"

Louis's voice. Louis had finally come home.

"Is my aunt okay?"

Judith's voice.

Then everyone seemed to be talking at once, and Charlotte lost track of the conversation. Maybe if she closed her eyes again, everyone would just go away.

Not likely. You know better than that.

She did know better, and she also knew what was coming. Judith and Louis were going to read her the riot act, and probably rat her out to Hank as well. Stomach-tightening dread filled her. Once her son found out, he was going to have a hissy fit. Then she'd have to listen to him give her a lecture as well.

"Should have minded my own business," she grumbled. "Should have left the stupid watch there and let the police take care of it."

Yeah, and you might be dead now if you had.

Remembering the tan Toyota, she shivered, knowing that she wouldn't be able to feel safe again until Price was caught. As for Judith and Louis, sooner or later she was going to have to face them, so she might as well get it over with and be done with it.

Taking a deep breath, she eased off the sofa and got to her feet. Though she still felt a bit shaky, she forced herself to walk to the front door. She was almost to the door when she heard a distant flurry of muffled pops that sounded like several cars backfiring at once.

Suddenly, all conversation on the porch ceased, and Charlotte froze. Not cars backfiring. Gunshots.

With that realization, she suddenly felt weak all over again. But why gunshots? The younger officer had found Price's gun in her hedge.

Chapter 17

When Charlotte opened the front door, she'd decided that the gunshots she'd heard must have been warning shots. Suddenly, the radio belonging to the older officer crackled to life. The report coming over the radio sounded like a bunch of numbers gibberish, but after a moment, the officer's face split into a wide grin. "That's a big ten-four," he shouted into his radio. Turning to the others standing around him, he said, "Perp's in custody! They got him."

When the others cheered, Charlotte grabbed hold of the door frame and cried, "Thank the Lord."

Judith jerked her head around, and when her gaze connected with Charlotte, her expression grew tight with concern. Separating herself from the others, Judith hurried up the steps and over to Charlotte. "You okay, Auntie?"

Out of the corner of her eye, Charlotte saw Louis climbing the steps. Charlotte smiled at Judith and gave her niece a brief hug. "I'm okay now—a whole lot better than a few minutes ago, that's for sure." She paused and her smile faded. "Hon, I know you're probably upset with me, but, please, no lectures, at least not tonight."

"If you ask me, what your aunt needs is locking up for her

own good," Louis said as he walked across the porch to join them. "Good thing I'm retired or—"

"Nobody asked you, old man, so put a sock in it," Judith retorted good-naturedly.

"Little girl, you need to learn respect for your elders," he shot back with a grin.

Judith turned and smiled at Charlotte. "Don't mind him, and no lecture this time." She laughed and shrugged. "Don't see that it would do much good, anyway." Her laughter died and her expression grew serious. "I do have to ask you some questions."

Charlotte sighed. "Yeah, I guess you do. And I've got some information you need to hear." Charlotte stepped back from the doorway and motioned for Judith to come inside. Though Judith had said "no lecture," Charlotte knew that Louis would have no compunction about putting in his two cents. Once Judith was inside, Charlotte blocked the doorway. Giving Louis a saccharine smile, she said, "Not now, Louis." Then she firmly closed the door in his face.

Behind her, Judith snickered. "Guess you showed him, huh?"

"I'll deal with him later," Charlotte responded. Much later, if she were lucky, she added silently. "For now, though, guess what?" When Judith frowned, Charlotte pointed to the bird-cage. "Sweety Boy came back."

"No kidding!" Judith shook her head in amazement as she stared at the cage. "I thought he was a goner for sure. Just goes to show, miracles still happen." With another shake of her head, Judith walked over to the sofa and Charlotte followed her.

Once they were both seated, Judith pulled a notebook and pen out of her purse. "Okay, Auntie, why don't you start from the beginning?"

Charlotte nodded, and starting with her visit from Flora

Jennings and her claims of being a real estate agent, Charlotte explained about the missing watch and seeing Joyce come out of the pawnshop. Then she talked about her first trip to the hospital, her conversation with Delbert O'Banion, and what she'd learned about the theft ring going on there. Albeit reluctantly, she also told Judith about her run-in with Daisy.

"I swear, Auntie. One of these days, you're going to get yourself killed." Judith pursed her lips. "Okay, okay, enough said. Please continue."

With a slight smile, Charlotte talked about her second trip to the hospital and what Bert O'Banion had said about the bluebird diamond, and then she finished up detailing her ordeal in the Quarter with Flora Jennings, and later, with Roy Price.

Charlotte tilted her head first to one side and then the other, stretching her stiff neck muscles. "That partner of his, Flora Jennings, was definitely in on the whole thing," she said, reaching up to massage the back of her neck. "And I'm pretty sure that she was Joyce's outside contact as well. I figure that Joyce decided to go it on her own and cut out Jennings and Price. That's when things got nasty." Suddenly, she frowned. "Speaking of Price, he's got my spare house key that's been missing."

"How do you know that?"

"Because after I locked him out, he used it to unlock the door. Thank the Lord, the dead bolt held, though. But don't you see? The only way that he could have gotten that key was from Joyce, *after* she'd used it to get back inside my house."

Judith stared into space for a moment as she tapped her pen against the notebook. "Yeah, well, I suppose that's one possibility." Then she looked Charlotte straight in the eyes. "I'm afraid it's not definitive proof, though. Sorry. Besides, he's probably tossed it by now."

"Whatever. Doesn't much matter now. That baby-faced officer found Price's gun in my hedge. And another thing." She snagged her purse from the coffee table and pulled out her father's watch and the receipt. Handing both to Judith, she said, "This should help you prove they were dealing in stolen property."

Judith eyed the receipt, and when she spotted her name on it, she said, "I should run you in for impersonating an officer of the law." Then she laughed. "Just kidding, Auntie."

Charlotte rolled her eyes. "About my key. If Price does still have it, I'd like to know. And once y'all are done with it, you can toss it. I've got a locksmith coming tomorrow to change my locks."

At the sudden knock on the front door, both women turned their heads. "It's just me," Louis called out as he opened the door. "Okay if I come in now? I figured you'd be about through," he said to Judith.

Judith nodded. "Yeah, we're just about through here."

Normally, upon just the sight of Louis, Sweety Boy would squawk and thrash around in his cage, but to Charlotte's surprise, the little parakeet didn't react at all to Louis's presence when he stepped inside and closed the door behind him.

In Louis's hand was a plastic bag, and Charlotte's mouth watered when the smell of food drifted her way.

Then Louis turned and stared at the birdcage. "Well, I'll be a son of a gun," he said. "Your bird came home." He motioned toward the cage with his free hand. "Hey, that's great." Pulling his gaze away from the bird, he walked over to the sofa. "I thought you could use a bite to eat." He handed the bag to Charlotte. To Judith, he said, "Have you ever noticed that your aunt gets a little cranky when she's hungry?"

Judith held up her hand, palm out. "I plead the Fifth on that one."

"Coward," Louis teased, and chuckling, he turned to Charlotte. "If I remember right, your favorite sandwich is a shrimp po'boy."

Charlotte stared up at him for a second, hardly believing that he had been so thoughtful, especially after she'd so rudely shut the door in his face. "Ah—thanks—thanks a lot. I'm starved."

Judith reached out and touched Charlotte's arm with her fingers to get her attention. "Auntie, if you're sure you're okay, I really need to leave now. I want this Daisy person and Flora wrapped up tonight."

"I'm fine now, Judith. You go do your job. If it helps, the last time I saw Flora, she was still at the pawnshop. As for Daisy, the hospital should know where she lives."

"Yeah, go to work, little girl," Louis quipped. "I'll make sure she behaves."

With a snort, Judith stood. "Yeah, right, in your dreams," she retorted. Then she bent down and hugged Charlotte's neck. "I love you. Get some rest."

"Thanks, hon, and you be careful."

As soon as Judith closed the door behind her, Louis said, "Want to take that to the kitchen table?" He motioned to the sack of food. "While you eat, I've got some news about Aubrey Hamilton. Besides, if you feel up to going over it again, I'd like to hear the scoop on that Price dirtbag."

"Maybe tomorrow," Charlotte responded. "I'm tired of even thinking about it."

Louis shrugged. "Sure. Whenever."

In the kitchen, Charlotte fixed them both a glass of tea. Once settled at the kitchen table, Charlotte bit into the still-warm shrimp po'boy. "Mmm, manna from Heaven."

Louis nodded and grinned. Then his grin faded. "Seems I was all wrong about Hamilton."

Charlotte frowned as she chewed. With everything else going on, she'd forgotten all about Aubrey Hamilton. Swallowing, she said, "Yeah, what about him? What was he doing here?"

"Well," Louis answered, "he showed up at the station this morning to turn in a man he'd taken into custody—a hit man hired by the Russian mob to take out Joyce. Don't ask me how, but Hamilton was able to track him down here in the city. Turns out that Joyce was a snitch for Hamilton, after all, but then, we already knew that. Hamilton came here originally to track *her* down, but not to kill her. He was after her to warn her about the hit."

"Well, Hamilton should have said something to begin with. And why didn't that contact of yours out there tell you that's what was going on?"

"The reason my contact didn't say anything was because he didn't know anything at the time."

"What about all that stuff they told you before? I thought Hamilton was being investigated by Internal Affairs and was suspected of committing a murder similar to Joyce's murder."

"Turns out that Internal Affairs investigation was a setup. Hamilton suspected that someone in the department was a rat on the mob's payroll, so the mob's rat tried to get rid of him. At the time, Hamilton didn't know who to trust, so he went off on his own. And he was right to do so. The hit man is singing like a canary, and the SFPD has already arrested the rat."

Charlotte chewed a moment more as she digested what Louis had just told her. Then she swallowed. "Just goes to prove, nobody is all bad or all good," she said gently. "Poor Joyce. I can't imagine being under that kind of pressure."

"Can't you, though?" Louis shot back. "You've been in some pretty sticky situations yourself. And as I recall, one of those situations was with the mob."

"Yeah, but I've never had a hit put out on me."

Louis rolled his eyes. "Oh, yeah, right. Maybe it wasn't exactly a hit, at least not an ordered hit, but one of the mob's hired guns did try to kill you."

Deciding it was time to change the subject, she asked, "Has the coroner released Joyce's body yet?"

Louis nodded.

"So when are you holding her funeral?"

Louis didn't answer immediately, but lowered his gaze and stared at the tabletop.

"What's wrong?" Charlotte asked, frowning with concern.

"No funeral," he replied.

Charlotte's frown deepened. "What do you mean, 'no funeral'?"

"It wasn't my decision. Believe it or not, Joyce had a will and requested that her body be donated to science."

"Oh, Louis." Charlotte reached out and covered his hand with hers. "That was a really noble thing for her to do."

Still staring at the tabletop, Louis turned his hand beneath hers and squeezed, then simply shrugged.

Since it seemed to bring him comfort, Charlotte left her hand in his for the moment. "You can always hold a small memorial service," she suggested gently.

"Stephen and I talked about that. He's arranging it for Sunday afternoon around four-thirty, just before sunset. It will be mostly just family and a few close friends."

"Where?"

"When Stephen was a little boy, Joyce used to take him to a particular spot on the levee nearby and let him play. It's one of the few good memories he has of her. Since Joyce never belonged to any church, he thought we would all gather there on top of the levee. The pastor of Stephen's church has agreed to say a few words, and afterward, we'll go back to Stephen's house for dinner."

"That sounds lovely," Charlotte told him. "I don't remember you or Joyce ever mentioning her family. Did she have other family?"

"Her parents died several years ago, but she does have a sister and a niece and nephew, who live near Shreveport. I called her to let her know about Joyce, but I doubt if she'd come for the service. She and Joyce have been estranged for years."

"That's a shame," Charlotte murmured. Though she and her own sister, Madeline, had had their differences, she couldn't imagine her life without her sister in it.

Louis lifted his head and stared into her eyes. "Will you be able to come?" Then he quickly added, "After everything that's happened, I wouldn't blame you if you didn't want to."

"I wouldn't want to intrude or anything, but, yes, I'll be there."

Louis nodded. "Thanks." Releasing his hold on her hand, he pushed back his chair and stood. "I don't know about you, but I think I've had about all of this day that I can stand."

"Amen to that," Charlotte replied.

"See you tomorrow." Turning, he headed for the doorway leading into the living room.

"Thanks again for the sandwich," she called out.

At the doorway, Louis paused. "You're welcome. Now, make sure you use the dead bolt tonight."

A minute later, after Charlotte had locked and bolted the front door, she turned to Sweety Boy's cage. "I sure have missed you, you little squirt." When the little bird sidled over to the edge of the cage, Charlotte reached through the wires with her forefinger and gently rubbed his head.

"First thing tomorrow, you're going to the vet and get all checked out," she told him. Withdrawing her finger, she covered the cage for the night.

* * *

Later, restless and unable to fall asleep, Charlotte stared up at the dark ceiling above her bed. Though she couldn't quite put her finger on it, something about the whole mess with Joyce's murder still bothered her.

Charlotte groaned, and closing her eyes, she turned over so that she was half on her stomach and half on her side. She should be relieved that the whole mess was over, she thought. After all, she was safe now. Roy Price was in custody, and she was sure that by now Judith had probably arrested Daisy and Flora. So why couldn't she put it all out of her mind and go to sleep?

Overtired and too much excitement. Maybe that was the problem, but somehow she didn't think so.

Chapter 18

On Thursday, when Charlotte finally crawled out of bed, it was almost eight o'clock, a lot later than she normally slept. Even so, she figured that she'd only gotten about six hours of sleep.

You could have slept longer.

"Yeah, yeah," she muttered. In spite of Thursday being one of her days off, Charlotte knew that once she woke up, that was it. Once awake, there was no going back to sleep.

Charlotte yawned, then stretched. The old saying, "rode hard and put up wet" came to mind as she headed to the bathroom. Then she decided that "run over by a Mack truck" was an even more appropriate description of how she felt.

After uncovering Sweety Boy's cage and making sure he was still okay, she headed for the kitchen. She'd just poured herself her first cup of coffee when the phone rang.

Taking her coffee with her, she hurried back to the living room.

"Hello," she said into the receiver, "Maid-for-a-Day, Charlotte speaking."

"Hey, Aunt Charlie, it's Judith."

"Hey, yourself," Charlotte retorted. "You sound pretty chipper for so early in the morning. What's up?"

"For one, I finally got a day off, but mostly, I wanted to let you know that we arrested that nurse and the woman at the pawnshop last night. Turns out that Flora Jennings wasn't her real name, after all. She picked the name from a real estate ad in the newspaper, just in case you decided to check up on her—"

"Which I did," Charlotte interrupted. "For all the good that did."

"Yeah, well, it even gets better. She even made sure that the real Flora Jennings wouldn't be in the office on the day that she came to your house. Pretty devious, huh?"

"Yeah, devious, all right. And a lot smarter than I gave her credit for being."

"Anyway," Judith continued, "the woman's real name is Nora James, and she has a rap sheet as long as my arm."

"Hmm, Nora James, Flora Jennings. Do you think it's possible that Nora James purposely picked the alias because the first names rhymed, and the last names both started with a *J*, the same letter that her real name started with?"

Judith laughed. "Anything's possible, but I think that's really stretching it. I'm not sure I'd give her that much credit."

"Yeah, you're probably right," Charlotte agreed. Besides, it wouldn't have mattered, anyway. There was no way that Nora could have known that she would ever show up at the pawnshop; thus, there would be no reason for her to connect the name of the pawnshop with Nora James or Flora Jennings. "What about the other one—the nurse?" Charlotte asked.

"We had to do some digging on that one, and turns out, she's no angel of mercy, that's for sure. With the city being so desperate for medical personnel, she somehow slipped through the cracks right after Katrina. She was fired from her last job up in Arkansas for the same type of scam, but she got off on a technicality. She even admitted that she'd figured that with everything a mess down here, no one would be the wiser.

"She won't get off this time, though," Judith vowed. "She's caught, and caught good."

"One thing about her I haven't figured out," Charlotte said. "That first time I met her down in the Quarter, why did she try to get me to complain to the police about Price, especially if she was using him to fence the stolen property?"

"That one's easy, Auntie. Greed. Splitting the profit from the diamond two ways would be better than splitting it three ways. Oh, yeah, and another thing, Auntie. Louis told me what he found out about the syringe. If you'll come in and file a complaint, we'll get her on attempted murder, as well as theft. It might not hold up, but the ADA thinks he has a good shot at it. Who knows? She might even confess if she's offered a deal for less time in prison."

What goes around, comes around, Charlotte thought. And people do get paid back for what they do in this life, one way or another.

"One last thing, Auntie," Judith added. "The results aren't in yet, but if the bullet that killed Joyce matches the gun that was found in your hedge, that, along with the loose key we found in Price's pocket, should put him away for good."

"Thank the good Lord," Charlotte whispered.

After Charlotte hung up the receiver, she stared thoughtfully out the front window. In spite of all of Judith's assurances, she just couldn't shake the feeling that something was still not quite right, that something was missing. But what? All the culprits were in custody.

With a shake of her head, and a silent admonition to be thankful for her blessings and forget about it, she phoned the vet's office and made an appointment to bring Sweety Boy in for a checkup after lunch.

"One more call," she murmured as she dialed her son's home phone number. Surprised when Carol immediately answered, Charlotte said, "Hey, hon. How are you?"

"I'm just fabulous," Carol answered. "I actually got to sleep a whole six hours last night without being interrupted."

Charlotte frowned. "Aren't the twins a little young to be sleeping that long?"

Carol laughed. "Yes, of course they are. But I took your advice, and after talking to their pediatrician and getting his okay, I switched them to formula. It seems to agree with them, and they do seem more satisfied now. Between that and the new nanny we hired, I feel like I'm almost human again. And, Charlotte, just in case I haven't said so already, I so appreciate your help and your support."

Charlotte smiled. At least someone appreciated her and still thought she had sense enough to come in out of the rain. After talking a few minutes more to her daughter-in-law, she hung up the phone and headed for the kitchen. Time for breakfast and time to figure out what chores she needed to get done before Sweety Boy's vet appointment.

While Charlotte ate her standard breakfast of oatmeal and drank a glass of orange juice, she mentally reviewed the chores she'd been meaning to do. Ever since the first cool spell a few weeks earlier, one of the chores included cleaning the closet in her bedroom and switching out her summer clothes with the winter clothes she kept stored in the guest room closet.

"No time like the present," she murmured.

After hand washing the few dirty dishes she'd used for breakfast, Charlotte headed for her bedroom to get dressed. After she'd dressed, she made up her bed, and then went to her closet.

Opening the closet door, she stared at the clothes inside.

She didn't have all that many real summery-type clothes. Other than her work clothes, most of the outfits she had could be worn year-round. Even so, at least once a year, she liked to go through what she had and get rid of anything that was worn or didn't exactly fit right.

It didn't take long to remove the few summer outfits from her bedroom closet and deposit them on the bed in the guest room. Once most of the clothes were out, she removed all the shoes and other various items from the bottom of her bedroom closet as well. Then she thoroughly vacuumed the carpet.

Once she'd put the shoes back, she headed for the guest room and started the procedure all over again. Instead of shoes in the bottom of that closet, she had several boxes of other things she kept there. When she pulled out one box in particular, an unexpected spurt of anger erupted within.

On top of the box was the tote bag that Joyce had borrowed that first day when she had supposedly gone looking for an apartment.

"Stupid tote bag," she whispered. Knowing Joyce, she'd probably left crumbs from a sandwich inside it or something else equally nasty for the roaches to feast on. Though she was tempted to simply throw it in the garbage and be done with it, she couldn't see wasting a perfectly good tote bag because of one ugly memory.

Unlike a lot of tote bags, this particular one was made of a nice grade of canvas on the outside and had a thin waterproof-type insulated lining on the inside. If nothing else, she could drop it off at one of the many thrift shops in the neighborhood.

Charlotte placed the box on the bed and sat down beside it. As she reached for the tote bag, suddenly, like a blinding light of revelation, she realized what had been bothering her all along. Yes, all the culprits connected with Joyce's death were in custody. All, but one. The real culprit—the bluebird diamond—was still out there somewhere, and as far as she knew, it was still missing.

She pulled the tote bag out of the box and placed it in her lap. So why hadn't anyone—least of all the police—said anything about it or even mentioned it, for that matter? After Joyce's murder, the crime lab people had turned her house upside down looking for clues.

Charlotte shook her head. No, that didn't matter. All of that happened before either she or the police knew anything about the diamond brooch. But later . . .

Was it possible that they had simply assumed that Price had already fenced it?

"I want that bluebird brooch. Now, where is it?"

Recalling Price's demands when he'd forced her to drive him to her house, Charlotte shook her head. It didn't make sense that the police would assume such a thing, or else what reason would Price have had for kidnapping her in the first place? But had she even told the police that was the reason he'd kidnapped her to begin with?

This time, she nodded yes. She distinctly remembered that she'd told Judith all about it last night.

Charlotte sat for several minutes staring into space, her fingers clutched around the tote. Of course there was another possibility. The police could have assumed that Joyce had already fenced it, and Price didn't know that she'd fenced it. At least that made more sense.

But Charlotte knew better on both accounts. The bluebird diamond was still missing, still up for grabs. But where?

"Where else?" she murmured, glancing around the guest room. It had to be here, somewhere in her house.

Suddenly, yet another revelation hit her. It was because of the bluebird diamond that Joyce had come back to the house after she'd been kicked out. Not to trash the house, but to collect the brooch she hadn't been able to take with her because Charlotte had watched her every move while she'd packed.

Only problem, Price had somehow caught up with Joyce and followed her. When she'd refused to tell him where the brooch was, he'd killed her.

Afterward, Price, not Joyce, was the one who had trashed the house while searching for the brooch. So why didn't he find it? Where had Joyce hidden it?

Charlotte dropped her gaze to stare at the tote bag, then her eyes narrowed. Was it possible? Could she have hidden it in the tote bag?

There was only one way to find out, she decided. Opening up the bag, she peered inside it. Contrary to her suspicions, and to her disappointment, there was nothing in it but an empty sandwich bag and a half-full water bottle.

Charlotte reached inside and took out the sandwich bag and the bottle, and then she laid the tote bag out flat on the bed. Using her palms, she pressed them against the canvas, feeling for anything out of the ordinary.

Suddenly, her hands stilled. "Why, Joyce, you devious little devil." Yes, there it was. She pressed her fingers around the small lump near the bottom of the bag. Had to be, she thought.

With excitement rushing through her veins, she picked up the bag and closely examined the top of the inside where the lining connected with the outer part of the bag. Sure enough, there was one place, not more than two inches long, where the lining was loose.

Using her fingers, Charlotte started at the bottom of the bag and worked the lump up toward the small opening. When she had it close to the top, she reached in with her finger and was able to wiggle out the small black velvet pouch. She opened the pouch and pulled out the brooch.

The bluebird diamond. She stared down at the sparkling piece of jewelry in awe. The base of the brooch was lacy gold filigree fashioned in an oval shape that looked to be about two to three inches in diameter. The large blue diamond, which was worth so much money, was actually the body of the bird. There were several smaller blue stones positioned around the larger one to shape the bird's head, beak, and tail, and a tiny black onyx had been used for the bird's eye. Surrounding the bird were several tiny white diamonds. It was absolutely the most gorgeous piece of jewelry that she'd ever seen.

And worth a million bucks.

Charlotte swallowed the lump in her throat. It might be beautiful and it might be worth a million dollars, but it wasn't worth Joyce's life.

Choking up, she quickly slipped it back inside its velvet pouch. Now what? she wondered. For one thing, she'd have to turn it over to the police. The sooner, the better, as far as she was concerned.

In the living room, the cuckoo clock cuckooed twelve times, and Charlotte suddenly stiffened. "My goodness, how time flies," she grumbled. She'd have to hurry to get Sweety Boy to his vet appointment on time.

But what about the brooch?

With a grim smile, Charlotte placed the velvet pouch back inside the tote bag. The brooch could wait. She would eventually turn it over to the police, but for now, she had another little bird that needed her attention more. After placing the bag back on top of the box, she headed for the living room. For now, she intended on giving Sweety Boy some much-needed, much-deserved extra TLC.

"Hey, there's my hero," she crooned to the little parakeet as she approached his cage. "Time to get you ready to see the vet." She reached inside the cage with her forefinger and rubbed his head. "And when we come back home, I just might let you fly around a while in the house, but only if you promise not to fly away again."

For several moments more, she continued rubbing his head; then, with a shake of her head, she withdrew her finger. "I missed you, you silly bird. And I think it's high time that I taught you a few new phrases."

Charlotte stared out the front window a moment, then grinned. "Hey, I know. How about I teach you to say, 'Reach for the sky'?"

A Cleaning Tip from Charlotte

At least once a year, everyone should clean his or her clothes closet. You wouldn't believe how much dust accumulates on the walls of a closet over time. You should also go through all of the hanging clothes. It's a good rule of thumb that if you haven't worn a particular garment or pair of shoes in a year or more, then get rid of it. Donate the item to Goodwill or some other charity. But if you can't bring yourself to do this chore in one fell swoop, then make it a rule that each time you buy a new garment or new pair of shoes, you have to get rid of an old garment or an old pair of shoes.

CHARLOTTE'S CHICKEN POTPIE
Makes 4 to 6 servings

Pastry for 2-crust pie or 2 frozen pie crusts (thawed)
½ cup chopped onion
3 tablespoons butter or margarine
2 cups cubed cooked chicken (white meat preferred)
¾ cup chicken broth
1 can cream-of-chicken condensed soup
8 ounces frozen mixed vegetables
1 four-ounce can of mushrooms, drained
salt and pepper to taste

Preheat oven to 400 degrees.

Divide pastry in half. On lightly floured surface, roll out half of pastry to ¼ inch thick. Cut to fit the inside of a 9-inch square casserole, or 9-inch pie plate (sides and bottom). Cook onion in butter (margarine) till tender. In a bowl, combine onion/butter, cubed chicken, chicken broth, cream-of-chicken condensed soup, frozen mixed vegetables, drained mushrooms, salt, and pepper. Stir until blended. Pour mixture into pastry-lined casserole. On lightly floured surface, roll out remaining half of pastry to ¼ inch thick. Cut to fit top of casserole. Adjust top pastry and seal edges to bottom pastry. Cut slits in top pastry to let steam escape. Bake pie for 35–40 minutes or until top crust is medium brown. Remove pie from oven and let stand at least 10 minutes before cutting and serving.